"Want me to start a h

"A long bubble bath can be so relaxing. planning on having one when I get home. It's the least I can do for you before I leave."

When Daisy licked her lips, which were red from the cold, an image flashed in his mind. Daisy in the bathtub, wet and surrounded by a mound of bubbles. Finn squeezed his eyes closed. A fantasy like this had happened once before. His brain needed to get it together and knock this off.

Back when Daisy had been their boss, Finn had no choice but to keep things completely chill because he and his brothers had needed the job on her horse ranch. Once they'd saved enough and bought Four Star Ranch next door, he'd briefly considered asking her out for a bit of fun, but Daisy Dalton was the girl-next-door type—both figuratively and literally. If he let his mind go down a dangerous path, it could ruin everything.

Daisy expected—and deserved—a committed relationship, and that was something that was not part of his DNA. He never did it on purpose, but he always wound up breaking hearts. Finn wasn't the kind of guy who settled down with one woman.

He cleared his throat. "I think I'll just get in the shower. Seems faster."

And safer.

Dear Reader,

Welcome back to Channing, Texas! *Her New Year's Wish List* is the third book in my miniseries, The Women of Dalton Ranch. In this story, the second Dalton twin gets to live out her greatest romance. I had a lot of fun writing this book because Daisy and Finn have such a playful and passionate relationship.

When Daisy and Finn—best friends and neighboring Texas ranchers—spend the days between Christmas and New Year's snowed in together, Finn sees her wish list. He can't fulfill her desire for a brief romance. Or can he? He doesn't do forever, but he can do temporary. He discovers that unexpected challenges can lead to a beautiful life he never dreamed possible.

I hope you enjoy *Her New Year's Wish List*. As always, thank you for reading!

Best wishes,

Makenna Lee

HER NEW YEAR'S
WISH LIST

MAKENNA LEE

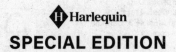

H Harlequin

SPECIAL EDITION

Harlequin®
SPECIAL
EDITION™

Recycling programs
for this product may
not exist in your area.

ISBN-13: 978-1-335-40215-8

Her New Year's Wish List

Copyright © 2024 by Margaret Culver

Harlequin Enterprises ULC
22 Adelaide St. West, 41st Floor
Toronto, Ontario M5H 4E3, Canada
www.Harlequin.com

Printed in Lithuania

MIX
Paper | Supporting
responsible forestry
FSC® C021394

Makenna Lee is an award-winning romance author living in the Texas Hill Country with her real-life hero and their two children, one of whom has Down syndrome and inspired her first Harlequin book, *A Sheriff's Star*. She writes heartwarming contemporary romance that celebrates real-life challenges and the power of love and acceptance. She has been known to make people laugh and cry in the same book. Makenna is often drinking coffee with a cat on her lap while writing, reading or plotting a new story. Her wish is to write stories that touch your heart, making you feel, think and dream.

Books by Makenna Lee

Harlequin Special Edition

The Women of Dalton Ranch

The Rancher's Love Song
Her Secret to Keep
Her New Year's Wish List

Home to Oak Hollow

A Sheriff's Star
In the Key of Family
A Child's Christmas Wish
A Marriage of Benefits
Lessons in Fatherhood
The Bookstore's Secret

Visit the Author Profile page
at Harlequin.com for more titles.

To Kitty.
Thank you for cheering me along on my writing journey.

Chapter One

"Is that a baby goat in your rowboat?"

With a hip bump, Daisy Dalton closed the door of her new sapphire-blue truck, zipped up her heaviest winter coat and looked past the three cowboys standing at the edge of the pond. Their arms were crossed over broad chests, and their heads were tilted in what she recognized as their thinking pose.

"Yep. That is in fact a baby goat." Finn Murphy glanced over his shoulder with a shrug and a half grin. He was the tallest and blondest of the brothers, with wavy strands brushing the tops of his ears below a black cowboy hat.

The ice-tipped blades of grass crunched under Daisy's boots as she joined them at the edge of the oval-shaped pond. This wasn't the first time she'd found them involved in something unexpected. "She's so tiny. Where in the world did you get a goat?"

"You'll have to ask our big brother about that," Jake said, and punched Finn's shoulder. Jake was the youngest Murphy brother, always quick with a comment and very outgoing.

"I didn't have a choice." Finn rubbed his fingers through his blond beard, which had grown thicker over the winter months. "Someone abandoned the goat at the feed store. The second we got home, she sprinted down the hill, hopped into the rowboat, and it slid down the frosty bank and launched into the pond before I could catch her. I've decided to name her Rascal."

"Seems like an appropriate choice." Daisy smiled at the man who had become one of her best friends. He was a tough as they come cowboy, but it didn't surprise her that Finn was the one who'd brought home the orphaned animal.

A gust of wind rustled the cluster of bare-branched trees that grew along the edge of the water, and the musical sound of tiny ice shards tinkled onto the rocks below. Sleet began to fall from the gray sky as the tiny brown-and-white goat jumped up onto the center bench seat, making the boat rock in the frigid water.

Daisy's heart sprang into her throat. "What if she falls into the water?"

"That's what I'm worried about," Finn said. "I'm hoping the wind will blow the boat to the edge of the pond."

As if the universe was laughing in his face, another gust blew the boat farther into the middle, but at least Rascal hopped down from the seat into the center of the boat and propped her chin on the side. The little animal was bleating excitedly and looking around as pleased as could be with her grand adventure.

"So...how are you going to get her back to shore?" Daisy asked the three brothers.

"I guess we need another boat," said Riley, the quiet middle brother who only talked when necessary. His extra deep voice was a low rumble in contrast to the goat's high-pitched bleating.

Daisy's long hair blew across her face, and she tugged her red stocking cap lower to cover more of her ears. As she watched Finn pace along the bank, an idea took shape. The two of them were always on the lookout for a challenge to issue to the other, and this was something he wouldn't be able to do. In one of his recent dares, she'd ended up with her butt in the mud, and it was payback time for Finn.

"Too bad there isn't anyone brave enough to swim out there and tow the boat back to shore," she said.

Three sets of blue eyes snapped in her direction.

"Are you offering?" Jake sat on the open tailgate of an old black truck and lifted his hat to brush back his dark blond hair.

"Absolutely not." She shivered at the mere idea of torturing herself in such a way. "You know I don't do cold water, but your big brother is always bragging about how he used to jump into the river in the middle of a Montana winter." Finn's playful scowl made her grin. He hated it when she came up with a dare that he couldn't complete.

"You don't think I'll do it?" Finn asked.

"Nope. I think you're going to drive next door to my ranch and borrow my boat."

He shrugged off his coat, tossed it over the truck bed and then started unbuttoning his flannel shirt. "Shows how much you know, Daisy Maisy," he said, using the nickname he'd given her.

This was a dare she would've refused and assumed he'd do the same, but she was getting a bad feeling. "You cannot actually mean to jump into that ice cold water."

"Sure I can." Now bare chested, he walked out onto the wooden dock, hung his shirt and his hat on one of the posts and pulled off his cowboy boots and socks.

Heat blossomed in her belly. She'd learned to think of Finn as a close friend who just happened to be good-looking, and her initial lust had been safely tucked away, but when he paraded his perfect male body like this… She sighed and shook her head.

I really need to start dating again.

Every once in a while, he did something that re-sparked her libido. He'd say something that made butterflies dance or he'd touch her in an innocent way, completely unaware of the tingles rippling across her skin.

His full-body shiver snapped her back to the danger of what he was doing. This could go wrong in a hurry, and it would be all her fault. Who was going to rescue him when he cramped up in the middle of the pond?

"Okay, you win. You don't have to turn yourself into a human Popsicle to prove how tough you are. I believe you swam in the ice-cold river as a kid."

"It's the quickest option to get the goat back to shore before she falls in." He started working on the top button of his jeans.

She spun to face Riley and Jake. "Guys, tell him not to do it."

They both shrugged, not appearing the least bit concerned.

When she turned back to Finn, he was standing at the end of the dock in a pair of black boxer briefs—his powerful physique framed by the gray winter sky. And it was quite glorious.

He glanced over his shoulder with a mischievous grin and then dove into the water.

"Finn!" She gasped and rushed out onto the dock, holding her breath until he surfaced and began swimming with long powerful strokes toward the boat. "Is he going to be all right?"

"He'll be fine." Riley stepped up beside her and handed

her a heavy wool blanket. "We always keep a few of these in the truck."

"Now I understand why." She'd always wondered if Finn kept the blankets there so he could take his dates out "stargazing" in the bed of his truck.

Finn grabbed the front of the rowboat and began towing it in. The goat peeked over the side, bleating noisily in-between attempts at trying to eat his hair.

As he reached the shallows, each step revealed chilled skin so taut across his muscular body that he resembled a marble statue. And with water droplets clinging to his blond beard and his breath pluming into the icy air with each huffed breath, he looked like a painting of a Viking warrior of old.

Shivering and scolding the noisy goat, he pulled the small boat onto dry land. "This is the thanks I get for saving your scrawny little butt?"

Daisy rushed forward with the blanket held open and wrapped it around his shoulders. "Crazy fool. I can't believe you did that."

His teeth chattered behind lips that were tinged blue. "Payback is g-going to be a b-b-bitch."

There was no doubt that she'd set herself up for something awful.

Riley scooped up the tiny animal before she could bolt again and tucked her into the front of his coat. "I'll take her back to the house." He started walking up the hill while Jake pulled the rowboat farther up the bank.

"Get in my truck. The heater is already running full blast." Daisy put a hand on Finn's back and urged him forward and was relieved when he didn't argue. "I'll grab your clothes."

Jake handed over Finn's coat. "Tell my brothers that I'm

driving down to the barn to put out a couple more bales of hay for the cattle."

"Be careful. It's icier than you think," she told him.

Daisy followed the path of Finn's striptease and put his hat on her head, her stocking cap making it fit and not slide down over her eyebrows like it normally did. Lifting his black flannel shirt, she caught the scent of his soap and cologne and brought it closer to her nose before she could stop herself. Why did he have to smell as good as he looked? Stepping around icy patches on the dock, she made her way carefully to his discarded jeans.

At least I don't have to pick up his underwear.

With her arms loaded, she made it back to her truck without incident, until she reached for the door handle. Her feet slipped in two different directions and his clothes tumbled to the ground. The only thing that saved her from going down completely was her one-handed grip on the door frame.

"Graceful as always," Finn said with a chuckle.

"Shut up, Jack Frost." Daisy still had a hold of one boot, and once she righted herself, she tossed it his way before collecting the rest of his belongings.

"Sorry I laughed. Are you okay?" he asked.

She scoffed. "You're not the least bit sorry about laughing at me."

"That might be true." He put the boot on the floorboard and leaned his face close to a heater vent. "Why did you come over this evening? I thought you were excited to have the house all to yourself while your niece and sister's families are away for the week."

"I am, but some of your mail was in my box again." She flicked an unpolished fingernail across an envelope sticking up from a cup holder. "It's postmarked from Montana. Maybe it's from one of your family members?"

"We don't have any relatives left in that part of the country." He scrubbed a hand roughly over his face.

Daisy wasn't sure if it was to warm up his skin or to brush away his past. He didn't like talking about his life in Montana, and she regretted bringing it up. "What are your plans for New Year's Eve? Hot date?"

"Jake wants to have a party and invite everyone we know, and not surprisingly, Riley wholeheartedly objects to a house full of people. But the bad weather and icy roads might prevent any kind of big celebration." He wiped water droplets from his hair with the blanket. "What about you? Got any big plans?"

"No. It will be a chill New Year's Eve for me." She didn't want to admit her lack of a date, and since he hadn't answered her question, maybe he didn't have one either. But that seemed so unlikely, and he'd no doubt have his choice of gorgeous dates by New Year's Eve. A hint of melancholy settled over her, and she sighed. She'd been looking forward to her time alone, but now…the idea of ringing in the new year all by herself wasn't as exciting as it had been only a few hours ago.

It only took a minute to drive up the hill from the pond to his house, and Finn Murphy's skin was prickling painfully as the heater began to thaw him from the outside in. He'd never been this cold. Ever. But letting Daisy know the extent of his misery after plunging into glacial water was out of the question.

When she grinned at him, he playfully scowled. "You lost. I took your dare and did what you thought I wouldn't. So, you're enjoying this more than you should be."

"Not as much as I would have if you'd kept your clothes *on*. Now I have to wash my eyes out."

He barked a laugh. "I've never had a woman wish I'd keep my clothes on."

"Okay, Casanova." She angled another heater vent in his direction. "I had such big plans to endlessly tease you when you refused to swim in an ice bath, but you foiled my evil plan."

"Don't mess with the master. My brothers learned that lesson years ago."

She parked beside the row of hawthorn bushes and turned off the engine. "I'll bring in your clothes and boots, so you don't drop your blanket."

"Good idea. We can't risk you getting another look at me without my clothes on," he said. "It's too cold to have you fainting like a wilting flower."

"Hey, my name might be flowery, but I'm…" Her voice trailed off as her brow crumpled. "Not."

Why had that made her good mood fall away? Did she wish she was more…flowery? She was pretty, but not turn-your-head-gorgeous. He'd only seen her in a dress a few times, and her face was usually free of makeup. She was more tomboy than feminine. But did she want to be seen differently? For some reason, anytime Daisy was sad, it made his chest tight.

It's just because I'm protective of her like I am with Riley and Jake.

He grimaced and instantly knew that was not the reason. She might not be some party girl he was dating, but he definitely did not put her in the sister category.

She moved his cowboy hat from her head to his. "Maybe this will keep you warm."

"You're such a giver." He grabbed the mail, took a deep breath and stepped from the warmth of the truck's cab.

"Holy hell." He hissed as his feet touched the ice-cold gravel and every step was like walking on a pile of Lego bricks.

Why the hell didn't I put my boots back on? This was yet another time he wasn't willing to admit a weakness. All that did was give people an invitation to use it against you.

The sounds of chaos met them before he'd even opened the front door of the sprawling one-story log ranch house he shared with his brothers. When the front door swung open, the scene that greeted them was his own doing. He'd been the one who brought another animal home. Their black dog was barking his head off at the baby goat who was bouncing across the back of their old sectional sofa. They seemed to be competing to see who was louder.

"Enough, Astro!" Riley knelt beside the dog. His deep voice could bring a rowdy room to attention, but he rarely used it at full power.

Daisy dropped Finn's things onto one of the recliners and scooped up the miniature goat. "You really do live up to your new name, don't you?" She laughed when Rascal headbutted her shoulder and then snuggled into her arms like it was nap time. When the animal was curled up, she was no bigger than a puppy.

Finn rushed across the cold hardwood floor of their living room to stand on the rug in front of the fireplace. Flames blazed in the stone hearth, and he flung open the wool blanket to let in the heat, but in his haste, he forgot he was holding the letter from Montana. The envelope slipped from his cold fingers and sailed right into the fire. The center blackened immediately, and the edges curled as they were caught in a flash of flames.

"Damn. I hope that wasn't important."

Daisy came up beside him with Rascal curled up in her arms. "Did you just burn that letter?"

"Not on purpose. For some reason, my fingers are too numb, and I couldn't hold on to it."

She winced. "I feel partially responsible for your discomfort, and I know you're—"

"A hero?" he suggested.

She smiled wide enough to show her one dimple, which was low on her right cheek. "I was going to say freezing, but now that you mention it, yes. I'm sure the goat will agree with your hero status." She snuggled the animal under her chin. "Do you have any idea what kind of goat she is? She seems smaller than other baby goats I've seen."

"She's an African Pygmy goat. The old farmer who brought her to the feed store said she was orphaned, and he didn't have time to supplement her food with bottle feeding." He shivered.

"Want me to start a hot bath for you? A long bubble bath can be so relaxing, and I'm planning to have one when I get home. It's the least I can do for you before I leave."

When she licked her lips, which were red from the cold, an image flashed in his mind. Daisy in the bathtub, wet and surrounded by a mound of bubbles. He squeezed his eyes closed. A flash like this had happened once before. His brain needed to get it together and knock it off.

Back when she'd been their boss, he'd had no choice but to keep things completely chill because he and his two brothers had needed the job on her horse ranch. Once they saved enough and bought Four Star Ranch next door, he briefly considered asking her out for a bit of fun, but Daisy Dalton was the girl next door type—both figuratively and literally—and his tastes ran more toward party girls who had no interest in anything serious. Plus Daisy was his first female friend, and she meant a lot to him. If he let his mind go down a dangerous path, it could ruin everything.

Daisy expected—and deserved—a committed relationship, and that's something that was not part of his DNA. He never did it on purpose, but he always ended up breaking hearts. He wasn't the kind of guy who settled down with one woman.

He cleared his throat. "I think I'll just get in the shower. Seems faster."

And safer.

Chapter Two

The winter ice storm raged across the whole Dallas Fort Worth area, but Daisy was safe inside the white farmhouse that had been in the Dalton family since it was built by her great-great-grandparents.

"Brrr. Thank heavens for central heating." Daisy sat on the wooden bench right inside of her front door and slipped off her boots. They were wet from the sleet that was quickly forming into slick sheets of ice, and her toes were numb from the below freezing temperature. She set them on a mat to protect the narrow-plank oak floor.

The walls of the wide entryway were eggshell white with an eclectic mix of artwork. Watercolor landscapes, black-and-white family photos in antique frames and a collection of McCoy pottery wall pockets holding dried flowers. The entryway led from the front door to the center of the house, where a staircase went up to the second floor. On each side of her were identical archways. To the left was a cozy living room with a fireplace. To the right was a dining room where she remembered family dinners and lively conversations with lots of laughter.

The jingle of the cat's collar reached her a moment before the white fluffball hopped onto her lap. "Hello, Lady. I hope you're ready for a cozy night indoors. There will be no sneaking out for a midnight hunt." Stroking Lady's long fur, Daisy stood with the purring animal in her arms and went down the center hallway past the stairs and into the kitchen for a hot drink.

She fed the cat and groaned at the stack of breakfast dishes in the sink. Instead of washing them right away, she opened a cabinet and moved aside her nephew's sippy cup to grab a mug. It was her sister's favorite pink one, but it was the biggest and Daisy often used it. While water heated for hot chocolate, she rinsed and put the dishes into the dishwasher. For the next five days she had the place all to herself.

Her identical twin and business partner, Sage Dalton De-Luca, was on a post-Christmas trip with her husband, their teenage daughter and baby girl. Her niece Lizzy, who also worked on the family horse ranch when she wasn't singing with the Fort Worth opera company, was with her husband and son visiting grandparents. Sage's family lived with her on the horse ranch when they weren't at their house in town, and her niece's new house was so close she could see it from the front windows. This led to the main farmhouse being a hub of activity with lots of people in and out on a regular basis, and she didn't mind a bit. It had once been just her and Sage on their ranch, and now having so much family around was wonderful, but she told herself that a few days alone was going to be good for her. A chance to recharge.

And she had big plans to start her evening with a long, hot bubble bath, and then complete control of the television remote and the freedom to eat junk food without judgment. She could even walk around the house in the nude if she wanted to—not that she'd ever do such a thing. But first, she wanted to make a list of goals, wishes and dreams for the new year. Lots of options had been spiraling around in her mind, and she wanted to get at least the important ones written down before her bath.

With her hot chocolate in hand, Daisy made her way to the living room and plugged in the Christmas tree lights so she could enjoy them for a little longer. The festive decorations they all loved so much would likely stay up until well into January, mostly because no one wanted to be the one to remove the decorations and pack it all up. The house was too quiet, so she also turned on the television. An old movie about a group of misfit cowboys was playing. She'd seen it many times but left it playing in the background.

Daisy grabbed a thick sheet of pale blue stationery and her favorite pen, then sat in her comfy blue velvet chair beside her sister's matching pink one to begin her list.

Daisy's New Year's Wish List

She'd been planning to make number one something really important, like donate to a children's charity or learn a new language, but after watching a few minutes of the movie and letting her mind drift into thoughts of real-life cowboys, she decided to start with things that were more fanciful and save the serious stuff for the end of her list. She glanced back at the TV just as one of the cowboys pulled his shirt over his head and revealed a killer physique, and she wrote down the first thing that came to her mind.

Sleep with a hot guy/Brief fun affair.

There was a tug low in her belly, but she rolled her eyes at her own line of thinking. She didn't just want some meaningless hookup. She wanted to fall in love and be loved in return.

On the TV screen, cowboys were stacking bales of hay, and it made her think of the Murphy brothers working around her ranch or theirs. The brothers had strikingly similar features, with big blue eyes, square jawlines and full mouths that smiled often. But none of them were dating options.

The thought of reentering the dating field once again came to mind. Her last date had been months ago and had been a disaster. A nice guy at the horse auction had asked her out, and she was starting to think she should stop giving him excuses and say yes.

Number two on her wish list really should be something with more substance, but before she could complete the thought about falling in love, the lights flickered, and she was plunged into darkness.

"Nooo." She groaned into the quiet, dark room. "Is this seriously happening?"

In the blink of an eye, all her plans disintegrated. Normally in a situation like this she could go out to the efficiency apartment behind the horse stable where a backup generator powered their high-tech horse facility, but the new to town and very cute veterinarian was temporarily living there until his new house was ready. Dr. Dillon Cameron was also a possible dating option, but going out with him while he was living on her property seemed like a recipe for trouble.

Maybe Lizzy's house, right across the fence, had electricity. She folded her list—that was something she didn't want anyone else to see—and slipped it into the back pocket of her comfy jeans and went to look out her front window. The outdoor security lights that usually shone across the metal roof of Travis and Lizzy's log home were dark. It was a good thing they had remained in Austin because having no electricity in an ice storm with a toddler would be no fun at all. But the lights at Finn's house glowed in the distance, sending out halos in the icy air.

Her phone rang, with the veterinarian's number appearing on the screen, and she answered. "Hi, Dillon."

"Is the electricity off up at the main house?" he asked.

"I'm afraid so. Do you know how to start the generator?"

"I do. I'll get it running and check all the horses."

"Thanks. I appreciate it."

"If it doesn't come back on soon, come stay out here in the apartment with me."

Her mouth dropped open. What was Dillon suggesting? Skipping a first date and going straight to sharing a bed, or an I'll-take-the-couch kind of thing? "I'll get back to you on that. I'm going to call the power company and see if I can get any answers. Let me know if you have any trouble with the generator."

"Will do, Daisy."

She got a recorded message about downed power lines, and because of the weather, they had no idea when they would be repaired. Her next call was to Finn.

He answered on the third ring. "Hey, Daisy. What's up?"

"I see that you have electricity on at your ranch."

"I take it this means that you don't."

"Sadly, I do not."

"At least you have a generator and an empty apartment behind the stable."

"It's not empty. Dillon moved into it yesterday. He'll be here until his house is ready."

"Dr. Cameron? You can't stay there with him," he said in a quick, sharp tone.

She held back a laugh. He sounded scandalized by the thought of her staying in the one-bedroom apartment with a man—even though she was in her midthirties. "Why not? It's a safe, warm option."

He was quiet for a few heartbeats. "Pack a bag and come over here. This isn't a night to be without power."

So much for a bubble bath and all her other leisurely plans. Instead of having a relaxing evening, she'd have three rowdy guys, a dog, a goat and the cat she'd have to take with her. "I guess you're right."

"Don't get out on the icy road. Come through the gate between our properties."

"Like I don't already know to do that? I always come that way even in good weather. First, I need to make sure everything is good in the stable and that Dillon has everything he needs." When you had horses that were worth as much as theirs, you had to take precautions.

"Dr. Cameron is a grown man. He'll be fine. Need my help with anything?"

"No, thanks. I'm a grown woman. I'll be fine," she said, mimicking his words with a chuckle. It was comforting to know he had her back, but his sudden papa bear protectiveness was also a bit entertaining. "I'll see you in a bit."

She packed a small suitcase, and tote bag of all the snacks she'd planned to hoard for herself. She'd be lucky if Finn, Jake and Riley didn't eat everything within an hour. She bundled up and rushed to her truck with first her bag and a litter box and then the cat inside a carrier. After double-checking that all was good at the stable, she drove over to Finn's.

When she arrived at Four Star Ranch, the sleet was coming down faster and the wind was whipping. The brothers kept the new truck in the garage, but there was no sign of their old black truck that was normally parked in front. Surely Jake wasn't still out working with the cattle. She walked in their front door to only the dim lighting of the fire, the television and the Christmas tree she'd helped them decorate. Finn was kicked back in one of the recliners with the dog at his feet and the goat asleep on his lap.

"Where are your brothers?"

He turned down the volume on the movie he was watching. "Both in town with women they're dating."

Warmth swirled inside her, and she pressed a hand to her stomach, willing away the butterflies caused by their seclusion. What was wrong with her? They were frequently alone. But something about this stormy-night setting made it feel like they were the only two people on earth. "So, it's just you and me here?"

"Plus a dog and a goat."

She lifted the cat carrier. "And one feline."

On cue, Astro got up and bounded over to sniff the cat. Lady hissed and made the carrier shake in Daisy's hand. The dog always wanted to play and never tried to hurt her, but the cat had other ideas. When Daisy opened the carrier, Lady hissed once more and then rapidly pranced away with her head held high and her fluffy tail swishing. Astro followed her into the kitchen.

She put her tote bag on the couch and opened it. "At least the snacks will last longer without Jake and Riley here."

"Please tell me you brought junk food?"

"I did." She put a bulging plastic grocery bag on the battered square coffee table.

Shifting the sleeping goat to the warm spot where he'd been sitting, Finn got up to rifle through the bag.

Daisy moved closer to his chair and laughed at the small animal wearing a child's diaper with a hole cut out for her little tail. "Where did you get a diaper?"

"We have a couple different sizes of them for when Rose and Davy are here with their fathers when y'all have your ladies' nights," he said about her niece and nephew. "I put one on the goat after cleaning up a puddle. I also looked it up, and apparently, you can potty train a goat."

"That's good news."

"I wrote down the important points, and I can start working on it tomorrow. But for tonight, I'm going to put Rascal in the big dog crate."

"Good idea." She sighed and flopped onto the threadbare couch.

He pulled out a bag of chips from the grocery bag and sat in the corner of the sectional couch. "What's wrong? Did you not get your bubble bath?"

"No, I didn't."

"I have that huge tub in my bathroom that I never use, but you can use it if you want to."

"Too bad I didn't bring any bubble bath."

"The best I can do is dish soap."

She laughed. "I think I'll pass, but I will take you up on using the tub."

"My bathroom door doesn't close all the way and needs to be fixed, but no one will bother you."

She paused on her way out of the room. "Don't eat all the food while I'm gone."

Finn sprawled across the couch with the chips and grinned. The bag crinkled as he opened it. "I'll try, but no promises."

"Remind me why were friends?"

"Because I'm so much fun and totally irresistible."

Daisy rolled her eyes—even though his assessment was true. "Says you."

His ego was big enough without her confirming it. Resisting Mr. Irresistible would remain at the top of her list.

Daisy rolled her suitcase down the hallway, the wheels softly bumping over the hand-scraped hardwood floor.

She peeked into the youngest brother's room and shook her head. Jake was definitely the messy one of the bunch. Clothes, boots and random items were tossed across his bed and most pieces of furniture. The next bedroom was filled with workout equipment and the third was Riley's tidy room and the one she chose. She glanced toward the open door at the end of the hallway. Being the oldest, Finn had claimed the largest room with the attached bathroom.

In Riley's room, she put her suitcase on the navy spread of his neatly made bed and unzipped it. Her cosmetics bag was bulging and heavier than she remembered, and she was pleased to find the products her sister had added. And luckily, one of the little bottles was cherry blossom scented bubble bath.

"Thank you, Sage." Her twin was so good about restocking the travel-sized products for both of them.

She took what she needed into Finn's room, where there was not much more than the king-size bed without a headboard, one nightstand and a dresser that didn't match. One wall was made of logs that had been stripped of their bark and varnished with a satin finish and had a row of tall windows with an excellent view of the ranch. Instead of curtains, several sheets were tacked up above the windows and held back with string. He'd stripped off the floral wallpaper from the other three walls and left them in great need of paint.

The bathroom had a granite countertop in shades of gray around the double sinks, sage-colored walls and a large sunken Jacuzzi tub beside the walk-in shower. It was uncluttered with nothing more than a toothbrush and tube of paste in a plastic cup. She pulled the door, but as he'd warned, it wouldn't close all the way.

She started filling the large tub and poured a generous

amount of bubble bath into the running water. After undressing and twisting her hair up into a knot on the top of her head so it wouldn't get wet, she eased into the deliciously scented hot water and sighed as her muscles began to relax. But every time she closed her eyes, she pictured Finn standing on the end of the dock in a pair of fitted boxers. He was perfectly formed. Not like a bodybuilder who spent all day in the gym, but rather sculpted from hard work and good genetics.

She'd only been in the tub for five minutes when the bathroom door squeaked open a crack and she sucked in a breath, but it was only her cat prancing into the room. It wasn't uncommon for Lady to sit with her or her sister as they bathed, but Daisy wasn't in her own bathroom and the thought of someone coming in made her jumpy.

What would she do if Finn opened the door? Yell at him to get out or… She shivered. Or invite him to join her?

She groaned and blew out a long slow breath. Starting her New Year's list had put foolish ideas into her head.

She reached out to let the cat bat at a pile of bubbles on the palm of her hand. "Are those other two rowdy animals getting on your nerves, Lady?"

Before the cat could even meow her irritation, the door burst all the way open and banged against the wall. Daisy gasped and sunk deeper into the mound of bubbles as the dog and goat bounded into the small space.

"Are you kidding me?"

The goat spotted her and kicked up her back hooves as she headed her way.

"No! Stop!" But it was too late. The goat gave one final hop and plunged into the tub. A wave of soapy water hit her in the face with a splat, but Daisy quickly scooped her up to make sure her head was above the water. Rascal had a mound of bubbles on her tan-and-white head, and if a goat could smile, that's exactly what this little girl was doing.

"Astro, get out here," Finn called from his bedroom. He appeared in the open doorway but came to a sudden halt, covered his eyes and turned around. "Sorry, Daisy. I promised no one would bother you, and you didn't get more than a few minutes to yourself."

She was too busy holding on to the wiggly creature. She was far enough under the bubbles that he couldn't see her, but she appreciated his discretion. She yelped as the goat attempted to jump from her arms up onto her shoulder. Daisy's butt slipped across the bottom of the tub, her head went under, and one leg curled beneath her as the other went straight up into the cool air above the bubbles. She came up sputtering and wiped her face with her free hand.

She met Finn's eyes right as her soggy topknot of hair flopped over her forehead, and he burst into laughter. With the wily animal clutched against her, she tossed her head to flip back her hair and laughed along with him when the goat sneezed.

"Get the dog out of here, and I'll deal with this one."

With his gaze averted but his chest still shaking with laughter, he picked up the dog and left her to her ruined bath.

With one arm curled around Rascal to keep the goat from splashing her in the face, Daisy pulled the plug to let the water out. "You are on the naughty list, girlfriend."

Rascal nuzzled her cheek and tried to nibble on her ear. "Stop that, silly girl."

The water drained quickly, so she stood, grabbed a towel and wrapped it around herself before getting another and lifting the animal from the remaining water. She bundled her up so only her head was visible. When Rascal was basically dry, she carried her to the bathroom door.

"Finn," she yelled. "Come get this little beasty."

"Coming."

"Rascal, the next time you want a bath, I better not be in it." She kissed the top of her head that now smelled of cherry blossoms, put her on the bedroom floor and closed the bathroom door the best she could.

"Come here right now," Finn said from the other side of the door. "I couldn't figure out why anyone would leave you behind, but now I'm starting to suspect I know the reason. You're a handful and a half for someone who's smaller than Daisy's cat." The animal bleated in response. "But you do smell better now. Kind of like…flowers."

Daisy sniffed her own hair as she studied herself in the mirror. Even with her best intentions to keep it dry, it was dripping wet.

What does Finn see when he looks at me?

Her hair needed a trim, and she didn't pamper her skin like her sister did, but maybe she should start. She didn't wear a lot of makeup like most of his dates. Mascara and lip balm were her go-to items. She didn't wear the high heels or short skirts he favored. She wasn't Finn's type at all. But she had his true friendship, and that was worth protecting.

Finn might be good-looking, but he was not an option for the hot guy who could help fulfill number one on her list. He would laugh his head off if she suggested sleeping together and would probably think she was pulling a prank on him. It was clear that he wasn't into her in that way. Sure, he had a flirty nature, but he was that way with every adult female, even if they were ninety years old.

Lady came out from her hiding place behind a wicker laundry basket and brushed against her legs.

"It's been a very eventful day, hasn't it, girl?"

She dressed in the new pajamas her sister had given her for Christmas and brushed out her long blond hair. But when she picked up the tubes of pink lip gloss and mascara—also courtesy of Sage—she stopped herself. There was absolutely no reason to put on makeup for Finn Murphy. It was clear that he thought of her as a buddy, or worse, like a family member.

She tossed the tubes back into her cosmetics bag and marched toward the living room.

Chapter Three

When Daisy came into the living room dressed in a black tank top and a pair of fuzzy red pajama pants covered with pink hearts and lip prints, Finn smiled and grabbed the bag of chocolate candy from the coffee table. He leaned back against the couch cushions. With her wet hair and bare feet, she looked way younger than midthirties. Sometimes he forgot she was five years older than him.

"That was way more entertaining than when you almost slipped getting into the truck." He flashed her a wide grin.

She held out her arms and curtsied. "Happy to be the evening's entertainment."

"Somehow…that's not what I pictured you sleeping in."

"Well, now I have to know. What *did* you picture?"

An image popped into his head. Daisy naked with her long limbs stretched out on soft sheets. Heat surged through his body. Although the moment had been brief, when she'd popped up in the water after being dunked, he'd seen most of her breasts. Only clinging bubbles had preserved some of her modesty. He rubbed his eyes and hoped his beard would hide the heat creeping onto his cheeks.

He had to say something before she guessed where his wayward thoughts had gone. "I'm thinking you wear one of those head-to-toe, long-sleeved granny nightgowns."

"For your information, those are very comfortable." She

snatched the chocolate candy out of his hand and fished around in the bag.

She was no doubt looking for her favorite dark chocolates and was going to be so irritated when she discovered that he'd hidden all of them. "I gave Rascal a bottle and put her in the dog crate." He motioned toward the fireplace where the dog was stretched out alongside the crate.

"Wow. You got that done fast. I put my things in Riley's room because he's the neat freak." She sat on the couch, tucked up one foot and put the other on the coffee table.

"Good call. Picking up after himself is not one of Jake's strong points. When we interrupted you, I couldn't help but notice the bubbles. Did you end up using dish soap?"

"No. I found a bottle my sister put in my suitcase. Hey, where are all the dark chocolates?" She shot him a thunderous glare that made her look like a disgruntled little girl.

He grabbed his drink from the side table and took a sip to keep from laughing. "You know I don't eat the dark ones. Maybe they messed up at the candy factory and forgot to put any in this bag."

"What did you do, Finnigan?"

"You know that's not my name. It's just plain old Finn."

"You're trying to change the subject. Where'd you put them?"

"They're around." He circled his hand to encompass the whole room. "Somewhere."

Her sigh was long and overly dramatic. "I guess this is payback for your cold swim. At least I won't eat them all at once. Aha." She leaned forward to grab a foil-wrapped chocolate that he'd hidden under a remote control.

"Want to watch a movie?"

"Sure. Let's watch that classic holiday movie we started the other day."

Daisy fell asleep thirty minutes into the movie. She was curled up on one end of the couch with her head on a green pillow. He'd always considered her pretty in a girl-next-door kind of way. She wasn't all made up and pushed up and overtly sexy like most of the women he dated, but with firelight flickering on her ivory skin and her full lips relaxed in sleep, she was very attractive.

Daisy stretched out her legs and her feet pushed against his thigh. For a woman her height, her feet were small, high arched and narrow. For some reason he was surprised to see her toenails painted a shimmery red with silver snowflakes on her big toes. Her sister must have talked her into a holiday pedicure because he'd never seen them painted more than a barely there pink, and she never painted her short, neat fingernails.

He couldn't resist running the pad of his thumb back and forth across the sole of her foot.

Her toes spread, and then she jerked her foot away. "Sage, I don't want to wear high heels," she mumbled in her sleep.

He grinned, finding it unsurprising that she'd say that and fitting that she talked in her sleep. He had a thing for a pair of long legs in sky-high heels. He'd only seen Daisy in heels a few times, whereas her twin sister wore them often.

He yawned and turned off the TV. "Daisy, time to go to bed."

She tucked her hands under her cheek. "Later. I'm not hungry."

He chuckled. Her sleep talking was something he could have some fun with. There was no telling what information he might learn and be able to use later. He curled his fingers around her foot and used his thumb to knead the high arch, and this time, she didn't pull away. Daisy moaned and arched her back in a way that made his stomach flip.

"So-o-o good."

When she sighed, long and breathy and sweet, he was hit with an urge to discover what other spots gave her pleasure. He jerked his hand away before he could slide it under the leg of her fuzzy pants.

What is going on with me?

Daisy was his friend. The first real female friend he'd ever had. She was his next-door neighbor for life—not the next woman whose heart he'd no doubt break if anything happened between them.

Picking her up off the couch and carrying her to bed was completely out of the question. Especially if she made one of those moaning sounds that made his body tighten. Finn stood and linked his fingers behind his head, backing slowly away from the surprisingly tempting female curled up on his couch.

He never meant to make women cry, but it too often happened, usually when they discovered he was not kidding about never marrying or having kids. The revolving door of people in his childhood home, plus the times he and his brothers been left alone to fend for themselves, had taught him many hard-earned lessons. He'd seen too many examples of the many ways relationships went wrong.

His friendship with Daisy was important and had to be protected, because if he let romance enter the picture, she would want more than he had to give. It would end badly, and then he'd have to share a fence line with a woman who hated him. He shook his head, pulled a blanket off the recliner and covered her before heading to his room. She was the kind of woman who expected—and deserved—a committed relationship.

Continuing to think of her as a buddy was the only way to protect both of them.

* * *

Shadows moved in a fitful dance across the ceiling every time the wind blew the trees outside Finn's bedroom window. His insides felt as rattled as the branches, and sleep wouldn't come because he couldn't stop thinking about his best friend Daisy. When he'd offered her dish soap for her bubble bath, his brain had created an image of her in the tub. Like a muted, fuzzy watercolor that left a lot to the imagination.

But getting a real-life glimpse of her in a mound of bubbles had put a clear, vibrant picture in his head. One he couldn't shake. He kept replaying the way that one long leg had popped up into the air when the naughty goat dunked her. She'd come up sputtering but had laughed along with him. Even with the splashing, noise and complete chaos, he'd seen enough to add the word sexy to a description of his best friend.

This is not good. Not good at all.

He considered stepping out into the freezing night air for a blast of cold to clear his thoughts, but he'd had enough of being frozen after his icy dip in the pond.

With his door cracked open, he'd heard Daisy go to bed shortly after him. She was probably once again sleeping soundly. But he couldn't. He got out of bed and went to check on the baby goat. Rascal saw him and headbutted the door of the crate.

"Are you hungry, little girl?"

He unlatched the door, and Rascal bounded out, bouncing in a circle around him and causing Astro to get up from his bed in a corner of the kitchen and join in on the fun. He tried to shush them before they woke Daisy but wasn't having much luck. He grabbed a bottle of the milk replacement he'd mixed up earlier, picked up the baby goat and carried her into the living room.

* * *

Loud barking and Rascal's answering high-pitched calls had awakened Daisy. For a couple of minutes, she'd stayed perfectly still, hoping they would settle down.

Lady had been asleep at her feet but was now trying to work her way under Daisy's pillow as if that would protect her from the chaos.

"All right, scaredy-cat, I'll go check it out." Before she could open the bedroom door, the noise died down. She was about to go back to bed, but Finn's voice stopped her. She tiptoed down the hallway and stood in the shadows to watch him kick back in a recliner with the goat.

Rascal bounced from one of Finn's thighs to the other, and he winced. He adjusted her on his lap, and she practically attacked the bottle. "I hope you plan to sleep through the rest of the night," he said to the goat.

Astro hopped onto the couch, turned in a few circles and then settled down to sleep.

"What am I going to do with you, Rascal? What are the chances that someone left you at the feed store right before I get there? I think they must've seen a sucker coming."

The tiny animal butted her head against his arm.

"We need to have a conversation about this potty train-ing thing. Daisy brought a litter box for the cat, and to-morrow we are going to try the technique I read about. I'll make a deal with you. I'll wake up in the night to feed you if you promise to be easy to house-train."

Daisy stayed where she was and watched the tender scene. He claimed he didn't want to be a father, but from her point of view, he had the skills and instincts needed to be a really good parent.

Now, he just needed to realize that for himself.

Chapter Four

The baby goat bounced around in a patch of morning sunlight that was streaming in across the terra-cotta tile floor, and then she hopped up onto the low kitchen windowsill.

Daisy followed her and looked out at the backyard. "Oh my gosh. Finn, come look. It's snowing. Everything is a sea of white."

He joined her at the window with a mug of steaming coffee. "It sure is."

She took the coffee from his hand and took a sip. "Why aren't you more excited? It's so beautiful."

"Because I grew up in Montana and have seen more than my share of snow."

"Well, for a Texas girl, even an inch is exciting." He barked a laugh, and she smacked his shoulder, sloshing a bit of coffee onto the floor. "Your mind is in the gutter."

"I'm a thirty-two-year-old single guy," he said in way of explanation.

She wasn't actually bothered by his humor. It was just fun to mess with him. "Guess it comes with having a guy as a best friend."

"Are you done with my coffee yet?"

"I suppose." She took one more sip and handed it over with a grin. "It's your own fault for taking your coffee with heavy cream just like I do."

The cat ran over to lick the milky coffee off the floor, then hissed and ran away when the dog nosed in on her territory.

"I think you just enjoy taking my stuff," he said. "My coffee and my favorite T-shirt. And always my french fries."

"If I order my own, I'll eat too many of them."

The oven timer rang, and he crossed the room to pull biscuits from the oven. "Come eat your breakfast, and then I'll take you out to play in the snow, Daisy Maisy."

Once they'd fed themselves and the animals, they attempted the first suggested steps for house training a goat—with little success. Daisy dressed in layers, and they both bundled up before going out into the cold, crisp morning air. But Finn had refused her suggestion to wear a stocking cap and insisted his winter cowboy hat was enough.

Astro darted past them and barked at Rascal when she attempted to hop onto his back. Her cat tiptoed onto the snow and then darted back into the house, wanting no part of the unusual conditions.

Daisy tipped her face up and let snowflakes land on her cheeks. "You have to admit that this is beautiful."

"It's nice. This is the first time I've seen Four Star Ranch covered in snow."

"Over my lifetime, there have been a number of times it has snowed here, but it's rare enough to be special." Daisy stuck her finger down into the snow, then looked at the level of white on her red glove. "Looks like it's about an inch so far."

The goat and dog were darting back and forth across the yard and didn't seem the least bit concerned about the cold.

While she admired the snowy landscape, he scooped up enough snow to make a snowball. "Be careful walking. There's still ice under the snow."

"I will." She carefully lay down on the ground and swept out her arms and legs to make a snow angel.

"Enjoy it while you can. The temperature will be dropping again in the next few hours, and more ice is expected," he said. "With our horses in your stable during the storm, the cattle are the only animals that need tending on my ranch. Without my brothers here, I could use your help, if you don't mind."

"Of course I'll help you. Where do we start?"

"First, I have to get feed from the barn and drive it out to the pasture. And I'll probably have to break the ice on the water tanks, so remind me to grab the sledgehammer from the barn."

"After I help you with the cattle, I need to go over to my ranch. Dillon is there to watch over the horses, but I still want to check on him."

"You want to check on *him*? Shouldn't he be able to handle it?"

She bit her lip to hide a grin. If she wasn't mistaken, Finn sounded a little...jealous. But it had to be her imagination. "It's the first time Dillon has looked after my animals, and I want to make sure everything is good. And make sure he is comfortable in the apartment," she added just to get his reaction.

He made a sound in his throat. "Since my horses are there too, I should go with you."

After Astro and Rascal were back inside the warm house, they got into his truck and headed for the barn. To keep from sliding on any patches of ice, he drove slowly along the dirt road. When she opened the big sliding door, he backed inside the barn, and they put bags of feed into the bed of the vehicle.

"Daisy, will you drive so I can hop in the back when we get out there and pour the feed in the troughs?"

"Sure." She got in on the driver's side and drove out to the pasture where the cattle were wintering.

Wire fencing was stretched between cedar posts, and it had a large section of one corner walled off with corrugated metal walls. It blocked the cold north wind and had a roof to keep the rain off. Most of the Black Angus herd was gathered in that corner, munching on hay and waiting for their morning feeding. The mooing started the second they spotted the truck. Daisy drove very slowly beside the long metal feed trough that stretched across the front of the windbreak, and Finn poured in the feed.

She smiled when she saw Finn pulling his scarf up to cover his exposed ears. He was a tough as they come cowboy on the outside, but at the heart of him, more and more every day she was discovering a sensitive side. A part of himself he kept so carefully hidden around most people.

From what she had pieced together, she had a strong feeling he was guarding a wounded part of himself. Protecting it from more damage. The tough guy swagger was his armor.

He jumped down from the truck bed and got in on the passenger side. "Pull over there and wait for me while I break up the ice on top of their water."

She pulled forward. "I can help you."

"There's only one sledgehammer, and it won't take me long."

"If you insist, but don't say I ever shy away from the hard stuff." A tingle zipped across her skin as the words "hard stuff" made her think of his bare chest. She hadn't meant for it to sound sexual, but he'd no doubt be unable to pass up the opportunity for a comeback.

"No one can say that you shy away. It would be untrue to say that about Daisy Dalton." His smile was genuine, and his tone was serious, without a hint of teasing.

The sincerity of his comment was so unexpected that she didn't know what to say. She'd totally been expecting his usual style comment—as if she was one of the guys.

When she put the truck in Park, he got out and retrieved the sledgehammer from the back.

As he swung it high above his head and down to crack the ice, she was once again taken back to the moment he'd emerged from the pond. The Viking warrior moment. But today, dressed in flannel, denim and leather and wielding a hammer the size of an axe, it brought to mind lumberjacks.

Why does he have to be so damn good-looking?

She just needed to set her mind to other contenders, and everything would be fine. Dr. Dillon Cameron came to mind. He was tall and sturdily built with dark hair and structured features, and although he could look slightly intimidating, his frequent grin gave away his kindness and fun personality. And judging from his recent behavior, he certainly seemed interested in exploring what could be between them. She had to admit that she was intrigued.

More and more, she'd been thinking about asking the handsome veterinarian out to dinner, but something always stopped her. She hated the thought that somewhere deep inside she was holding herself back because of Finn. When they got to her place, she would pull Dillon aside and talk to him and see if he sparked anything inside her. Any little thing that could catch her attention enough to make her forget about something happening with Finn.

Smoke curled from the little chimney off the rear of the apartment attached to the stable. Finn knew the veterinarian was staying there, and he hoped he would stay put and not come out to talk to them. He didn't dislike the man. There was just something about the way Dillon was extra attentive with Daisy that bothered him.

I'm being ridiculous.

As they went into the high-tech stable on Dalton Ranch, Finn blinked to adjust to the dim lighting that was necessary to save on the pull on the generator. The scent of hay and horses greeted them, and several horses stuck their heads out of their stalls and whickered.

"Hello, my beauties." Daisy grabbed the red treat bucket and stopped at Titan's stall to stroke his long sleek neck. The stallion was their sought-after stud horse whose breeding capabilities had financed this stable and led to Dalton Ranch becoming famous and extremely profitable.

The high ceiling was vaulted with heavy timber framing and lighted fans that were fancy enough to be in a house. The large stalls along one side of the barn had solid wooden walls of horizontal boards between them so the horses could not see one another. The opposite side's stalls had smooth, round metal bars on the top half of the walls so the horses could look across to see other horses.

The aisle down the middle was red bricks laid in a herringbone pattern that matched Daisy's patio at the back of the farmhouse. Most stalls had a door that led to an outdoor area that was half covered by a roof so the horses could choose sun or shade while getting fresh air. But with horses that were worth as much money as these, the danger of one of the animals slipping on ice was too risky to let them outside until the storm cleared.

Finn walked over to his horse, Maverick, and rubbed the heart-shaped white spot right in the center of his brown forehead. "We'll get you back to our place as soon as the storm is over, big guy. You're much better off here than in our drafty old barn."

While he was more than happy for the Dalton twins' success, he couldn't help but compare the way he and his brothers struggled to make ends meet on their own ranch. Daisy looked his way with her usual happy smile before moving to the next stall. Something weird shifted inside his chest. Why was her smile suddenly affecting him in an unusual way? He took a deep breath and glanced upward while counting to ten.

Daisy went farther down the aisle while he stayed at his horse's stall.

A door closed behind him, and Finn turned to see pretty boy veterinarian Dr. Dillon Cameron coming from the back door that led to the apartment. He walked past the tack room and raised a hand in greeting.

"Morning." Finn nodded. He had no problem with the other man. He'd never been anything but nice and respectful as far as he could see, but the way he looked at Daisy made his teeth ache.

Daisy came from the far end of the stable, past him and headed straight toward Dr. Cameron. "Good morning, Dillon. "How's everything going here?"

"Great. The stalls have been cleaned and everyone is fed according to the list you gave me. But I do have bad news about the electricity. I called and they said a bunch of lines are down along with other issues, so it will probably be a couple more days without power."

"That's a bummer."

For some reason, Finn wasn't upset by the news. No electricity meant Daisy would need to continue staying with him. At his house. But it was only because he'd be lonely with his brothers not there. At least that was the excuse he was going to stick with.

She spread her arms. "This building is insulated enough that the horses will be okay even if we run out of fuel for the generator, but what about you?"

Dillon braced a hand high up on the wall and grinned at her. "I'll be fine. The wood-burning stove in the apartment heats it up nicely, and it makes me feel like I'm at a secluded cabin in the mountains. And the offer to stay in the apartment with me still stands."

She blushed and nibbled one corner of her full lower lip. "I'll keep that in mind. I really appreciate you being here 24-7 with the horses."

"Not a problem. It's part of our agreement in lieu of rent."

Finn couldn't help but wonder what the rest of the agreement entailed. His stomach tightened without warning, and he had a strange urge to growl. He did *not* like his own reaction.

What is this feeling? Jealousy?

Maybe it was, because he didn't like the way the other man received her sexy smile. One that he did not. When it came to Daisy, this sudden shift of emotions was a new phenomenon.

I need to get out of here.

"Daisy, I'm going to go get the milk and other perishables from your refrigerator," he said on his way out the small side door where they'd come in. Cold wind hit him when he stepped outside, and snow was once again coming down in soft flurries. Daisy was going to love it.

"Finn, wait for me," she called after him, and promptly slid on a patch of ice but caught her balance just in time.

"Nice save. I thought maybe you'd decided to stay with the doc."

On her way to the passenger side, she ran her gloved hand across the snow-dusted hood of his truck. "Trying to get rid of me already?"

No! His brain answered, but thankfully he had better control of his mouth. "Not yet, Daisy Maisy."

Chapter Five

The second they got back inside the ranch house, Daisy built a fire while Finn worked on house-training the goat. She sat on the geometric patterned rug in front of the stone hearth, rubbed her hands together and shivered when the fire's heat reached her chilled body. Even with the central heating unit running, it was having trouble keeping up with the unusually cold conditions. The fireplace was a bonus, and the giant stack of logs on the back porch would last for weeks if necessary. Courtesy of a lumberjack cowboy who she knew looked good while swinging an axe.

She grinned at the mental image and wrapped her arms around her drawn-up knees, but then she frowned.

Her little experiment in the stable to see if she could create a spark with Dillon had been a failure. No lust or unbridled excitement had been generated by the handsome man with thick dark hair and moody brown eyes. Not even when he'd touched her arm and dropped his voice to a low rumble.

The whole time she'd been talking to Dillon and searching for something between them, she'd felt Finn's eyes on them. Returning to her over and over, the heat of his gaze making her blush. She'd also felt a little thrill because Finn had seemed—maybe jealous wasn't the right word—

bothered by her full attention on another man. And she hadn't even been flirting.

The good-looking vet who appeared to want more than friendship with her was not the one who gave her tingles in all the right places. Not the one who gave her foolish fantasies about skinny-dipping in the summer and what it might be like to be in his arms and—

"I'm starving."

She jumped and clasped a hand to her heart at the sound of Finn's voice.

He quirked up an eyebrow. "What's got you so jumpy?"

She ignored his question. It's not like he knew what she was thinking about. "I'm hungry too. Let's go see what our options are."

Because it was suddenly too hot in front of the fireplace.

They reheated bowls of nine bean soup they'd grabbed from her refrigerator and sat at Finn's round kitchen table. It was a well-used chunky piece with four chairs from several different eras in time. A cane-back chair was older than the table, while a diner-style metal one across from it was flanked by two swivel chairs meant for an office. The mismatched grouping was positioned in front of a bay window that looked out over Four Star Ranch. Just looking at the snowy view made her happy.

"What should we do for the rest of the day?" he asked.

"Good question. Too bad we can't get out on the icy road."

"Where is it you want to go in weather like this?"

"Well, your bedroom is in serious need of painting, and a trip to the hardware store for supplies would have given us a project to work on."

"I already have paint. It's in the garage."

She put her spoon in her empty bowl. "No kidding?"

"I bought it a few weeks ago along with brushes and stuff."

"Excellent. I'm up for painting. What do you think?"

"I'm not turning down your help."

After they finished eating, she went with him to help get everything from the garage. A wooden workbench ran along one wall with large tools neatly lined up and smaller ones hung on the pegboard behind it.

"Does Riley organize your tools?"

"How did you know?" he said with a chuckle.

"Just an educated guess."

"If you'll grab those two bags of supplies, I'll get the paint." He carried a can of paint in each hand and a roll of plastic sheeting under one arm.

"What color did you pick?" she asked as she followed him back inside through the laundry room.

"I don't remember."

The outer log wall wouldn't need paint, but the other three walls were made of Sheetrock, and they were in desperate need of attention. He pried open a can and let paint drip off the lid and back into the can.

Her nose wrinkled. "Finn, you cannot paint your bedroom that color. It looks like mustard."

"I like mustard."

"On your walls? I'm sorry, but this is the color of a spoiled condiment. Did you pick it out?"

"Not exactly. You know that rack in the paint section where you can get really cheap paint that's been mixed but no one bought?"

She laughed. "That explains it. And you have two cans of this unfortunate color?"

"No, that one is different." He pointed at the other can by the bathroom door. "It's light gray."

"That sounds much better. You were planning to use two different colors in here?"

He shrugged. "A couple different colors sound better than the way it looks since I stripped off the wallpaper. And what's the worst that can happen? I have to repaint it? I have two more colors still in the garage. Want me to get them?"

"Yes, please. We'll see if we can salvage this project." While he was out of the room, she tuned the radio on his dresser to a country station and hummed along with the number one song of the week.

He came back into the room and put two more cans of paint on the bedroom floor beside the gray. "Check these out and see if any of them meet your strict standards, Daisy Maisy."

She knelt beside him and looked at the lids, which had a smear of paint indicating the color. One was a blue that was a bit too bright for a man's bedroom. The other was a light shade of green. "These three are way better than the mustard. That's for sure."

"What color do you suggest?" he asked.

"I have an idea. One can isn't really enough to paint all three walls, but if we mix two colors, we might be able to make something nice. Do you have some disposable plastic cups we can use to test out a few different options?"

"I have red plastic cups in the pantry."

"Perfect."

Once they had several options mixed, they painted a swatch of each color on the wall, then stood back to look at them. She tilted her head to catch the light in different ways. "I like the gray mixed with the blue. It reminds me of the Texas sky right before a storm."

"I agree," he said. "But where can I use the mustard paint, Ms. Designer?"

"In very small doses. Maybe the barn or the back side of one of the wooden fences."

He laughed. "Damn. You really hate that color."

"Hey, I'm just being honest with you."

They scooted the furniture into the middle of the room and laid down plastic. He found a bucket, and they mixed the color they'd chosen. She started with a brush and painted around all the edges and in the corners, while he used a roller on the center of the walls.

"You already have paint in your hair," he said.

"Of course I do. Maybe I'll just claim it's the new fashion. That's the kind of daring thing Maleficent would do."

"The Angelina Jolie character in that movie you made me watch?" he asked.

She chuckled. "Yes. But it actually started with the animated version of *Sleeping Beauty*. You know how people talk about the angel on one shoulder giving good advice and the devil sitting on the other? Well, Sage and I saw that in a movie when we were about ten, and we were also really into *Sleeping Beauty* at the time, so we named our angel and devil after the movie characters."

He dipped his roller into the paint tray. "That's pretty clever. I can't say that I've ever thought much about what mine would be."

"Probably a cowboy dressed in white and one in black."

"I wear a lot of black."

She pointed her brush at him. "What does that say about you?"

He let his smile grow. "That I'm the fun one."

A couple of hours later, Finn stood back to survey their work while Daisy was on her hands and knees touching up a spot above the baseboard. The way her curvy bottom swayed from side to side along with the beat of the music was very distracting—in a good way. His eyes moved to the tray of paint beside her, and he couldn't resist. The tight, faded denim stretched across her butt became an irresistible canvas. He quietly knelt beside the paint tray and dipped the palms of both hands into the blue-gray paint. In one swift movement, he pressed two handprints to the denim. One on each cheek.

She stiffened and froze, then shot a startled look over her shoulder. She gaped at his paint-covered palms. "Finn! What did you do?"

He shrugged and walked into the bathroom to wash his hands. "It had to be done."

"You're lucky these aren't my favorite pair." She followed him into the bathroom and gasped at her reflection. "Why didn't you tell me I have paint on my face too?"

"That part was not me." He held up his wet hands in surrender. "I swear."

"I think this is a good excuse to leave you with the cleanup while I get to take a shower."

"I suppose that's fair." His mouth trembled with the urge to laugh.

She shooed him out the second his hands were dry. The door shuddered against the frame as she tried to force it closed. "Your next project should be to fix this door," she called from the other side.

"Hand out your jeans and I'll take care of them."

A minute later, the door opened enough that her arm slipped through, jeans dangling from two fingers by a belt loop.

Daisy was holding a towel across the front of her body, but obviously didn't realize he could see her reflection in the mirror behind her. The sight of her nicely proportioned bare backside made his mouth go dry.

Without his brain's permission, his eyes took in her

beauty. Long blond hair trailed halfway down her back, almost to the graceful curve where her waist met her hips. She might have only one dimple on her face, but now he knew she had two more low on the small of her back. And long legs, toned from riding a horse.

He stood there like a dummy as she closed the door and cut off his view. All that feminine beauty had been hiding under the denim and T-shirts.

A very unhappy meow and hiss followed by barking pulled him from his thoughts, and he rushed out into the hallway and followed the cat and dog into the living room.

"You two, knock it off." He draped her jeans over a ladder back chair by the fireplace.

Astro trotted over to him and sat at his feet with his tongue lolling out of the side of his mouth. Finn rubbed his head. "You like having someone to play with, don't you? Let's go see if Rascal is awake from her nap."

After he let the goat out of the crate and got the animals settled down, he went back to the fireplace and saw a folded piece of paper on the floor below Daisy's jeans. Without thinking much about it, he picked it up and unfolded it.

Daisy's New Year's Wish List
1) Sleep with a hot guy/Brief, fun affair
2) Fall

His body started to awaken. He couldn't believe he was seeing this right after seeing her half naked. He shouldn't even consider it, but technically, he could grant her first wish. That's if he was willing to gamble with their current relationship. But if number two on her list was the start of what he thought it was, he could not help her with falling in love.

His head snapped up.

Was Dr. Dillon Cameron the guy she had in mind to fulfill her New Year's wishes?

Chapter Six

Daisy had just put conditioner on her hair when the bathroom lights went off. She sighed and tipped her head under the water. Her first thought was that it was just Finn messing around with her, but the radio had gone silent as well as the small space heater she'd set up on the granite countertop. Only the dimmest of evening light came in through the long narrow window above the shower.

"Well, shoot. This can't be a good sign."

She quickly rinsed her hair and fumbled for her towel. It helped that she always stacked her clothes in the order she put them on, with her panties on top. She dressed in her pajamas and wrapped a towel around her head before opening the door.

In his bedroom, the large bank of windows gave her a view of the gray stormy night. The trees swayed like contemporary dancers in the strong wind as snow flurries swirled about like fairies. It felt like one of those nights that was made for ghost stories and warm drinks and snuggling with someone. But the only cuddling she was going to get tonight was from either a cat, a dog or a tiny goat.

She ran her hand along the wall until the flickering glow of firelight helped light her way into the living room.

Finn closed the fireplace screen and looked up. "Our

luck just ran out. I already checked and found out another power line was pulled down when an ice-covered tree fell."

"I was afraid it was something like that."

"I got a couple of lanterns out of our camping gear." He pointed to the green metal lanterns on the coffee table. "Tomorrow we'll probably have to move some of the things in the refrigerator to an ice chest and put it outside."

"Guess we won't be baking the lasagna and garlic bread we had planned for dinner."

"I have a cast-iron pot and know how to cook over a fire. But the easiest thing would be roasted hot dogs and s'mores."

"Yum. I could go for that. Do you actually have s'mores makings?"

He thought for a minute. "I do. But now that I think about it, I don't have any hot dogs."

"You're such a tease." She laughed. "If you provide dessert, I'll get out the stuff we brought from my house and put together a picnic style meal."

He gazed into the flames for a couple of seconds before answering. "Deal."

She sat on the stone hearth, pulled the towel from her hair and began to dry it. "Did the paint wash out of my jeans?"

"Um. I didn't wash them." He pointed to her pants still hanging over the chair.

"Finn! Do you expect me to walk around with your giant handprints on my butt?"

When his mischievous grin appeared, she knew she'd said the wrong thing.

Finn couldn't believe the great opportunity that was being handed to him on a big, shiny serving platter. "I dare you to wear those jeans with my handprints. In public."

"Oh, man. I walked right into that one." She dropped her head forward in a dramatized show of defeat. Firelight filtered through her curtain of golden hair, the drying strands swaying in the waves of heat from the flames.

"Told you I was the master."

"I'm not crowning you king of anything just yet."

With the goat in the lead, all three animals raced in a circle around the room and disappeared down the hallway.

"I suspect Lady is starting to enjoy the companionship." No sooner had she spoken than the cat bounded back in and jumped into Daisy's arms. The disgruntled feline looked over Daisy's shoulder and growled at the other Astro and Rascal. "Or maybe not so much."

"Your cat sure has got some sassy attitude, but at least she never uses her claws."

"She doesn't get the attitude from me," Daisy said.

"I don't know about that. I think you have your sassy moments." He could think of a few right away.

"What about my claws?" She raised her hand and curled her fingers. "Do these worry you?"

It had not taken him long to figure out that Daisy was a protective mama bear when it came to those she cared about. And he felt like he was lucky enough to be counted in that group. "I think for someone that you love you would use your claws to eviscerate the bad guy."

"You're right about that. It used to be just me and Sage, and we had to be tough."

"I remember." When he and his brothers had first arrived in Channing and started working on Dalton Ranch, the twins had both been single and living alone in their family farmhouse.

"It was such a wonderful surprise when Lizzy returned

to us, and then fell in love with Travis and brought Davy into our lives."

"Your niece came in like a singing whirlwind." Travis, their business partner who owned half of the Four Star Ranch, had had his life upended by an opera singer and an orphaned baby with Down syndrome. Finn had to admit that his friend was happier than ever.

He just couldn't relate to being that happy about taking on the responsibility for other human lives.

He'd somehow gotten his brothers well into adulthood without major damage, and the memory of the overwhelming stress from when they were young was a big part of the reason that he'd chosen a bachelor life.

Daisy ran her fingers through her hair to untangle it. "And then Sage found her happily-ever-after with Grayson. Now, because of Lizzy and Sage, I have two beautiful nieces and an adorable grandnephew."

The sadness in her eyes and the longing in her voice kept him from teasing her about being old enough to have a grandnephew. He knew she wanted a child of her own. A family of her own.

The exact opposite of his goals.

She shivered and moved closer to the fire with Lady still on her lap. "Without electricity, it's going to get really cold in here fast."

"We'll both have to sleep in front of the fire." When her eyes widened and her lips parted, his gaze was drawn to her mouth. How had he never noticed how full her lips were?

Seeing her reflection in the bathroom mirror and then her handwritten wish, the idea of sleeping side by side in front of the fire was making him lose his grip on what was between them. Keeping some level of distance was the only safe choice. Sex wasn't worth ruining their friendship. "I should go have a shower before there's no hot water."

Don't be a dumbass and screw this up.

Daisy set the cat on the floor and got up. "Take your time. I'll work on our fireside picnic."

Finn's eyes widened, and he rushed from the room. She stood perfectly still. Something had made the fun-loving attitude disappear from his eyes, and then he'd bolted. Maybe it was the term fireside picnic? It sounded too romantic, and she'd probably freaked him out.

What she'd thought would be a relaxing but boring few days alone had certainly taken an interesting turn. First, Dillon had offered to share the one-bedroom apartment with her, and now, Finn was talking about both of them sleeping in front of his fireplace. Was this happening because she'd written down a New Year's wish and put the thought out there into the universe?

"I'm being ridiculous," she whispered, and shook her head.

She grabbed one of the lanterns and went into the kitchen to prepare their meal. She didn't want to have an awkward discussion while she was feeling so off-kilter. If he took a long shower, she'd have time for Sleeping Beauty on her right shoulder to give her a pep talk about being a good girl.

Why did her BFF have to be a Greek god? Being his friend was wonderful, but also confusing and sometimes difficult. Especially since she'd worked hard to overcome and put aside her initial attraction to him. At times like this, her dedication to stick to the smart choice was tested.

She opened the refrigerator and pulled out a variety of food. The Murphy brothers didn't own any fancy wooden charcuterie boards or pretty trays, so she got out a cookie sheet and covered it with foil. She sliced cheese and dried meats and added the fruit they'd grabbed from her house.

While she was standing at the kitchen island cutting an apple, she caught a glimpse of him as he walked past on his way to the living room with his arms piled high with sleeping bags and a stack of blankets. He hadn't been kidding about making a bed in front of the fire. The thought of sleeping beside her sexy, younger best friend was exhilarating and scary. And way too tempting.

"Don't even think about it," said Sleeping Beauty.

Finn Murphy had always been very clear about what he wanted in life. He was not at all a good choice for her in any romantic sense. He didn't plan to make any permanent commitments and had made no secret of it. He had no interest in a serious relationship and zero intentions of ever having a wife or child. Not to mention no romantic interest in *her*. Sure, he sometimes flirted with her in his usual way, but he did that with everyone.

Her cat pranced into the kitchen and rubbed against her leg. "Hello, Lady. How did you get away from the rowdy duo?" She'd spoken too soon. Her words were immediately followed by the clip-clopping of teeny-tiny hooves, dog paws clicking and cowboy boots making a familiar shuffle against the floor.

"Everyone wants to eat," Finn said. "Maybe if this crew is fed, they'll give us some peace."

"Here's hoping."

"Rascal ate a little of the goat feed earlier, but she is probably ready for another bottle."

"I'll make the bottle." While he fed the cat and dog— each on opposite sides of the kitchen—she mixed the milk replacement formula with the tiny goat perched on her foot.

"Come with me, little miss." Finn scooped up the goat

and took the bottle Daisy held out. Rascal started sucking on it right away. "She's happy with this, but for us, wine, beer or hard liquor?"

"With the—" She bit her tongue. She'd almost used the words fireside picnic, again. "With the kind of food I'm putting together, I think red wine sounds best." She ducked her head to continue her work, unwilling to let him see any emotion her face might show. She was *not* setting up a romantic evening.

"Red wine. Got it. I'll take this one into the living room to feed her where it's quiet and see if she'll go to sleep."

It suddenly felt like they were playing house, and it was messing with her mind. Tending the ranches, painting a bedroom and now meals by the fire.

Why am I doing this to myself?

She had worked so hard to bury her attraction to him. She shook her head and pushed the thought away before turning back to her original task of food prep.

In the living room, he had spread out and layered everything in one bed that was big enough to sleep two, and she set the tray on the center of their bed.

"My brothers and I used to sleep in front of our fireplace when..." His voice trailed off.

The pinched look on his face hinted at a painful memory. She hoped he would someday share some of his past. But...she had secrets too, so she understood and had never pushed him to share.

"I forgot the wine. Be right back," he said, and hurried away.

Both of them seemed to be doing a lot of running away this evening. She sat on one side of the bed and got comfortable. He returned with a bottle of bourbon, an open bottle of wine, two mismatched glasses and a couple of shot glasses from their trip to the San Antonio Rodeo. He'd barely filled hers with burgundy liquid before she grabbed it and took a big sip.

"Better slow down or tonight's nickname will be Dizzy Daisy."

"Hey, you're the one who brought wine and hard liquor."

"I thought we might need it to keep warm."

This evening could go a couple of different ways, and she wasn't sure which one she was hoping for. Maleficent's red lips curled into a grin.

Finn put another log on the fire and adjusted it with a rustic poker that was topped with a star, kind of like the one they used as part of their Four Star Ranch cattle brand. "Do you know Tim, the new guy at the hardware store?"

"I've met him a few times," she said.

"He recently got a huge surprise. Fatherhood."

Daisy rolled onto her side and propped up on one elbow. The way he'd said it sounded like this was one of his worst fears. "He is going to be or already is a father?"

"The baby is two months old." He returned to his spot beside her on the sleeping bags.

"That would certainly be a big shock."

"No doubt. At least a woman knows for sure whether or not she has a kid."

Her heart was hit with a quick, sharp jab. "That's not always true." The second she said it, a knot formed in her belly.

"What do you mean? How can that be?"

"Never mind. You're right. The wine has already gone to my head."

Finn stretched out on his back beside her and tucked his laced fingers under his head. "Tell me a secret, Daisy Maisy."

The request startled her. But...this was her chance to learn more about him and his past. To get a deeper peek into that part of himself he kept shuttered behind layers of cockiness.

"If I tell you a secret, you have to do the same."

"Deal," he said.

Finn was a private guy, so his rapid agreement surprised her. But she'd forgotten how talkative he could get while drinking. She was right on the edge of grasping that nice, warm, fuzzy feeling that came with being tipsy, and one more drink would be just right.

And one more drink for him would make him even more talkative. "First, pour a couple of shots, please."

He did as she asked, they clinked shot glasses and drank. She shuddered as the bourbon burned its way down her throat and warmed her chest and belly. "Okay. My secret is that I like to eat ice cream right out of the carton. In bed."

He chuckled. "I could've guessed that. You also talk in your sleep."

"That's a well-known fact. Stop stalling. What's your secret?"

"I like to sleep in the nude."

"Not a surprise." She used this moment as an excuse to look him over from his head to his toes, possibly lingering longer than necessary on the black T-shirt pulling taught across his chest. "Thank you for being appropriately clothed this evening."

He grinned. "It's only because it's so cold."

"Rascal sure is cozy by the fire." At Finn's feet, the baby goat was tucked into the size of a football on their nest of sleeping bags. The firelight made the animal's white-and-tan hair glisten, and she looked more like a child's toy than a real live animal. Of course, Finn—the ladies' man that he was—would be adored even by a female goat.

"How old were you when you had your first kiss?" she asked him.

"I was thirteen. And I know for a fact that I'm a great kisser."

She chuckled. "I'm sure you think so, Casanova."

"I've been assured that it's true. Multiple times." He propped up on his side to face her. "Now tell me something real. Something few people know about."

Taking her own opportunity to stall for time, she bit into an apple slice and chewed. Only her sister knew about the sacrifice she'd made to save their ranch years ago. When she had given the gift of parenthood—to someone else without really thinking it through.

Over the last couple of years, she'd told Finn a lot about her life, but she didn't want to put a downward spin on tonight by bringing up something that made her sad. Reliving it aloud would make it all too real. So, she decided to tell him her second most regrettable decision.

"I was married."

"For real?"

"For six months. When I was eighteen years old. We spent a lot of our time together in high school and both thought it was love, but it was only lust that burned out way too quickly. We were a disaster in the bedroom and much better friends than lovers."

This important lesson was something she needed to keep at the forefront of her mind in her current situation. Friends didn't always translate into lovers.

"So, you just decided to split?"

"Well…he sped things along when he cheated. I think he lives in Houston now."

Finn bit into a cracker and studied her. "Is getting burned like that the reason you've never married again?"

"No. It sounds cliché, but I just haven't met the right one, I guess." She swirled her wine and took a sip. "Your turn. Tell me something about your childhood. You started to say something about you and your brothers sleeping by the fire."

"It's a long story."

"Do you have somewhere you need to be?"

He chuckled. "Well, no. I suppose I have time." He scratched his head as if choosing where to begin his story was hard work. "I had to start taking care of Riley and Jake when I was nine years old."

"Like babysitting?"

He plowed his hand through his hair. "It was more than that. Our mom was gone by then. She was in a boating accident with a group of her wild friends."

"Oh, no." She had known his mother died when he was young, but she hadn't known how tragic it had been.

"Our dad was rarely around. He was a long-haul trucker. Sometimes we didn't see him for days at a time."

Daisy's chest ached at the thought of three little boys all alone and scared. This was heartbreaking and explained why the three brothers were so close. "Did he leave you with enough food and money?"

"Most of the time, but not always. When the electric bill didn't get paid is when we slept by the fireplace to stay warm. I did odd jobs for neighbors. Raking leaves, walking dogs and stuff like that. Thankfully, it was enough for some food, and the grocery store was within walking distance. We ate a lot of sandwiches and cereal."

Daisy clasped her hands to keep from putting her arms

around him to comfort him like she would do with Sage or Lizzy. "Did you have to move from place to place?"

"No. Thankfully we owned the house. It had been my grandparents' house."

"It doesn't surprise me that you stepped up and took such good care of your little brothers."

"Somebody had to." His brow furrowed, making the faint lines of his early thirties more pronounced. "But I'm not so sure good describes it. I did the best I could. Getting us all to school on time was a challenge, but I couldn't let us be late all the time and have anyone discover we were alone. I couldn't stand the thought of us being separated."

This explained more about his in control personality. "That must have been so stressful. Especially for someone so young."

"It was. It's a big part of why I plan to remain childless."

That made her sad. "I'm sorry to hear that because you are naturally good with kids. You're wonderful with Rose and Davy when you babysit."

"It's not so bad when it's just for a few hours at a time. But anything longer than a day or so is too much. I'm not built to ever be a full-time father." He reached one hand across to his opposite shoulder and kneaded the muscle as if it was suddenly tight. "Give me one more secret," he requested.

He had shared some hard stuff, so maybe she could too. She was just tipsy enough and comfortable enough to consider letting someone other than her sister in on the secret that haunted her. Maybe it would be cathartic to talk about it.

"Well, there is something no one other than Sage knows. Remember when Loren announced that Sage was the surrogate who carried and gave birth to her and was now going to be her stepmom?"

"Who can forget something like that?" He sat up suddenly and looked at her waist. "Wait...were you a surrogate too?"

She shook her head as her pulse raced. "No. I was not a surrogate." The lump in her throat made it difficult to speak. Bringing this up was a mistake. She should have listened to her first gut instinct.

I should have chosen something embarrassing or funny. Think. What can I say instead?

Before she could think of something that would match up with what Loren had said, Finn sneezed, and the goat's head popped up a second before her whole body sprang into the air. She bounded up the space between their bodies.

Finn picked her up with one hand, and Rascal's little legs churned in the air like she was running. "Wish I could wake up this perky," he said.

"I'm surprised you don't."

He shot her a sexy smirk. "My brain takes longer than that to fire up and tell my body to get out of bed. But there are times when the mind and the body have different ideas."

That was certainly true. Her mind, body and heart, plus Maleficent and Sleeping Beauty, were all arguing about what to do with Finn Murphy. What box did he—or should he—fit into?

She reached out to rub the goat's soft ear between her fingers, and Rascal tried to suck on her pinkie. "Looks like someone is ready for another bottle."

"I'll go get it." Finn handed over the tiny animal and walked around the corner to the kitchen.

Daisy cuddled Rascal, rubbed her tummy and whispered, "Thanks for interrupting right when I needed you to."

Sharing too much while drinking had been a problem for her more than once. She crisscrossed her legs and closed her eyes.

When she and Sage had needed the money to save their horse ranch a little over fifteen years ago, she'd come up with her portion of the money before really thinking it through for the long-term. In desperation, she had donated her eggs so some other woman could have a baby. But even now, she too often wondered if she had a child out there somewhere in the world. A boy? A girl? More than one?

This was the reason she'd started going to hold babies in the NICU at the hospital. Even though she'd never know for sure, there was a chance she might've held her own baby.

Chapter Seven

It wasn't until Finn was moving around the kitchen and slightly off balance that he realized he had more than a buzz going. He put water and two scoops of powdered formula into the bottle, screwed on the top and shook it.

The kitchen was cold now that the central heat had been off for a few hours, and a chill was seeping through his socks, but he knew right where he could find some warmth. And he was feeling just relaxed and playful enough to be slightly dangerous.

Even though he knew he couldn't see Daisy, he glanced toward the living room. It wasn't the fire that was drawing him in. It was the woman he was having fun with. The woman he could be himself around. He waited for the panic to hit him...but it didn't come.

That's because there is nothing wrong with what we're doing.

It had felt good to share some of his childhood struggles with her after keeping it locked inside for so long, and he was glad she had encouraged him to talk about it. Daisy couldn't seem to understand why he wanted to remain an unencumbered bachelor. Knowing him better would help her understand.

Back in the living room, Daisy was sitting cross-legged,

eyes closed and swaying from side to side with the goat in her arms. She looked ethereal in the flickering light. What Mother Nature must look like if she was young and beautiful.

He shook his head. *What is going on with me?*

She opened her eyes, smiled and held out her hand. "I'll feed her."

"Thanks. I'm going to let the dog out. Don't forget to set Rascal directly into the litter box when she finishes eating."

"I will. I think she is already making progress with her training."

"I certainly hope so. She's way too little to be outside or in the barn. I don't know what I was thinking when I offered to bring her home."

"Why did you?"

"Because if someone didn't take her before close of business, the feed store owner said he was going to take her to the pound."

"Do they even take goats at the pound?"

"I think he was just blustering, but I didn't want to find out. I swear I don't know how someone who owns a business that sells feed and supplies for animals can have such a dislike for them."

"He really is a grumpy old man. I'm glad you brought her home." She kissed the top of the animal's head as Rascal devoured her bottle.

By the front door, Finn pulled on his coat and boots and went outside. Astro whimpered. "I know, buddy. Do it quick and then we'll go back inside."

He remained on the front porch while the dog went to the very edge, gathered his courage and then went a couple of steps into the yard. A sudden gust of wind jerked at his coat and went right through the material of his black-and-gray-plaid pajama pants. He shivered, and it brought on a strong craving to live on the wild side. A craving for the woman he was snowed in with.

Astro didn't take long to do his business and then dashed back into the house the second the door was open enough to squeeze through.

"The conditions are not getting better out there." He stood on the hearth and held his hands out to the warmth.

Daisy pulled the bottle from the goat's mouth, then got up and took her over to the litter box by the front door. She put her in and said, "Okay, Rascal. Show us what a smart girl you are."

The little animal bleated happily and did exactly what she was supposed to do, and they both praised her. But just to be safe, she put a diaper on her for the night.

"I'll go wash this bottle. Need anything?" she asked.

"No, thanks."

When she returned, he was sitting at the foot of their makeshift bed with his forearms braced across his drawn-up knees.

Rather than sitting beside him, she settled behind him. "I should've put my socks on. My feet are freezing."

That was all the warning he got before she slid her Pop-sicle feet up under the back of his T-shirt to the small of his back. He sucked in a sharp breath but remained as still as possible. "I charge extra for warming services." He looked over his shoulder and into her smiling face.

"I'm sure it will be worth every penny." She slid her feet up higher to torture a new spot on his back.

But he didn't really mind. She didn't know he was more than willing to warm her up for free. He was enjoying their playful, flirty banter. Having this closeness was helping him relax and let go of some of his worries—if only for a little while. Being with Daisy felt comfortable and...safe.

"Who said it's money that I want as payment?"

"I probably don't want the answer to that question. Do I? It's bound to be something embarrassing or cause me to need several showers." She moved to his side, stretched out her legs and propped herself up on her elbows to gaze into the flames like he was doing.

"It's nothing bad. Just a little bit of light housecleaning. Bathrooms, kitchen, bedrooms, living room and my laundry. And windows."

"I think that's where the shower part comes in. For maid services, we're going to have to spend a whole lot more time with my feet on your warm skin."

He opened his mouth to issue a witty comeback, but the image of any part of her against any part of his bare skin made him momentarily lose his words. He jerked his gaze back to the fire.

"I'm open to negotiations."

She shivered. "Let's talk about it under the covers."

He grinned at her soft gasp and horrified expression. It was right on brand for his Daisy Maisy. She often said something that she didn't mean to sound suggestive, but it did, and it presented a perfect opportunity for a comeback that would make her blush.

"Because I'm cold," she hurried to say in answer to his grin. "I need to stay warm until we can negotiate a reasonable exchange of services."

"I'll sleep on it and have it figured out by morning." He pulled the blankets up over them.

They'd never discussed boundaries between them. It had just always been understood as friendship, because that was safe. But they'd never stated any specific rules. At least none he could think of at the moment. He and Daisy were adults and deserved to enjoy themselves. But what exactly would that look like or mean for them? Flirting was one thing, but what was the point of no return?

He'd sleep on this as well and see if he found answers in the light of day. Or maybe in his dreams. In companionable silence, they fell asleep side by side.

A log shifted and crackled in the fireplace, and Finn half-opened one eye, still hovering somewhere between that fuzzy dream state and reality. A soft, warm, sweet-smelling woman was spooned against the front of his body. The scent of flowers lingered in her hair, and he pulled her closer, letting his hand slide from her curvy hip up to a full—

He froze and his eyes popped open.

Daisy.

She sighed and arched her back, simultaneously pushing her breast into his palm while wiggling her bottom against him. He groaned and fought against the urge to pull her closer and touch every part of her.

He should roll away from her. He really should. Except that she was on his side of the bed, and if he rolled, he'd end up on the floor. But before he figured out a way to let her go, it wouldn't hurt to hold her for just a little while longer.

He slowly eased his hand down to her waist and breathed in her scent. He would take this small moment in time. Just for himself. And he'd imagine what it would be like if he knew how to love a woman.

Daisy turned in his arms and snuggled against his chest with her head tucked under his chin. He once again froze. There was no way she could miss the physical effect she was having on his body. But she wasn't pushing him away. In fact, her hips shifted forward ever so slightly, but it was enough that he noticed. Inner heat built.

"Daisy, are you awake?"

Chapter Eight

The deep rumble of Finn's voice pulled Daisy from a deep sleep. Hovering in a dreamy state, his musky scent filled her head and swirls of stardust danced across her skin.

"Daisy?" he whispered.

She wasn't sure what made her do it, but she didn't want him to know she was awake. "I'll have the chocolate cake," she mumbled, hoping he would believe she was talking in her sleep.

His chest rose and fell with a deep breath, and he remained still, but his body was giving away his excitement about being pressed so closely together. He tightened his arm around her and smoothed a hand over her hair as he kissed the top of her head.

His tenderness made her heart do a cartwheel.

He seemed to like holding her as much as she was enjoying being in his arms, and their cozy cocoon was too good to give up. Everything felt right, and there was no harm in remaining right where she was.

Snuggling didn't cross a line. Not like kissing or making love would. If there was any fallout, she'd deal with that when she wasn't living out part of a fantasy.

Daisy needed this small haven of security. She closed her eyes and relaxed into his warm embrace.

* * *

A few hours later, the goat was making a racket in the dog crate and woke Daisy once again. It only took a few seconds to realize that her head was still on Finn's chest. She popped into a sitting position like a cork bobbing in the water.

He chuckled. "You wake up just like Rascal."

Not normally. She thought to herself. She was not a morning person. "Sorry about using you as a pillow. I've been told I'm a bed hog."

"No worries." His voice was still gravelly from sleep, but he was chuckling. "Hard times, desperate measures."

"Hard...what?" She was still too groggy to fully comprehend what he'd said, but his comment made something flutter in her belly.

He tried to hold back a smile but gave up. "The hard time was the freezing temperature. The desperate measure was you seeking my body heat."

"Oh." She chuckled. "Now I really owe you for your warming services."

"I have no doubt we can work something out that will make both of us happy."

She tried to smooth down her bedhead. "You know, I did return the favor of warmth last night, and now that I think about it, who is to say you weren't the one who pulled me over to keep you warm?"

"Fair point." He stretched and his T-shirt rode up to reveal his lower abs and the V of blond hair that disappeared into the waistband of his pajama pants. "I guess your tab is forgiven. This time."

She quickly got to her feet and pulled off the top blanket to wrap around herself. "I'll go start the coffee."

"No electricity," he said, reminding her.

"Shoot. I forgot about that."

"Never fear. I have a camping coffeepot and a small propane stove."

"Thank goodness. I'll make Rascal's bottle while you do that." She was smiling as she stepped over the cat and crossed the room to the front windows to pull back the curtains that they'd drawn to help keep out drafts. "There's a fresh layer of snow. My snow angel and all of our footprints are covered."

This meant they would likely be without electricity for even longer, but rather than being upset by the likelihood, it put an even bigger smile on her face.

The idea of extending their ice storm seclusion was very appealing.

They followed much of the same routine as the day before. But this time breakfast was by lantern light and the dim morning sun trying to make its way through the storm clouds. After tending to his cattle, they went over to her ranch.

In her stable, the familiar scents of molasses feed, hay and horses always made her smile. Ever since she was a toddler riding in the saddle with her dad, horses had been one of her favorite things in the world.

Dillon was walking up and down the aisle between the stalls with his cell phone to his ear.

He paused his conversation when he saw her. "Morning, Daisy. I'm talking someone through delivering a calf. But all of the horses are fed, and the stalls are mucked out."

"Thanks for keeping on top of that. Don't let me keep you from your important call."

He turned and headed toward the apartment. "Call me later," he said over his shoulder.

Finn was coming in the side door and the two men waved to one another.

"Phone date?" Finn asked her.

The idea of him being jealous was kind of fun. "We just didn't have a chance to catch up because he is being a virtual veterinarian. Since he can't get out on the road, he is walking someone through how to deliver a calf."

"I checked all the outdoor water faucets to make sure the weatherproofing is still in place, and they all look good." Finn's phone rang, and he pulled it out of his jacket pocket to look at the screen then started walking toward the tack room while answering. "Hi, Connie. What's going on with you?"

A twinge of jealousy stirred to life in her belly, and she hated it, especially since she'd just been enjoying the thought of him being the jealous one. Connie was a woman he'd gone out with several times, but Daisy didn't think she was right for him. She wasn't the least bit outdoorsy, and of all things, she was afraid of cows. That made her grin, wondering what Connie would think of a goat in the house.

The other woman's fear of animals was the kind of information she learned when she listened to him talk about his dates. She always listened, occasionally offered advice and never complained because she wanted to be a good friend. But she hated hearing about how this lady or that one couldn't keep her hands off him.

She grabbed the red treat bucket and started down the center aisle, giving each horse some attention along with their favorite treat. An apple for Titan, Lou, Zeus and Lizzy's horse, Misty, and carrots for the rest of them.

"Hello, handsome," she said to Titan. He nuzzled his nose against the red stocking cap on her head, then took the small apple from her hand. "I know it's hard being stuck indoors. I'll turn on the radio before I go so you can have some entertainment."

She moved along to the next stall to talk to their youngest stud horse, Cinder. He was a jumpy one and let few people other than herself touch him. It annoyed Finn that Dillon was one of the other people Cinder allowed near him. Was that another sign of jealousy?

Something small and light kept thumping against the back of her head and shoulders.

"What is that?" Not for the first time, she looked up to make sure it wasn't one of those spiders that drops down on a long strand of web to float in midair as if ready to land on her face. There was no sign of an arachnoid or any other critter such as a raccoon moving around in the rafters or running along the top rail of the stalls. She caught movement from the corner of her eye and spun to see the cause of it.

"Finnigan Murphy! I should've known it was you."

He stepped out of his horse's stall and dropped the pieces of feed he'd been tossing. "Took you long enough."

"You are such a man-child. A big man-child."

"I'm choosing to focus on the big man part."

"Of course you are." She turned to go—and to hide her grin.

"Daisy, freeze. Don't. Move."

His tone of voice hinted at danger and brought her to a sudden halt. Every muscle tensed. "Please, tell me it's not a spider."

Chapter Nine

Even in harsh weather, the Dalton Ranch stable made a cozy winter home for the small, harmless barn spiders. The only animal that Daisy couldn't stand.

"Hold still while I untangle the little beast from your hair," Finn said.

Daisy stiffened, her hands fisted at her sides. "Get it out. Quick!"

Rather than tell her there really was a spider on her head, he removed it from her red hat then tugged on a lock of her hair. She didn't need to know that there really had been a creepy crawly on her.

"Gotcha. Can't believe you fell for that."

Daisy spun on him with an adorable scowl. Her big green eyes flashing. "No fair tricking me like that. You know how I feel about spiders."

He cleared his throat to keep from chuckling. "Sorry. You're making it too easy to mess with you today."

You could use a good spanking, Finn Murphy."

. "It's debatable who needs the spanking." He turned up the wattage on his slow grin. The one that occasionally triggered female giggles.

Daisy's high cheekbones turned a rosy pink as she thrust the red bucket out to him. "Help me out with this, please."

They tended the rest of the horses for a few minutes and managed to avoid any more spider encounters.

"Let's go home, and I'll make another pot of coffee by the fire." He wanted to get out of the stable before Dr. Cameron came back out to chat up Daisy. The idea that his thinking was going in that direction made him frown. He had zero right to keep Daisy from dating anyone she wanted to. Especially since he couldn't be the one who gave her what she was looking for. He could not be her husband or the father of her children.

She hung the bucket on its hook. "I could use the caffeine and the warmth. And Rascal is going to be ready to get out of her crate."

When they got back to his ranch house, he built up the fire. They spent the rest of the day playing with the animals, reading books, eating and napping. The snow turned to sleet and chased away any chance of sunshine. With the conditions even worse, no one would be traveling, and their seclusion was safe from his brothers' return for a while longer.

"I cannot go to bed without a bath or shower," Daisy announced. "I guess I'll have to go to the apartment since it's the only place that has the generator to keep the hot water heater running. I'm sure Dillon won't mind at all."

He was *sure* the doc wouldn't mind. A sharp jab punched him in the gut. After seeing her in the bubble bath, he didn't want her showering with Dillon on the other side of the door. And what if… He shook his head.

She was trying to hide a smile but not doing a very good job of it.

Is she teasing me? Does she know I'm…jealous?

"Seems like a long way to go in this weather," he said.

She laughed. "Because it's sooo far to my place? We can see the stable in the distance from your front yard."

"I mean because of the sleet that has mixed in with the snow. It's slick and more dangerous now." Sounded like a good excuse to him. "I can give you a hot bath right here."

"How?" Her smile was challenging but sweet.

"Remember those two huge pots we used for the crawfish boil? I can put them on the gas grill on the porch and heat enough water for a bath in the small tub in the hallway bathroom."

"Okay. I'm game for that. Who gets the water first? You or me?"

"While the water heats, we can play a game of cards, and the winner gets the bathwater first."

"Deal," she said.

He let her win because he knew how much she disliked being in cold water, and the bathroom wasn't going to be warm.

When he went into the bathroom carrying the heavy pot of hot water, Daisy was standing there in his black bathrobe. Did she have any idea what she was doing to him? On the counter beside the sink, her pajamas were neatly folded with a pair of red panties on top. He smiled when he saw that his flannel pajamas were stacked neatly beside hers.

She twirled one end of the robe's belt. "I wanted to be ready to jump right into the tub, so we don't waste any of your hard work heating the water."

"Very thoughtful." He carefully poured the second pot of water into the tub. "Have at it, Daisy Maisy."

"I'll be quick."

"Give me a shout when it's safe to come in."

He closed the door and then leaned against the wall to wait. He could hear her splashing and humming. Mother Nature bathing under a waterfall came to mind, and he smiled despite the sexual dilemma he was getting himself into. Only a couple of minutes later, the splashing grew quiet and shortly after, she called out to him.

"Your turn."

He opened the door just as she was cinching the belt of his robe, but her pajamas were still on the counter. Which meant she still wasn't wearing anything beneath. He inwardly groaned.

"It's still hot. I'm going to go make us a snack. Meet you by the fire." She picked up her pajamas and slipped past him.

His self-control was going to be tested tonight, but he was up for the challenge.

While she was in the bedroom talking to her sister on the phone, he used the propane camp stove to heat a coffeepot of water. He made two mugs of hot chocolate and set them in front of the fire to stay warm. He'd set a bottle of rum on the coffee table earlier. Now he grabbed it and added some to his mug.

Daisy entered the room, and as she walked past the dark Christmas tree, she brushed her fingers over its branches. "It still smells good. I wish the Christmas tree lights worked on batteries. I love sitting and staring at the colorful lights."

He'd been wondering what he could do to make their New Year's Eve special, and her wish gave him an idea. He had an AC inverter in the garage that could power the strands of lights. Tomorrow, he would put the inverter in the sun with the solar panel to catch any rays of sun that slipped through and make sure it was charged. He could surprise her with a lighted tree for New Year's Eve.

"The best I can do for you tonight is this fire," he said.

"Oh, I'm not saying the fire isn't wonderful." She sat crisscross beside him. "I'm just being greedy and want both."

"Nothing wrong with that." She reached for the mug of hot chocolate in his hand—rather than the one on the hearth in front of her. "This one has rum in it," he said in warning.

"Is it the dark sweet rum?" she asked.

"Yes."

"That sounds yummy." She took the mug and sipped. "Mmm. I like it."

He chuckled. "Guess I'll add rum to the other mug as well."

"Good plan."

She was wearing his favorite black flannel shirt over her pajamas. She'd had to roll up the sleeves a few turns but left the top three buttons open enough to tease him, and now he wanted to see her in nothing but his shirt. Just like she'd been in his robe. There was an odd pitching in his stomach. Something…different.

He rubbed his eyes to get himself right, then added rum to the second mug. "I see that you've found one of my shirts to keep you warm."

"I did. Hope you don't mind. It's supersoft." She lifted the collar to her nose. "It smells good too."

For some reason it made him happy that she liked the smell. "I should be used to you taking my stuff by now," he said with a grin.

"I'll let you borrow my stuff anytime you want to."

They talked and laughed as they drank their hot chocolate and then climbed under the covers.

Finn tucked one arm under his head. Daisy was on her back with her eyes closed, but her face wasn't relaxed enough for her to be asleep. "Are you awake?"

"Yes." She rolled to face him. "I'm just thinking."

"What are you thinking about?" That sounded like something a girl would say, and he mentally chided himself.

Plus did he really want to dig into her nighttime thoughts while they were side by side in bed?

"Lots of things."

"Is my shirt still keeping you warm?" He'd meant to tease, but it didn't come out that way. He was flirting with her.

"Not warm enough." And she was flirting right back.

She bit her lip in a way that made him want to nibble on it himself. He lifted the layers of blankets. "Come over this way."

Without hesitation, she slid over to share his pillow.

They were so close. Close enough that he brushed back a long lock of her hair and let his fingers linger on her cheek for a moment longer than necessary. "You smell like flowers. It's nice. I told you that you can be flowery."

"I suppose I can. Cherry blossom mixes well with your leather and warm spices."

"That's a very specific description of my scent."

The dimple on her cheek deepened with her smile. "Don't be too impressed. I read it on your cologne bottle." Her tentative touch moved slowly up his arm, growing bolder with each inch until she curled her fingers around the back of his neck.

Sparks shot to every part of his body, and he groaned. "There are limits to what a man can resist."

"Same for a woman. What should we do about it?"

"I can think of several options worth exploring."

"Are we about to screw up our friendship?"

"Not if we don't let it." His thoughts snapped to her New Year's list.

Sleep with a hot guy.

At the moment, all of his worries and excuses about why they should be strictly friends with physical boundaries seemed useless. Fire was building beneath his skin, burning too hot to stop, and his body was battling with his mind.

Then he remembered the second part of her number one wish.

Brief fun affair.

She wanted hot and brief, and he could give her that. No problem. "If I'm not mistaken, we're both curious. He stroked her cheek with the pad of his thumb. "We could…"

"Scratch that itch?" She ran her tongue between her lips. "Just this once?"

"One time to get it out of our systems?" Thank God they were on the exact same page regarding this. He shouldn't do this. But he wanted to. He really wanted to.

Finn was well practiced and knew how to separate physical intimacy from his feelings. He'd been doing it for years.

But could Daisy handle something like this?

"We can try something simple and see how it goes," she whispered. "Finn Murphy, I dare you to prove you're a good kisser."

Chapter Ten

Daisy held her next breath. She had just dared Finn to prove he was a good kisser, and there was no taking it back. Good thing she didn't want to. Sleeping Beauty's delight and Maleficent's you-go-girl cheer seemed to agree.

Am I about to kiss my best friend?

The irresistible grin—that Finn had likely perfected in the cradle—was another vote for yes. The way he caressed her with his eyes made her feel like she was the most beautiful woman he'd ever seen.

He slid his hand into her hair and stroked her cheek with his thumb. "Challenge accepted."

"If we kiss and it's a dud, at least we will have answered the question of who is the better kisser. And I'll be able to tease you forever."

He chuckled. "You sound pretty sure of yourself."

She wasn't. She wasn't sure at all. Long ago she'd learned to keep Finn out of her daydreams, but with their bodies close enough to feel the other's chest move with increasing breaths, there was no way on earth to ignore the crackle of sexual tension.

"Don't be shy," she said with more courage than she was feeling.

Thank you, Maleficent.

The rough pad of his thumb brushed across her mouth, and he made an appreciative rumbling sound before his soft lips caressed hers.

An achingly slow, delicious tease.

Shimmers of longing danced over her skin, and she let her hand explore the solid breadth of his shoulders.

He didn't rush or go where he wasn't invited. He made sure they were both on the verge of molten before moving into a deep, searching, toe-curling kiss.

Cherishing. Savoring.

An ancient rhythm took hold. Their kisses began to explore, and their hands shifted clothing. Checking in with whispered words, they gave and took and shared.

And shared again.

Finn Murphy not only had bragging rights to being a great kisser, but he also had a whole list of delightful talents that she hoped to explore again.

The comforting weight of Daisy's upper body was draped across his chest, but Finn kept his eyes closed and replayed last night's highlights in his mind. But where to begin? The choices were plentiful.

He splayed his fingers wider on the bare skin of her back and inhaled against her hair.

He might have started their kiss, but Daisy's enthusiasm had catapulted them into something neither of them had wanted to stop.

Her softness. Her scent. Bodies pressed close. The way she used all of herself to share pleasure and welcome him. His Daisy was a real woman who didn't try to fake anything.

She sighed in her sleep, and her warm breath fanned across his skin. He shivered, and his blood began to surge as memories came to him.

One time had melted into two. Eager and passionate. Slow. Tender.

Their bodies tangled in an exhausted sleep.

His lips curved into a smile. Now that he thought about it, the whole experience had been one big highlight.

Finn opened his eyes to assure himself his mind wasn't playing tricks. Daisy's hand rested over his heart. Her long hair tumbled in a golden cloud around her shoulders, and her creamy skin looked iridescent in the firelight.

The fire had died down and needed to be tended, but he didn't want to move. She was comfortable in his arms, and this blip in their relationship would end soon.

There was no reason to rush it.

Daisy woke with her cheek resting on the warm skin of Finn's bare chest and his arm curled around her back—that was just as bare as his. The mood of the night had swept her away and there had been no resisting.

What have I done?

Her skin tingled, and she held her breath, trying to figure out if he was awake, or like her, too afraid to move and break the spell.

Please don't let sleeping with him be one of my worst ideas ever.

She'd made mistakes before and lived to tell the tale, but this had the potential to be crushing.

But…she had written down a wish to sleep with a hot guy.

She hadn't even finished writing her list, and she could already check something off. Well…almost. What about the brief fun affair idea she'd subconsciously tagged onto her first wish? Or was one night together as much time as she was going to get?

"I can hear you thinking."

She startled at the sound of his deep, sleepy voice rumbling under her ear. When she started to move off him, he tightened his arm to keep her close against his side. After gathering her wits, she lifted her head to meet his sleepy smile.

"Good morning." Her voice came out an octave higher than normal."

He grinned. "It sure is."

His words eased her worries about his negative reaction to their night together. "So...do we talk about this or pretend it was a dream or never happened?"

"It's kind of hard to pretend at the moment."

She had to agree. She rolled onto her back and pulled the blankets up under her chin. "Our friendship has to survive this, Finn."

With his arms crossed over his chest, he stared at the ceiling for a few heartbeats. "It will survive. This doesn't have to change us. We don't have to make more of this than it is."

That made her flinch. Their night together probably meant way more to her than it did to him. She had to keep in mind that Finn wasn't looking for a relationship like she was. In fact, it was the opposite. He was not an option for the guy she'd spend her romantic life with.

To her, their night had been a fantasy come true, but to Finn... Was she a conquest or just convenient?

"I guess you're right. It won't change us if we don't let it."

He traced his finger along her collarbone. "Since we're still in bed, this technically counts as one time, right?"

She smiled and snuggled closer to him. "Technically, if we continue, it will be our third time, so we already blew the one-time rule."

He wound a lock of her hair around his finger. "You know, it only makes sense for our *one* time to last the amount of time we're snowed in together. For as long as you stay here, we can temporarily explore the physical and satisfy our curiosity."

His promise that their friendship would be safe gave her courage. "Makes sense to me. Instead of only one time, what about one...tryst?"

"Tryst." He tried out the word and grinned. "And that is, what exactly?"

"A brief, fun affair," she said, quoting what she'd written on her wish list. She slid her arms around his neck and twined her fingers through his hair. "Can you do brief and fun, Finnigan Murphy?"

His smile was slow and sexy. "Casual with no strings?"

His words tugged at her heart, and she hesitated, but as he'd suggested, she wasn't going to try and make more of this than it was. "Sounds right to me."

"I can do that. No problem." He cupped her hip in his big hand. "The question is, can you? Can you separate our friendship from a physical relationship?"

Can I?

If she didn't do this, she would always wonder what could have been. She'd gotten through rough times before and could do it again if it came down to that.

Casual and without strings wasn't what she was ultimately looking for in a romance, but it had obviously been on her mind because she'd written down her desire for something brief and fun. Whatever this was with him, it was not and would not be a real romance. Remembering that fact was very important.

"To get myself back into dating, a tryst is actually something I've been thinking about trying."

"Trying a tryst." His lips quivered.

"Are you teasing me?" She pinched his forearm.

"No. That word just makes me want to do naughty things to you. I'm having fun, and according to you, that's a necessary part of a tryst."

"You catch on pretty quick."

"I'm a good student, but practice makes perfect. Plus I bet you're dying to know more details about what that word makes me want to do."

"You know me so well."

"Even better than I did yesterday."

That was certainly true in the physical sense. "I still have a few more secrets to show you. And just so you know, I'm a very tactile learner."

"That's good. So am I." He brushed his fingers over her stomach and made her giggle.

He sealed his mouth over hers, and there was no more talking after that.

While Finn was outside chopping wood, Daisy sat down at his kitchen table where the sunlight streamed in through the windows. Another perk was the very nice view it provided of him swinging an axe. He brought it down hard and split a log into three pieces.

Now that she knew what those muscles felt like under her hands and against her skin, this was even more entertaining.

Lady pranced in with her bell jingling and hopped up onto Daisy's lap. She stroked the cat's soft fur. "How am I ever going to go back to thinking of him as only a friend?"

She unfolded her wish list and smoothed out the creases in the blue paper. When her electricity had gone out, her second wish had only been partially written.

Should I complete my wish to fall in love or wait until our tryst is over?

Was there a chance putting it on paper could lead to a happily-ever-after? Like a little delayed Christmas magic. Maybe he would change his mind about long-term relationships, or what they had together might develop into more over time.

She stopped overthinking it and picked up her pen to add to her list, but then she stopped right away. If she completed the wish to fall in love, she might be the only one who fell in love and be even more hurt at the end.

She made the decision to complete that wish after their tryst. She drew a fill-in-the-blank line beside the word *fall* and then wrote out several more wishes.

2) *Fall* _____
3) *Learn a new skill*
4) *Have an adventure*
5) *Be a mom*

She wrote a number six but then tapped her pencil on the table while considering what it should be.

"Whatcha doing?" Finn asked.

Her heart sprang into her throat. "Nothing. Just a to-do list for later." She refolded the paper and shoved it into her back pocket. He would probably laugh if he saw it.

Chapter Eleven

Finn knew exactly what Daisy had put into her pocket. And he really wished he knew what she had added, but unless it was sitting out in the open, he wouldn't snoop. She was jumpier than normal, and he had doubts that she would be able to go through with their physical relationship.

Was he kidding himself that *he* could do this tryst thing with Daisy?

I do it all the time. I'm fine with this kind of thing.

He told himself this was just like every other time, but it didn't sound convincing—not even to himself.

The other women weren't your best friend, dummy.

She cocked her head and studied him as if she knew what he was thinking. "What's wrong?"

"Nothing. I hope." He moved closer. "I'm just trying to judge how you're feeling. Make sure you're okay. I don't want you to be uncomfortable or feel pressured or—"

She put her fingertips to his lips and smiled. "I want to be here with you. Like this. I'm not feeling any pressure."

He slid his fingers up the soft skin of her inner arm, rubbed his thumb in the center of her palm and kissed her fingertips. "Good. I'm happy you're here."

"Are you finished chopping wood?"

"Yes. Also, Riley called to see if I needed them to try

to get home to help me, but I told them to stay in town and not risk getting out on the icy road with tires that don't have snow chains." For once, he didn't want them to come home, and thankfully they'd both decided to stay in town.

"I think that was the right call." She hooked a finger in his belt loop. "For a several reasons."

He pulled her snug against him. "Tell me all about these reasons."

"Want me to show you instead?"

His blood surged and pulsed like a molten river through his veins. Maybe this arrangement was going to work after all.

"Give me all you've got." He clasped her hips and lifted her until she wrapped her legs around his waist. "Hold on tight, Daisy Maisy."

An hour later, they lay cuddled skin to skin in front of the fire, silently staring into the mesmerizing flames. The afternoon sun was barely cutting through the storm clouds, but they were cozy.

He played with her hand, letting his fingers trail through hers. "Does Sage have crooked pinkie fingers like you?"

"She does. So did our dad."

"Since we can't go out and no one can get here, our New Year's Eve is going to be a quiet one."

The cat skidded around the corner, jumped across their entwined bodies and then ducked under the coffee table. Astro and Rascal quickly followed.

"I don't know about that," she said. "It might get pretty wild since our only guests will be a bunch of party animals."

He chuckled. "A dog, a cat and a goat walk into a New Year's Eve party…"

She started singing "Old MacDonald." *"E-i-e-i-o."*

Astro howled while Rascal bleated, and Lady hissed before dashing from the room.

The sun glowed a rainbow of warm autumn colors as it set over the snow-covered landscape. While Daisy was enjoying another bath, courtesy of Finn toting huge pots of hot water, Finn turned on the battery-powered Christmas tree lights he'd rigged up. Now, she would be able to ring in the new year with the colorful lights she loved. He tuned the transistor radio to a Dallas country music station, then poked at the fire, even though it didn't need doing.

With a hand braced on the mantel, he looked at the photographs of him and his brothers. Riley was the sentimental one and had framed a few memories, ranging from when they were scrawny kids to the one they had taken not long ago at a county fair. All three of them, plus Daisy, had crammed themselves into a photo booth. He smiled at the memory of only Jake's head showing up while the rest of him had been on the outside of the curtain. And Daisy fit right in with the whole crazy lot of them.

His heart started to race. *Don't screw this up.*

"You did this for me?"

He turned at the sound of her voice. She was staring at the tree, and her eyes were as lit up as it was. "I thought you'd like it."

"Oh, I do." She joined him in front of the fire and wrapped her arms around his neck. "It's beautiful. Thank you."

He met her halfway for a tender kiss. It wasn't filled with urgent passion like their times in bed. It carried a calming playfulness, but there was also a sensation that sparked a flicker of panic inside him.

He slid one hand up the center of her back to keep her

body close to his, hoping it would make the scary feeling go away.

She relaxed against him, and they swayed to the music.

The living room was suddenly flooded with overhead lights. She groaned and he swore, then they looked at one another and seemed to be thinking the same thing.

"Turn off the lights," she said, echoing his thoughts. "I'm not ready for this holiday hideaway to be over."

"Me either. Save my dance and don't forget where we left off." He hurried around turning off lights and met her in front of the Christmas tree.

She finished texting someone and tossed her phone onto one of the recliners and welcomed him back into her embrace. "The power is back on at my ranch too. Oh, I love this song. Dance with me, cowboy."

"Yes, ma'am." He was going to make their last night together as memorable and special as possible.

They danced and laughed and toasted at midnight before cozying up in front of the fire where she fell asleep in his arms.

Finn brushed his fingers through the soft strands of Daisy's long hair. It was fanned out between them on the blue pillowcase, firelight dancing among the golden waves, making them multifaceted. Like her.

She looked so young and beautiful. He'd always considered her to be pretty, but now, there was a glow to her. A light that he'd overlooked in the past.

He shifted to ease the pressure on his spine. Three nights on a bed of sleeping bags was taking its toll on his body.

Daisy cracked open one eye. "Are you okay?"

Now that the central heat was working, they could get

off the floor and onto a soft mattress. "Let's move to my bedroom."

She raised her head and yawned. "Sounds good to me."

As they climbed into his bed, it struck him that he'd never brought a woman here. He'd kept it as a place all his own. But he'd just changed that.

"Go back to sleep," he whispered, needing a few beats to adjust to the shift.

"Good night." She spooned her back against his chest and was asleep within a minute.

He'd dated a lot of women, but none of them for very long. He was a keep-on-moving kind of guy. Daisy was the first woman he'd ever considered taking a chance on, but she was too important to "take a chance on" and risk breaking her tender heart. He knew full well that Daisy deserved more than him gambling that he could have a lasting long-term relationship. He didn't know what he was capable of giving a woman like her.

She mumbled in her sleep, sighed and smiled.

Was she dreaming about him? He wanted to wake her up with a kiss and make love to her again. But he stopped himself. What if his current feelings of...

He swallowed hard and pressed his fingertips to his closed eyes. A feeling he didn't know how to put a name to.

What if this passion and hunger was just a temporary blip before he reverted to his normal keep-moving response to emotional intimacy? If he didn't navigate this situation carefully and the lust burned away as it always did, this "tryst" had the potential to be the end of a valued friendship.

But for just a little while, he could hold her and imagine what it would be like if he knew how to love a woman.

* * *

Through Finn's bedroom windows, the first glow of sunrise peeked over the horizon, and it was beautiful, but Daisy wished it would freeze in time just for a little while longer. She wasn't ready for their frozen world to melt back into real life. But there was no stopping the dawn to extend their special moment.

Finn was spooned behind her, and he kissed her bare shoulder. "How are you this morning?"

"I'm really going to miss our holiday hideaway. It's been a nice respite from the real world. I'm not ready to go back to the daily grind."

"I know what you mean."

She turned to face him. "Now, I guess it's back to being just friends?" She'd meant for it to come out as a statement, but it had sounded more like a question, and she hoped he hadn't noticed.

"Always friends. You're the only one I can count on for certain kinds of advice." He studied her face as if searching for something. "But what about friends with a few extra benefits for a little while longer?"

Her stomach whooshed like she'd gone over a roller-coaster drop. This was what she had hoped for. More time to see what could develop between them. She tapped her thumb and pinkie together like she often did when she was nervous. "What benefits do you have in mind?"

"Occasionally doing exactly what we are doing right now." He expanded on that explanation by sliding his hands across her bare skin. "Something just between us. When no one else is around."

"A secret?"

"Private."

She liked the sound of that. It was best if their extended

tryst remained only between them because she knew it wouldn't last long-term, and then she'd be embarrassed if people knew it had ended and saw him around town with other women. "How do you see this working? Full-time friends and part-time lovers?"

"Yes. Until…" He scratched his head.

"How about a month? We can have all of January because I've always felt like I celebrate the new year for the whole month anyway."

"Good thinking, Daisy Maisy. Since we're both such good students and we're not done learning, we can extend our *tryst.*" He always chuckled when he said that word.

"And to set some limits, it can only happen here at your house." If she kept their romance away from her own ranch, it would hopefully be easier to separate their physical connection from everyday life. She wouldn't have the memories staring her in the face every single day.

"Not at your house or in any of the barns or stables," he added.

"And not in your truck."

He chuckled. "My truck? What made you think of that?"

"Well…" She blushed. "I figured that's why you have blankets in your truck."

He kissed the side of her neck. "Do you have a fantasy about making love under the stars?"

"I do now."

"Too bad the weather isn't cooperating."

"Too bad the truck is on the off-limits list," she said, reminding him.

"Damn. Rules are hard. Even when we are here at my house, it should only be when no one else is home."

"I agree. Otherwise, it won't remain private." And it needed to be, for everyone's sake.

"Because you do get kind of loud in bed," he teased.

She gasped dramatically. "I do not."

"I take it as a compliment, sweetheart."

Daisy's stomach fluttered. That was the first time he had called her sweetheart, but she couldn't allow herself to think it meant anything. She nestled against him with her head under his chin and just enjoyed being in his embrace.

She reluctantly accepted that she'd fallen 90 percent in love, powerless to completely stop it. But the other 10 percent of her love was a safety net for when his aversion to a wife or child eventually tore them apart. The impending heartache was something she would deal with later.

This secret benefits arrangement was probably going to be easy for him, but for her… Not so much.

She would borrow some of Maleficent's inner-badass energy. She was strong enough to do this if she put her mind to it. She would be his full-time friend, just like always, and his part-time lover for a month.

He kissed her shoulder and his hands started to roam. "Speaking of fooling around…"

"Were we talking about that?"

"We are now. Maybe we should take advantage of having the house to ourselves."

"Smart man." She hooked her leg over his hip and pushed him onto his back until she straddled him.

The front door slammed.

Daisy rolled across Finn and leaped from his bed. "Someone is here," she said needlessly.

"My brothers are home."

Chapter Twelve

Daisy's bare bottom was the last thing Finn saw before she disappeared into his bathroom. He chuckled and quickly closed his bedroom door.

Why in the hell did they have to come home so early in the morning?

He did not want his brothers to know about them sleeping together. Riley would tell him it was a mistake, and Jake would end up making a joke about it at some point and embarrassing Daisy.

He pulled on a pair of jeans and a long-sleeved blue Henley and then went into the living room. Jake was petting the dog and Riley was taking off his boots. Rascal was kicking up a morning fuss in her crate.

"The roads must be clear," he said to his little brothers.

"For us, yes," Jake said. "For Texas drivers, not so much."

Riley motioned to their bed on the floor. "I remember when we used to sleep in front of the fire."

Finn glanced back toward the hallway, wondering where Daisy was and what she was doing. Hopefully she wasn't freaking out.

Riley got Rascal out of her crate. "Is this little girl still causing trouble?"

"The dog has taken her under his wing and is kind of

helping. Astro seems to think she's a puppy, and he is responsible for training her. I'll have to tell you both about the house-training I've been doing with her."

Daisy came into the living room, sporting a smile that was a little too bright. "Hey, guys."

Jake spun to face her. "I didn't know you were here."

"Didn't you see her truck out front, Captain Obvious?" Riley said to Jake.

She ducked her head, and Finn knew she was gearing up to blush.

A band of tension cinched tight around his ribs. If she didn't pull it together in a hurry, she was going to give them away right off the bat. He was starting to doubt the sanity of what they had agreed to. He could do this part-time thing with no problem—well, not much—but in his experience, women were not built the same. Not on the outside or the inside.

The reality of the situation was suddenly hitting him. This was how it was going to be as long as they were sneaking around.

"The electricity went off at our ranch, so I came over here," she said.

"I thought you lost power here too?" Jake asked.

"It did," Finn said. "But not until the next day."

"I stayed because you guys have more firewood." She busied herself folding a blanket that had been tossed on one of the plush, brown recliners. "Riley, I hope you don't mind that I slept in your bedroom, so I'll change your sheets before I go."

"Sure. No problem." Riley sat on the couch and let the goat bounce around from one end to the other.

She cleared her throat. "Okay. I'll go do that, and then I

really need to get home." She spun on her heel and rushed back down the hallway.

Jake flopped into one of the recliners and turned on the TV. "What's up with her?"

"I think she's had about all of me she can stand," Finn said. "Guess I shouldn't pick on her so much."

"You two are like a couple of kids." Riley shook his head at Finn, got up and went into the kitchen.

Finn tunneled his hand through his hair. A couple of naughty kids all right. And he hadn't used very good judgment. He'd been blinded by lust.

I'm a fool for thinking this can work without anyone getting hurt.

Daisy set the cat carrier on her kitchen floor and then closed the door and pressed her back against it. She was being a total dork and freaking out—exactly like she'd promised herself she wouldn't.

"Meow."

"Sorry, Lady." She let the cat out and watched her race once around the island and then out of the room.

Her kitchen was bright and sunny, but she felt all quivery on the inside. And a bit sick to her stomach. She'd only left Finn's ranch a few minutes ago, but she missed him already.

"Why do I do these things to myself?" She groaned and folded her torso forward over the kitchen island's marble surface. The stone was uncomfortably cold under her cheek, so she pushed herself up and was glad no one was around to see her acting like a child.

They still had the whole month of January, but their un-interrupted time was over. It would never be quite the same as their magical holiday hideaway. Finding time to be alone at his house was going to be a challenge.

She was lonelier now than she had been before her sleepover at Four Star Ranch. What was this achy feeling in her gut? And then she realized what it was. Homesickness.

She was homesick for the bond they'd developed and shared during their time together.

"Well, this sucks even more than I imagined." Daisy started a pot of coffee and stared off into space while it brewed.

It was time to check on the horses, but she needed a few minutes to process her new reality. Ice, snow, power outages and even wild animals hadn't ruined their holiday. It was the best few days she'd had since she couldn't remember. No matter what plan or rules they made, no matter what she told herself or Finn, going back to being nothing more than best buddies in February was going to be a challenge. But she'd always have beautiful memories, even if they hurt at first.

She grabbed a mug, poured in some cream, then added the coffee and watched the colors mix into a creamy goodness. Lady wound around her legs. "Are you lonely too?"

Now she wanted someone she couldn't have. Not truly and fully. Finn would always keep a wedge of one kind or another between them. Just enough to let her know he wouldn't be held down and it wasn't permanent.

After her cup of coffee, she walked out to the stable. The radio was playing a George Strait song, and Dillon was singing along. His voice was surprisingly good. It didn't match the sight of him mucking out a horse stall.

"Happy New Year, Dillon."

He straightened and looked over the black horse's back with a smile. "Happy New Year to you." He rubbed his hand along the horse's flank on his way to the stall door, then stepped out and latched it behind him. "Did you make any resolutions?"

"No. More like wishes and goals."

"That's a good idea. You don't sound very excited about your wishes. Or is it that you drank too much last night?"

"No hangover. Just tired, I guess." Lizzy's horse stuck her head out of her stall, and Daisy put her cheek against Misty's neck as she patted her.

"What's really wrong?" he asked.

She couldn't tell him the truth of her self-imposed romantic pleasure with a side of angst. "Nothing. Really. I didn't get much sleep."

Dillon leaned his back against a post. "Have I ever told you that I have three younger sisters?"

"No, you haven't."

"For some reason they think I'm a good listener, and they always come to me. So, you can't fool me. I can see it on your face."

"What do you see?" She put her hands to her cheeks.

"I suspect there's a man involved, and I have a pretty good idea who he is. I've seen the way you look at one another when you think the other one isn't looking."

"Really?" Her cheeks were flaming now. How was she going to be able to keep their secret? She could not blow it on day one. "Dillon, you cannot say a word to anyone suggesting that there is anything romantic between me and Finn. Please."

His brow furrowed. "Okay. I promise I won't say anything you don't want me to." He braced an elbow on a stall door. "I'm sorry. I didn't mean to tease you. I didn't realize it was a secret."

"You don't have to be sorry. I just didn't know I was

being so obvious. And there is really nothing to even talk about."

"You don't have to say another word about it, but I'm here if you ever want to." He tapped the side of his head. "It goes in the vault."

She smiled and sat on the wooden bench beside her. "Are you a vet or a shrink?"

He chuckled. "A bit of both. I couldn't decide when I graduated from high school, and I took a lot of classes."

"Good for you."

"And if you want me to, I'll stop trying to make Finn jealous on purpose."

"You actually do that?"

"Maybe a time or two. I think that's why I've gotten a glimpse into your relationship. He doesn't like having me around you, but he seems to be having trouble recognizing what's right in front of him."

"You think so?"

"All the signs are there."

She tapped her thumb and pinkie together. "On second thought, it won't hurt him to be a little jealous now and then."

Dillon grinned. "Cool."

By lunchtime, most of the ice had melted except for a few patches in the shade. Daisy was too antsy to sit inside, so she went outside to gather the branches that had fallen onto her back patio during the storm. It would make good kindling for her fireplace.

When Finn drove up and parked beside her truck, her heart fluttered. They hadn't spoken since she'd rushed out of his house after almost being caught in bed by his brothers. She hadn't missed his silent pleas for her to be chill in front of Riley and Jake, but she'd been taken by surprise and totally unprepared to publicly hide their January tryst agreement that they'd made only minutes before.

She rearranged her face into what she hoped was a normal expression. His slow smile morphed into a full grin. Calmness settled over her, and she returned his wave.

I can do this. We *can do this.*

This was her Finn. Not someone she just met and hooked up with. He was one of the few friends she could talk with and laugh with. And bonus, for a limited time, they could occasionally revisit their physical connection. They could get through this, together.

"How is Rascal doing this afternoon?" she called out.

"See for yourself." He lifted the goat out of the truck and set her on the ground. At the end of a purple leash, the tiny animal was buckled into a pink harness.

She laughed as Rascal frisked along beside the tall, sexy cowboy dressed in head to toe black. She pulled her phone from her pocket and snapped a picture of them walking her way.

"What's got you grinning and taking pictures, Daisy Maisy? See something you like?"

"I do. A few things." To resist her urge to kiss him, she knelt to greet the goat. "Hello, sweetie. Where did you get pink and purple items? I know they weren't Astro's when he was a puppy."

"My brothers picked them up in town before they came home. She has taken to wearing it much better than I expected."

"She looks adorable. Almost like a child's toy." The cat ran up to see the goat and started licking her head. "Somebody wants to be friends. Good girl, Lady."

"She's already spoiled." Even though it was still forty degrees, Finn sat in one of the patio chairs.

She took the one beside him. "I was just thinking about calling you. I'm curious if your brothers suspect anything."

"I don't think so. They didn't say anything. And Jake for sure would have. Sorry they blindsided us and we didn't have a chance to say goodbye."

"It was an abrupt ending to our holiday hideaway, but I bet we'll look back on the moment and be able to laugh."

"I already can," he said, and chuckled. "You proved you can spring out of bed every bit as well as Miss Mess here."

Rascal tangled her leash around his foot and kicked up her hind legs.

A car horn honked as her sister's family drove up the gravel driveway.

Her niece Loren was the first one out of the car, and she came running their way. Her long, brown hair was loose and blowing in the wind. "You got a puppy? Oh, wait that's a goat." She hugged Daisy then dropped to her knees to pet her. "She's so adorable."

"Her name is Rascal," Daisy said. "She belongs to Finn."

"Where did you get her?" the teenager asked.

"I kind of came by her on accident when I stopped at the feed store."

Grayson waved to them but went into the house with luggage while Sage headed their way with Rose in her arms. "Finn, you pick up strays just like we do."

Daisy reached out the baby. "Hello, my sweet Rose. I missed you bunches and bunches." She cuddled her close and straightened her pink hat.

The baby babbled and patted her cheek.

"I have to go check on Mischief," Loren said, and ran toward the barn to visit her horse.

"Did you have a good trip?" she asked her twin.

"We did, but I'm glad to be home. Loren wanted to come out here rather than go to the house in town," Sage said about the house in the Old Town area of Channing that Grayson inherited from his great-aunt Tilly DeLuca.

Her brother-in-law, Grayson, joined them and put an arm around Sage. "Finn, do you have time to look at something with me?"

"I sure do." He stood, picked up Rascal and grinned down at Daisy, a secret smile in his eyes. "I'll see you later."

"Bye." She waved awkwardly.

The men started talking about cattle and headed for his truck.

"Ma-ma-ma," Rose said.

"Let's get her inside out of the cold," Daisy said.

Sage was looking at her curiously—too curiously—so she hurried toward the house with the baby cradled against her chest.

In the kitchen, she put Rose in the playpen near the table.

Sage stopped in front of her and held her by the shoulders, narrowed her eyes and then gasped. "You slept with him."

It wasn't a question, and Daisy palmed her face. "I knew I couldn't hide it from you."

"Spill it, sis. How did this happen?"

"Let's make tea and I'll tell you all about it." She heated water while Sage changed Rose.

Once the tea was ready, they sat at the round kitchen table that had seen countless family discussions. Hours and hours of laughing, crying, secrets and stories.

She told her twin about her snowed-in holiday hideaway and the deal they had made.

"Oh, Daisy. How are you going to do this?"

Chapter Thirteen

Finn grinned as Daisy moved around her kitchen. She was opening and closing cabinets and the refrigerator while chattering about there being nothing to eat that didn't take forever to cook. He sat back in his chair and sipped his iced tea. She entertained him, and even when she was buzzing around like a bee, she also calmed him.

When he'd brought the goat over on a leash the day before, he'd been unsure about how they should move forward. And second-guessing the wisdom of their intimate time and their January plan. But it hadn't taken long for her nervous expression to ease seamlessly into a genuine smile. The one that told him they would be okay.

She had a way of settling his jumpy nerves. It was one of the reasons he liked being around her so much. She wasn't demanding or too serious. Just his easygoing Daisy Maisy.

I just need to keep things playful and fun. And keep things from sliding into serious.

"Let's go get dinner at the Rodeo Café," he said.

"Excellent idea. I'm starving."

"There's a dress code tonight." He knew his grin told her he was up to something.

"No, there's not."

"There is for you. You'll be wearing a special pair of jeans."

She scowled and crossed her arms. "I'm not hungry anymore."

"Yes, you are. Be a good sport and go get dressed. Unless you don't accept the challenge?"

"Fine."

"Scoot." He patted her bottom.

She spun around and checked to make sure they were alone. "Grayson is in the other room," she whispered, but couldn't hold back her smile. "We're not at your house. And that's against the rules."

He sighed. "Sometimes I hate rules."

She chuckled. "I'll be back in five minutes."

He also liked that she didn't take a ton of time getting ready.

"Hey, look." Finn pointed at the new Italian restaurant. "Antone's is open. Want to try it out?"

"I'm not sure I'm dressed for that restaurant, thanks to you."

"You look beautiful." He wasn't just saying it. He meant it. He saw her differently now.

"Okay. Let's try it out."

He followed Daisy into the restaurant. The handprints on her back pockets shifted as she walked, and it looked like his fingerprints were squeezing her curves. He wanted so much to do it for real that he shoved his hands in his coat pockets.

He needed to find a way to get his brothers out of the house so he and Daisy could have some time alone. He stopped behind her at the hostess stand and looked up when she cleared her throat.

"Has something caught your attention down below?" she said over her shoulder.

He returned her grin. "It sure has."

There was a small bar area in the front corner separated from the main dining room by a wall of photographs. An intricate antique bar stretched across the back, and mood lighting gave it a cozy vibe. They were shown to a table for two near the back of the main dining room.

"I told you this place was too fancy for my handprint jeans," she whispered across the candlelit table. "Most of the other women have on dresses."

"Your ivory sweater is fancy with the beads around the neck." He moved a finger through the air to mimic the scooped neckline.

"I got it out of Sage's closet. And speaking of my sister, she knows about us."

His eyes widened. "Already?"

"I didn't even say a word. She just looked at my face. It's a twin thing."

"I understand. I should've expected that. She'll keep it to herself, right?"

"Definitely. She knows how to keep a secret when it's important."

While they ate, the natural effortlessness of their friendship took over.

"Finn, why don't you want to be a father? Truthfully."

He hated this question but would answer it anyway. When he thought of becoming a father, his palms always began to itch, and his throat tightened. "Because I've already done it with my brothers. I didn't care for it then, and I don't want to repeat it. I don't want to be responsible for anyone but myself. I know that sounds selfish."

She suspected it was a lack of confidence in his own

parenting skills and likely a touch of fear. Maybe he just needed time to realize it would be totally different doing it as an adult. "I know better than that. You are not a selfish person. Will you tell me more about being the one who basically raised Riley and Jake?"

"I had to raise myself too."

"You did a good job of it. You're one of the best men I know."

He made a sound in his throat. "Maybe you should ask my brothers about that before jumping to conclusions. I took on the responsibility of feeding them and keeping them safe. I was responsible for pretty much everything."

"That must have been so scary."

"That's one way to put it."

Every few days or weeks, their dad would show up with groceries and a little cash. But the few nights he did spend at home with them, he'd usually been drunk. Jake had always cried when he left again, and Finn had been the one to comfort his youngest brother until he fell asleep.

He'd already done the parenting thing, and it had been extremely hard. The crushing weight of failure when things went wrong. A child carrying an adult's fear. The worry about what the next day would bring their way. It was a miracle Riley and Jake had turned out okay and had lived to tell about it. He couldn't willingly raise another child. He couldn't risk being completely responsible for another person's life.

"Sometimes I would get so mad at one of them when they wouldn't listen and we'd end up wrestling in a pile on the floor."

She covered his hand with hers. "You were a kid, and they are your brothers. Not your children. I would imagine that lots of brothers get rough with one another. Right?"

"I guess. But the stress of keeping them fed and not flunking out of school and…" He took a drink of water. "It was incredibly hard and stressful, and now that they're grown men, I don't want to go through anything like that again."

"I can understand that. Thanks for telling me about it."

On the drive home, Daisy fiddled with the radio. It was dark with only the streetlights occasionally flickering across her face, making her blond hair glisten in the intermittent flash of lights. The truck was filled with the savory scent of leftover lasagna, the sweetness of her hand cream and the peppermint she'd popped into her mouth.

She worked the candy around in her mouth and licked her lips. "Where are your brothers this evening?"

It appeared her thoughts were headed in the same direction as his were. "Probably at home. Unfortunately. But… I could sneak you in through my bedroom window."

She smiled at him. "Didn't we say it could only happen when no one was there?"

Now that they were on the outskirts of Channing, it was darker in the truck. He stopped at a sign, then turned onto the farm road that went past their ranches. "Are you sure? I don't think we said that. I think I would remember."

She laughed. "Selective memory?"

"Only on a case by case basis."

"Rule breaker."

"Rule bender sounds better," he said. "Especially when it benefits both of us and hurts no one."

"You're the one who said I'm loud in bed."

"Grab my phone. My brothers and I have our locations turned on and shared between the three of us."

She opened the share your location app on his phone and softly sighed. "Looks like they're both at home."

That's what he'd expected, and it was probably for the best, but he had hoped. He drove past the entrance of Four Star Ranch and turned in at hers.

They didn't speak as he pressed in the code to make the gate swing open. He drove up her curving driveway that was lined with trees that were all bare branched and skeletal for winter. He pulled through the circular gravel drive near her front door.

"And now it's time to drop you off and say good-night."

He turned to look at her and tucked her hair behind her ear. "It's good practice."

She paused with her hand on the door handle. "Practice for what?"

"For the rest of our lives."

They shared a sad smile, and she got out of his truck.

The sun was bright when Daisy came out of the stable, so she shielded her eyes to see who was standing beside the corral. A young cowboy had one boot propped on the bottom fence board. There was a large military-style backpack at his feet, and he was stroking the neck of one of their most skittish horses. Hardly anyone could get that close to Cinder, but this stranger was having no problem.

"Hello, there," she called out. When he turned to face her, the expression on his face seemed to flicker through a whole range of emotions. He reminded her of someone, but she couldn't place who it was.

"Hi. I'm Adam Hauser." He extended his hand.

"I'm Daisy. Welcome to Dalton Ranch."

His hand trembled slightly in hers as if he was nervous, and this close, she realized he was only a teenager. He was at least an inch above her five foot nine, and leanly muscled with green eyes and a fringe of light brown hair peeking out from beneath his dark brown cowboy hat. She glanced around for an unfamiliar car or the other people who must be with him, but saw no one. "Are you here with your parents?"

"No, ma'am. It's just me. I heard in town that you're looking to hire a ranch hand."

"We sure are. Do you have any experience?"

"I do." Cinder stretched his neck over the fence and nudged Adam's hat with his nose. He took a step back so he could stroke the horse's neck. "I know a lot about horses."

"Cinder sure seems to like you, and he doesn't like anyone but me or my sister. And occasionally the veterinarian." She patted the other side of the horse's neck.

"My mother boarded and trained horses," he said. "I've been around them my entire life."

"Where does she live?"

He shuffled one boot in the patchy grass that surrounded the corral. "She passed away six months ago, and now it's just me."

The catch in his voice and sadness in his green eyes broke Daisy's heart. "I'm so sorry to hear that. I know this is a hard stage of grieving."

"Yes, ma'am. It is."

She looked around. "How did you get here?"

"I hitchhiked."

She gasped. "That's not safe these days."

"Well, technically, from the bus stop in Channing, I got a ride with an old guy from town right to your gate. So, it wasn't that daring on my part."

"I'm glad to hear you don't make a habit of hitchhiking. How did you get through my front gate?"

"I was standing outside of it when a young woman with long blond hair was leaving. I told her I was here about the job, and she said she was running late for her son's appointment and couldn't show me herself, but she told me to walk up the driveway and find you at the stable."

"That was my niece Lizzy. Can I ask how old you are?"

He straightened his shoulders as if trying to look taller. "I'm eighteen."

"I wasn't much older than you when I lost my mom. My dad was gone before that. What about your father?"

"Never had one. And no brothers or sisters. It's just me, for now."

She liked that he sounded hopeful for his future. "Where are you living?"

"At the moment, nowhere. But I grew up near Houston."

There was another strong tug on her heart. His clothes were clean and of high quality, so he wasn't destitute, but this sad young man needed her help, and she felt an immediate pull to take care of him.

"Grab your backpack and come inside so we can get to know one another and see if you are a good fit for the job." Her gut told her to hire him, but getting to know him better wouldn't hurt.

"That would be great." He hefted the pack onto his shoulders and followed her toward the farmhouse.

"Are you hungry?"

"I had lunch in town at the Rodeo Café, but I could use a cup of coffee to warm up."

They went in through the kitchen door. "There's a bathroom right around the corner if you need it while I make a fresh pot."

"Thanks."

When he came back into the kitchen, Daisy had put a plate of cookies on the table and was pouring coffee. "Do you need cream or sugar?"

"Just cream, please." He took a seat at the round kitchen table.

"That's how I take my coffee too. Those cookies on the table are peanut butter. You're not allergic to peanuts, are you?"

"No, ma'am. I love peanut butter."

"So do I. Please, call me Daisy. I might be almost old enough to be your mom, but I like to pretend I'm not." She chuckled, sat across from him and nudged the plate of cookies his way.

His eyes kept flicking back to her as if he was searching for something in her face. Was he trying to make up his mind about her like she was doing him, or as Finn would likely say, sizing her up to take advantage of her in some way?

It didn't feel that way to her. Nothing about this young man felt dangerous or dishonest. She wasn't nearly as gullible as her protective best friend thought she was.

Adam seemed to realize that he was staring and focused on the cookie in his hand.

"Tell me about growing up around horses," she said.

He swallowed a bite of cookie. "At our ranch outside of Houston, we boarded lots of horses for rich people. Many of the horses were worth a lot of money, so I know what it means to take care of expensive animals. It's serious business and nothing to mess around with."

"Are you familiar with what we do here on Dalton Ranch?"

"Yes, ma'am. I mean Daisy. I looked at your website and know that this is a stud farm."

"That's right. We have several stud horses, but our most famous is Titan. We also do some breeding with our partner Travis. He is married to my niece Lizzy, the woman you met at the front gate."

"You have a niece old enough to be married?"

"I do. I have a much older brother, and I was only ten when Lizzy was born."

"You are lucky to have so much family," he said.

Daisy had to admit that she was.

"I don't know much about breeding, but I know a lot about taking care of horses, and I'm a good rider. Someday I'd like to have my own place, and I would love the opportunity to learn from you." Excitement seemed to make some of his nervousness disappear. "I'd like the opportunity to prove I can be useful."

They talked for a few more minutes. "How did you end up in Channing?"

"I'll show you." He unzipped his pack, pulled out a small photo album and flipped it open.

The first picture was of a beautiful woman with blond hair and a huge smile and a young boy making a silly face. They were standing in front of a water fountain with a horse statue in the center, and she recognized it right away.

"That's Old Town Channing. Is that you?"

"Yes. When I was a kid, we came to Channing on vacation. We stayed at a place on the river, and we fished and canoed. It was lots of fun. My mom always said Channing, Texas, would be a great place to live, and it's where she would move if we didn't have our ranch." He cleared his throat and looked back at the picture.

"So, you decided to make her dream come true, for you. That's really sweet."

He shrugged. "She would like it. I figured while I was looking for a place to start over, this was as good a place as any to check out first."

"What were you going to do if you hadn't heard I was hiring?"

"I was hoping for a cheap motel room. And there are so many ranches in the area, I figured someone would be hiring or there would be a job somewhere around town." He flipped to the next photo and pushed it closer to her. "That's the ranch where I grew up."

"Beautiful. It looks like you had a really nice childhood."

"I did." His throat worked as he swallowed.

Normally, she would talk to her sister before hiring someone, but she had a feeling about Adam. She couldn't send him off to hitchhike around the country and have no one looking out for him. She'd always had a sense about people and was going to go with her gut instinct. "I like what I'm hearing. You sound qualified. We have an apartment behind the stable that has recently become available, and if you'd like, you can live in it as part of your pay."

"I got the job?"

"If you want it."

He sighed and seemed to relax as tension left his shoulders. "Yes, I do. That would be great. Thanks."

"Good." She stood and took her cup to the sink. "Let's go out to the stable and I'll show you the apartment and you can meet all the horses."

They went in through the small side door near the back of the stable. Daisy motioned to her left. "On this side is the tack room, and across from it are the collection room and the laboratory where we get the product ready to ship out."

"I wouldn't mind learning how all of that works."

"I'm happy to teach you." She walked down the aisle between the rooms. "Through this back door is the apartment where you'll be staying."

The one-bedroom was beautiful, because Sage had decorated it. It was an open floor plan kitchen and living area with a small bed and bath off to one side. It had a blue and tan color scheme and comfortable furnishings.

"Will this work for you?" she asked.

"Are you kidding? This is great." He put his backpack on the brown leather couch.

"Good. Let's go meet all the horses."

Back out in the stable, she pointed up to the ceiling as they made their way back past the tack room. "There are cameras all throughout the stable that monitor and record 24-7. The red button on that post will buzz the main house and can be used if there is an emergency."

"Good safety features. That's another thing my mom would appreciate."

"I'm glad to hear it. There are horses in here that belong to every member of the family. You've met Cinder, and next to his stall is Titan." She went down the row and introduced him to the rest of the stud horses, then all the horses the family rode, and the ones that belonged to Travis.

Lifting his hands, he moved them around to encompass the whole space. "It means a lot to me to have a place to stay. You're really going to trust me with all this?"

"Can I?" That he would ask made her believe she was making the right decision.

"Absolutely." He stood tall and put a hand over his heart. "I'll treat every animal and everything here as if I'm part of the family."

Chapter Fourteen

As Finn drew close to Daisy, who was standing on her back patio, he followed her gaze to the corral and saw a stranger exercising the feisty stallion that even he had trouble handling.

"Who's that kid working with Cinder?"

She looked over her shoulder and smiled at him. "That's Adam. I just hired him to be our new ranch hand."

"Seriously?"

"Yes. Of course seriously."

"He's just a kid. You should've let me check him out before you hired him."

Her eyebrows popped up. "I don't remember putting you in charge of hiring on my ranch."

He knew when it was time to shut his big mouth and did it in a hurry. They turned at the sound of Riley and Jake walking up behind them.

"What are you two staring at?" Jake asked.

Finn nodded his head toward the stranger. "Daisy hired that scrawny kid to be her ranch hand."

"Hey!" Daisy smacked his arm with the back of her hand. "Be nice. You don't even know him. Adam is smart and knowledgeable, and he recently lost his mom. He's all on his own."

"So, he's a charity case?" Jake asked, echoing Finn's own thoughts.

Daisy scoffed. "No, he's not. He knows a lot about horses and is really good with them." She motioned toward the corral and started walking that way. "As you can see. I haven't seen any of you three be able to do that with Cinder."

"He looks capable enough to me," Riley said in his deep, quiet voice.

The three of them followed her to the edge of the corral.

"What did y'all come over here for?" she asked. "Other than to pester me about my new employee."

Finn lifted his arm in a new automatic response to being near her, but he stopped himself right before wrapping it around her and shifted his hat instead. It was getting harder and harder to separate the friend from the lover. He watched the kid with the horse. It really did look like he knew what he was doing. "You haven't even put out an ad for the job. Who sent him to you?"

"His mother." Daisy smiled at him as if that settled everything.

A mother's recommendation made him feel a little better about him being here alone with Daisy. "Some of our cattle got out before we could repair a break in the fence, and we could use help rounding them up from the neighbor's place on the other side of us."

"Too bad they didn't get out on my side of your ranch," she said. "I'm happy to help."

The kid slowed the horse and led him over to where they stood.

Daisy propped her arms on the fence. "Adam Hauser, these are the Murphy brothers, Finn, Riley and Jake." She pointed to each of them in turn.

"Nice to meet all of you." Adam held out his hand.

Finn grasped it before either of his brothers could, and he was impressed with the kid's firm grip and use of eye contact.

"Adam, the brothers own Four Star Ranch next door, and they need some help rounding up cattle."

"I can help," Adam said.

"We need a real cowboy," Finn said. Daisy shot him a sharp look and then put a hand on his back and pinched him in warning. He almost laughed. She didn't understand how guys sometimes needed to take a man's measure and also allow him the opportunity to show you who he was.

Adam straightened his spine. "I am a real cowboy."

Finn looked the young man up and down. He had a feeling that he actually was, but another test wouldn't hurt. "What do you think, guys?" he asked his brothers. "Can we make a cowboy out of this kid?"

"I think it's worth a try," Jake said. "How old are you?"

"Eighteen. Almost nineteen."

"Let's see your driver's license," Finn requested.

Daisy mumbled under her breath.

Adam pulled out his wallet and dug out his ID. "I know I look young."

"Is this fake?"

The young man looked at him like he was stupid. "Don't you think if I had bothered with getting a fake ID that I'd make myself at least twenty-one?"

"He's got you there," Riley said.

Finn handed back his driver's license and propped his folded arms on the top railing. "You don't look old enough to shave more than once a week."

"Well, you certainly do," Adam quipped and then tipped up the front of his brown cowboy hat. "So how about it, grandpa? Are we going to round up some cattle or not?"

Jake and Rily laughed, and Daisy ducked her head to hide a smile.

Finn held back his own grin. He could not drop his guard with this teenager. Not yet. "Okay. You can show us what you've got."

"I'll put Cinder in his stall." Adam led the animal away.

He liked this kid's spunk, and later he would make sure Daisy knew why he was giving him a hard time. Every young man his age deserved the opportunity to prove himself. But because Adam would be around Daisy, he planned to keep an extra sharp eye on this young cowboy.

"Adam and I will ride over to your place as soon as we can get the horses saddled."

Daisy took Adam into the tack room. "For the horse you'll ride, grab that saddle, and I'll get your bridle."

He looked around and lifted the saddle from its stand. "My mom liked to keep a really neat tack room too."

"It makes things easier when everything is organized."

"That's the kind of thing she always said." He followed her out into the stable and down the center aisle between the stalls.

"Please don't let the Murphy brothers get to you."

Adam made a dismissive sound. "They're nothing I haven't dealt with before."

She smiled to herself. This young man was going to fit right in around here. He reminded her of the Murphy brothers. Tough with a little bit of sweetness hiding underneath. He'd proven that while sharing photos from his childhood. "You do seem to be able to hold your own with them."

"Don't worry about me."

"Good to know. You'll be riding Sandy. She's the palomino in the third stall."

Once Sandy and Lou were saddled, they led them outside, mounted up, then rode toward Finn's place.

"How long has this ranch been in your family?" Adam asked.

"My sister and I are the fifth generation to live on it."

"Wow. That must be so cool to be able to say that."

"Can I ask where you were living before you arrived in Channing?"

"With a bunch of other guys. Some of them were bad news, and it wasn't a good fit anymore." He reined his horse around a fallen tree branch.

"I'm glad to hear you got yourself out of a bad situation," she said. "Will you tell me about your mom?" She thought at first that he wouldn't answer, but then he let out a long, slow breath.

"She loved horses like you do."

"So, you inherited your horsemanship skills from your mother."

He studied her for a few seconds before glancing skyward. "I guess I did."

Daisy hoped being here would help heal some of his sorrow.

"This horse wants to run," he said.

"Are you up for that?" She hoped so, because for some reason, she really wanted Adam to impress the Murphy brothers.

"Absolutely. It's been too long since I've been able to ride."

"As soon as we go through the gate up ahead that separates our properties, there is a big flat pasture. It's a perfect place to run the horses."

From horseback, she leaned down to unlatch the gate, and her horse knew the routine of backing up to open it and did the same in reverse to close it. "Let's ride."

They started off at a canter and moved quickly into a gallop. The two of them kept pace side by side.

She was relieved that he was a good rider. For all of their sakes, she hoped Adam would work out as a new hire. She hated the idea of having to fire someone so young and vulnerable and unprotected from the world. Was this teenager the next person the Dalton family would take under their wings?

Finn was watching them as they neared his barn where three other horses were saddled and waiting.

She shared a smile with Finn. A silent I told you so.

Riley told everyone the plan and gave instructions, and Adam didn't have to be told twice. It didn't take the five of them long to round up the cattle and return them to Four Star Ranch, then patch the hole in the fence.

Finn gave Adam a slap on the back. "You did all right, kid."

"Thanks, old man."

Daisy smiled to herself. Maybe these three crazy brothers would be good for this sad young man who suddenly found himself alone in the world.

That evening, Daisy used an oven mitt to hold the handle of a cast-iron skillet while she cut the corn bread into triangles. A knock on her back door brought her out of her thoughts about the business calls she needed to make tomorrow. She could see Adam's nervous face through the windowpane on the top half of the door, and she motioned for him to come inside.

"You're just in time."

"Thank you for the invitation." He closed the door behind himself.

"Since I know you haven't been able to go grocery shopping yet, the least I can do is feed you."

"I have some snacks in my backpack."

"A growing young man needs better food than trail snacks. I expect you to come to the house for breakfast in the morning."

"Thank you. I appreciate it." He took off his cowboy hat and held it to his chest with one hand.

The movement struck her as protective, as if he needed to shield his heart. But his posture also seemed like a way of showing respect to her. "You can hang your hat on one of those." She pointed to the row of four polished wooden hat hooks that were mounted on the wall under a shelf.

He hung his hat on the far right hook.

"That's the one my dad always used. Most people come in and use the first one." She put the last piece of corn bread in the basket and covered it with a cloth.

He rubbed a hand over the smoothed knob end of one of the empty hooks. "They look old and handmade."

"They are. I believe my great-grandfather made them."

"You have real family history in your house."

"I guess I'm pretty lucky that way." The sadness on his face made her wish she hadn't brought up the family stuff to someone who had no family or home. She wondered what had happened to the ranch where he grew up, but she would wait to ask. It was a question with the potential to be painful. "I'll take you to the grocery store some time tomorrow. But for tonight, I hope you like taco casserole."

"Sounds good." He drummed his fingers against his thigh and tapped one boot heel.

She smiled in the hope of calming him, but instead of returning her expression, his eyes widened, and he rubbed his cheek.

She wasn't exactly sure what his reaction meant, but she chalked it up to him missing his mom.

He turned to study the photos on the front of her refrigerator and pointed to Lizzy and Travis's wedding photo. "That's the lady who let me in your front gate."

"Yes, that's my niece Lizzy. She is an opera singer."

"Oh wow. I like to sing, but I'm definitely not that good."

"You don't even want to hear me sing." She tapped a finger on the photo. "That's her husband, Travis. He partners with us on some horse breeding but is also a part owner of the Four Star Ranch next door, with the three Murphy brothers. And that cutie is their son, Davy."

"He was at their wedding?" Adam said, then grimaced. "Sorry. It was rude of me to say that. I didn't mean to judge. My mom always told me to run a question through my head before letting it come out of my mouth, but I obviously haven't mastered that yet."

"It's okay. No worries. Davy is adopted. He kind of helped bring them together."

"That's admirable of them."

Not for the first time, she noticed the way his speech and manners were a bit more formal than the average Texas cowboy.

"Who is this?" Adam touched a candid shot Sage had recently taken.

"That's my brother-in-law, Grayson, and his two daughters. You're about to meet them."

"Is he a cowboy here on the ranch too?"

"Grayson is an architect and part-time cowboy."

Adam's stomach growled. "What can I do to help with dinner?

"You can grab that basket of corn bread and follow me."

Daisy used two hot pads to carry the large casserole, and Adam followed her down the hallway to the dining room.

"Come and get it," she called to her family members in the living room.

Grayson entered first, and she introduced the two men.

"You're in for a treat," Grayson said as he took a seat at one end of the table. "I love this meal."

Sage came in right behind him with Rose cradled in her arms.

"Sage, this is Adam Hauser, the new hire I told you about."

Her sister tucked a curl behind her ear. "So nice to meet you. Welcome to the Dalton Ranch family."

"Thank you." Adam looked between them. "You're twins."

"We sure are," Sage said. "And this little one is Rose."

The baby waved her arms and blew a raspberry.

"Hi, Rose," Adam said, and then sat in the empty chair closest to him.

Sage swept around to her chair on the other side of the dining table and buckled the baby into her high chair.

As soon as Daisy sat at the opposite end from Grayson, Loren rushed into the room, and her steps faltered when she saw a stranger. "Hi. I'm Loren. Pronounced like Sophia Loren."

"I'm Adam. But I'm afraid I don't know Sophia Loren."

Her fifteen-year-old niece giggled and took her seat across from their visitor. "That's okay. She's a famous old Hollywood movie star. A lot of people our age don't know who she is."

Daisy smiled at their interaction. "Everyone dig in before it gets cold."

"Are you going to be the new cowboy here on Dalton Ranch?" Loren asked him.

"I guess I am."

Her niece flipped back the cloth and took a piece of corn bread, then held out the basket to their guest. "Soon, you'll meet my cousin Lizzy, her husband Travis and their son Davy."

"I met Lizzy, briefly. And I think her son was in a car seat in the back."

"Davy is two years old and has Down syndrome. He is so smart and so cute. And this is my baby sister, Rose." She leaned to the side and kissed the top of her sister's head. "She is just as smart and cute as Davy."

Daisy and Sage shared a smile. After years of it just being the two of them, it was so nice to have family around their dining room table. When all of them were here, they had to add one of the table extensions to fit everyone.

If I can show Finn that he would make a great family man, we'll need the second table extender.

She bit the inside of her cheek and reminded herself to believe Finn when he said he didn't want a wife or kids. Misplaced hope could lead to greater heartache.

After Adam went back to the apartment and her sister's family left for the ten minute drive to their house in town, Daisy took a long hot bath.

She went into the home office to check the monitor that would show her each of the horses. It was something she always did before bed. Adam was standing in front of Cinder's stall. She couldn't hear what he was saying but he was smiling, and the horse was eating up the attention. He put his forehead against the horse's, and it made her eyes sting with the urge to cry. No matter what anyone else thought, she knew she'd made the right decision hiring him. She watched until he dimmed the lights just like she'd shown him and went into the apartment.

Before climbing into bed, she pulled up her fluffy down comforter. Lady hopped onto the foot of the bed, turned a few circles and settled down by her legs. As she reached to turn off the bedside lamp, a text message came in. It was a sweet photo of the goat and dog cuddling. She replied that it was cute, but rather than responding with another message, he called.

"Good evening, Finnigan."

"What are you doing?"

"I just got in bed."

"I just realized what time it is. I'm glad I didn't wake you."

She snuggled farther down into her soft sheets. "Good friends are allowed to call in the middle of the night—on occasion."

"That's something I've been thinking about a lot lately."

"Calling me in the middle of the night?"

"Our friendship. Even though we have different future family goals, the importance of our friendship is something I think we can agree on."

"Yes, we can." She had a feeling he was about to work on convincing himself of the future he wanted. The one he thought he wanted. But the picture she saw forming had a fork in his road, and although she'd just this evening reminded herself to be cautious, she hoped she could urge him down the right one.

The sound of a television went off in the background. "Ultimately, we want opposite things. You want a kid, and I don't. You want to get married—"

"And you don't," she finished for him. "I'm well aware of your aversion to fatherhood and wedded bliss."

"I've witnessed a lot of the opposite of wedded bliss."

His bad opinion of marriage was sad, and no doubt partially explained his aversion. She might have failed at it in her youth, but that didn't mean she didn't believe in it, and she wasn't giving up on having a husband. "And that's why you don't want to be in a committed long-term relationship."

"In my experience, our curiosity will naturally burn itself out over time, and then we can get back to normal."

Her stomach clenched, and she was glad he couldn't see the look on her face. She understood what he meant, but it hurt to think that he would at any moment just stop desiring her. Most relationships hit a point when initial lust faded, but he'd made it sound as simple as extinguishing a candle.

"You'll meet a guy, fall in love and make it all happen."

He made it sound so easy peasy, like if she loved someone enough the rest would follow, like a wish granted. Her blood surged.

A wish granted.

Both parts of her first wish had come true. She picked up her list from the bedside table. Number two was still unfinished, but she'd decided to wait to complete her wish to fall in love, and she should stick to that decision. That wish would be written in February.

Learning a skill and having an adventure were fairly easy to accomplish. Becoming a mom would be a lot trickier. But just in case wishes really did come true, she now knew what she was going to add to her New Year's wish list.

Find someone who loves me the way I love them. The way I deserve.

Unaware of her tumbling thoughts, he continued. "Even after you're an old married lady, we'll still have our friendship."

"You'll be my cantankerous old bachelor friend."

"That's why we need to keep what we're doing just between us. That way there won't be any weirdness with someone either of us is dating. They won't have to freak out about us being alone together and fooling around. We will have already scratched that itch."

He was really sending her mood downhill. "Did you just call to remind me how much you don't want a family and why we're doomed?"

He was quiet for a moment. "No. Sorry. I didn't mean to get off onto that again. I just wanted to hear your voice… because I miss you."

She smiled as some of her happiness returned. "I miss you too."

Finn was fighting their relationship, and himself, but she could see a few rays of sunlight trying to break through.

Chapter Fifteen

Daisy and Finn had always helped one another on their ranches—when needed—but since their holiday hideaway, they'd fallen into a regular routine of working together as if the horse ranch and Four Star Ranch was one large property. Just like this afternoon when she'd helped him find a missing calf.

Finn unzipped his jacket. Today's weather had been mild, but in Texas, who could be sure what the next day would bring. "Thanks for helping me find that calf," he said to Daisy. "You have a knack for it."

"Happy to help."

They walked down the incline to the pond. The sun was just starting to dip behind the horizon, and the water glistened with warm colors. He let the goat off her leash so she could run with the dog. The rowboat had been securely tied so they wouldn't have another goat in a boat incident.

Finn wound up the purple leash and shoved it into his jacket pocket. "What does Adam drive? I didn't see a vehicle."

"He doesn't have a car. He took a bus to Channing and hitchhiked out here from town."

He stopped walking and turned to face her. "Hitchhiked? Where does he live?"

"In the apartment behind the stable."

"Daisy, you don't even know him, and you put him in there with all the horses?"

"What do you think he is? A horse thief or something?"

"Well, not really. He seems like a good kid. But still…" They started walking again.

"There are cameras everywhere, except for in the apartment of course, and Adam knows about them. Last night, I was in the home office and watched him on the monitor. He was out in the stable talking to the horses and all of the animals like him. And that says something about a person. I think he is really lonely, and he's still grieving for his mom. My heart aches for him."

"You have a soft heart."

"Yours is softer than you want people to know, Finnigan."

"Wait a minute. You said his mom was the one who recommended him for the job."

"In a way."

"In what way could that possibly be?"

"Adam's mom used to bring him to Channing on vacation, and she told him it was a place she'd like to live. He showed me photos of them by the horse fountain when he was a kid. He's all alone in the world and trying to start over. He's trying to live out his mom's dream."

He reached down to pet the dog's head before Astro darted off to play again. "I'll admit, I do feel for him. At least I had my brothers to keep me going and to lean on. Maybe Adam should come live at my house until we all get to know him better."

She hooked her arm through his as they walked. "Because you don't want him to be lonely or because you're worried that he is up to no good and don't want him that close to me?"

He shrugged. "A little of both, I guess."

They followed Astro and Rascal up the hill toward his ranch house.

He liked having her arm linked through his. It felt…comfortable. She'd occasionally done it before they'd explored the physical attraction between them, but now, along with the comfort there was a tingle. "Will you do me a favor and go with me to a barbecue tonight? It's a monthly mixer for a group of cattle ranchers that Riley wanted us to join. It has been good networking, but I really need you there."

"You need me to impress people with my witty personality or to chaperone?"

"Both, but actually, more of the second."

She laughed. "I was kidding about that."

"There's a woman who'll be there, and she can't take a hint that I'm not interested in going home with her. She has tried to get me to all three times I've seen her. I don't want to be mean or hurt her feelings."

"She's not your type?"

"Not exactly. I think Dolores is in her late fifties and expecting her first grandchild next month."

She chuckled. "You catch the eye of every woman from one to ninety-nine."

"She's still beautiful, but I think she's interested in only one thing from me."

Daisy was looking at him with a mixture of humor and curiosity. "Not ready to be a grandpa?"

"That's a hard no."

"So, tonight I'll be your what? Pretend girlfriend?"

His pulse jumped. "I hadn't really thought about it ex-

actly, but that could work. I don't think you'll know anyone else there."

"What about your brothers? Won't they be there?"

"We'll just tell them you're going to pretend to be my
date for the night."

"Sounds like playing with fire," she said.

It sure did, but it also sounded like a lot of fun.

"Want to know why else I'm happy you're going with
me?"

"Can't wait to hear it."

"I'm happy because…" He paused for dramatic effect
and grinned. "You're going to wear your handprint jeans."

She stopped walking and snapped her hands to her hips.
"I absolutely am not. I already accepted that dare when we
went to the new Italian restaurant."

"This time it's for a different reason."

"Why is this time different?"

"Because I like to watch you walk in them." He raised
both hands and made a squeezing motion. "It makes it look
like my fingers are cupping your butt."

She laughed and slipped her hands into her own back
pockets. "Now I'm definitely not wearing them in public,
but I will need to go home to shower and change clothes
before we go."

His front door opened, and his brothers came outside,
both dressed in their best jeans and boots.

"Are you ready to go?" Jake asked. "I promised to bring
ice and need to go into town to get it."

"No, we'll meet y'all there in a little while," Finn said.
"Daisy is going to pretend to be my date to keep Dolores
away from me."

Jake laughed. "This ought to be good."

"We're taking the new truck. See you there." Riley got in on the driver's side of their silver truck.

The second Jake and Riley drove away, he and Daisy grinned at one another.

"The house is empty," he said. "You said you wanted to take a shower, and I happened to notice that when you left in such a rush the other morning, you left your travel bag of cosmetics in my bathroom."

She tugged on one of his belt loops, then took off jogging. "Race you to the shower."

He whistled for the dog and goat and then followed Daisy inside with a big smile on his face.

An hour and a half later, they were late to the barbecue, but they were both relaxed and well satisfied. When they'd stopped by Daisy's house for her to change clothes, she had not put on the handprint jeans as he'd hoped. She'd rushed back outside dressed in a pair of slim-fitting black jeans, and a black sweater that fell off one shoulder and was sexy as hell. It was a good compromise as far as wardrobe choices went.

This month the meeting was at the home of the association's president. It was a massive red brick Colonial surrounded by cattle fields, with a big barn behind it. Someday he hoped to be half as successful as this rancher.

He waited for Daisy at the front of her truck, and they went up the brick pathway to the door. "Thanks again for coming with me."

"Let me know when you see your cougar."

"Dolores is not my anything. That's the whole point of this." He swept her hand into his and laced their fingers as they went in through the door behind another group of people.

Daisy gave his hand a squeeze. "Have I ever told you that I wanted to be an actress when I was a kid?"

"I don't believe you have."

"Now is my chance to give it a try."

"Oh, boy. Should I worry?"

She smiled, and there was a gleam in her eyes that hinted at mischief.

Pretend dating is going to be entertaining at the very least.

He introduced her to several people, and they got drinks at the bar. Daisy mingled easily with whoever she met. She seemed to fit in everywhere and was good with people.

Across the room, he spotted Dolores. She was lovely and didn't look at all like a classic grandmother type, and there was a time he would've taken her up on her offer, but lately he'd just needed a break from dating so many different women. Letting this woman down easy was certainly something he could've handled by himself in a perfectly tactful manner, but having Daisy here made it so much easier. He slid an arm around her waist.

Daisy turned to face him and put her arms around his neck as if she knew the reason. "Which one is she?" she whispered.

"The brunette in the red dress," he said against her ear. She shivered, and for added effect, he kissed her forehead.

Over Daisy's shoulder, Dolores smiled at him in a way that was sweet and accepting of their situation. He nodded and smiled back. There was now an understanding between them, but that didn't mean he could stop his pretend date with the woman in his arms. They had to keep up appearances.

"Want to get some food, Daisy Maisy?"

"Yes. It smells really good." She let her hands slide

slowly down his chest, and her eyes followed all the way to his belt buckle. "Something I did earlier has given me an appetite."

Before he could respond, she spun away from him, and he thought he heard her giggle. He hadn't realized until recently what a tease she could be. And he loved that about her.

Riley kept looking at them, and he had a feeling that his quiet brother was suspicious of him and Daisy. But like Sage, he wouldn't tell anyone. His baby brother was a different story.

There were tables set up inside and out, and they chose a standing table on the back deck where it was quieter and there was a good view of the night sky.

"Are you still driving into Fort Worth tomorrow?" she asked.

"Yes. I have a meeting, and I'm leaving at about nine o'clock."

"Can I catch a ride and get dropped off and picked up at the hospital?"

He almost dropped his drink. Panic was the first to hit him with a gut punch.

Oh crap, is she pregnant?

But just as swiftly, his thoughts flipped to worry. For her. He touched her bare shoulder. "What's wrong, sweetheart? Are you okay?"

She tipped her head to the side and grinned. "Yes, I'm perfectly fine. I figured we could carpool and save on gas. My nurse friend called and told me there's a new preemie baby in the NICU who needs some extra cuddling."

Relief made his shoulders drop. "You really like doing that, don't you?"

"I do. There is something so magical about a newborn."

She wrapped her arms around herself and glanced up at the starry sky.

He wasn't sure if it was because she was cold or needed a hug. Since they were pretending to be on a date, he pulled her into his arms. What did it matter that there was no one else around to see their display of affection? There was always the chance someone was watching them from the windows. Hopefully not one of his brothers.

She relaxed against his chest, and he let himself enjoy the moment. Everything else would be there to worry about tomorrow.

Daisy scrubbed her hands in the stainless-steel sink in the small room before she could enter the neonatal intensive care unit.

"Hello, ladies," she said to a doctor and her friend Tina. "Who do you have for me today?"

"A beautiful baby boy. He was a month early," Tina said, and motioned for her to follow. "Mom gave birth last night and had a rough time of it after her C-section. Dad is on his way home from a trip overseas, and he should be here sometime today."

"I'm happy to sub in for them. I would want someone to do the same for me." An old familiar ache crept in. Who had held her baby...or babies? She knew she shouldn't think of them as *hers*, but knowing and doing were two different things.

"It's almost time for the baby to eat," Tina said. "After I get you two settled, I'll get a bottle ready."

Daisy sat in one of the rocking chairs and let her friend place the tiny bundle in her arms. The baby was sucking on his little balled-up fist and starting to fuss.

"Hello, little darling. Welcome to the world." Swirls of

dark hair topped his head, and his big chocolate-drop eyes blinked slowly as he tried to focus.

Tina came back with the bottle, and she coaxed the baby to drink. While he ate, she let her mind wander from topic to topic, but she kept coming back to Finn.

Finn was such a contradiction. He was good with babies, and she knew he liked them. He'd proven that with the way he was with her niece Rose and her nephew Davy. And yet, he was adamant that he did not want any kids of his own.

From what she'd recently learned about his childhood, it had become pretty clear that it was because he'd been forced to be responsible for his little brothers at an age that was way too young. He didn't seem to understand that it would be different as a grown-up—with other adults around to help out.

She set the empty bottle aside, put the baby against her chest and patted his back. He emitted a soft burp. "That's it, sweetie. Good job."

All she could do was support and encourage Finn to see that he was a good man who could trust in himself and would make a great father. She sighed and rested her head back against the rocker. The last thing she needed was a guy who had a less than zero desire for a wife or child. *I'm too old to waste time.*

Sleeping Beauty sympathized with her dilemma, while Maleficent only shrugged with a mischievous grin.

Who had she been trying to kid that she would be able to keep her heart out of it when she was sharing a man's bed? It had become so much more than just physical for her. But for Finn? That remained to be seen.

Her tentative hold on the ten percent of her love she'd been reserving was starting to slip.

I should've taken Dillon up on his offer to share the apartment during the snowstorm.

At least then she would still have Finn's unblemished friendship, and possibly a tall, dark and handsome veterinarian as a future lover. She groaned. She didn't want to be with Dillon. He didn't give her the delicious tingles that Finn could with nothing more than a heated look or half smile. If she could write her future into existence, Dillon would be the one who remained in the "friend only" category, and Finn would be her...

Everything.

She squeezed her eyes closed. "No, no, no. I'm such a fool."

The baby stretched and grunted as if he was in total agreement with her self-assessment.

How was she supposed to give up her new connection with Finn just because the calendar flipped to a new month?

Daisy went out into the hospital parking lot and saw Finn's truck at the end of a row. He didn't see her as she approached, and she had to knock on the window for him to unlock the door. She got in and he started the engine. "I hope you haven't been waiting long."

"Not too long. How was the baby?"

She buckled her seat belt. "He was so small and precious. His dad arrived from out of town while I was there and was so happy to meet his newborn son that he teared up. It was so amazing to see his parents experience the moment together. I loved seeing their bond form right there in front of my eyes."

"That's cool."

"What were you thinking about so hard when I got in?"

"Something that keeps popping into my head now and

then. You never finished telling me about how you got your share of the money to save Dalton Ranch."

"It's funny you should ask me about that right now. It's the reason I started going to the hospital to hold babies." She pressed her teeth into her bottom lip.

"It's what made me think of it, too. I get the feeling it has something to do with a child."

"I wasn't a surrogate like my sister, but I did give a part of myself to help another woman be a mother."

"Huh?" He cocked his head and looked at her, clearly not understanding.

"I went to a fertility clinic and gave another woman a chance to get pregnant using my eggs."

"Oh, sweetheart." He reached across the center console and laced his fingers with hers. "That must have been so hard for you."

She took a moment to let the warmth of his touch soak in. "I have no idea if I have a child or children somewhere out there in the world. If I do, they are about Loren's age. Just getting started in high school." Her voice cracked, and she cleared her throat.

"You deserve the chance to have a baby of your own," he said.

That was something they could agree on. She just wished they agreed on the method to make that happen.

Finn's insides started to twist and cramp. He knew she wanted to be a mom. He also knew her well enough to know she wouldn't start dating anyone else as long as they were sleeping together.

What she'd had to do to save Dalton Ranch years ago went a long way to explain a few things about her. He was wasting Daisy's time and holding her back from finding a good man to start a family with.

She smiled but it faltered around the edges, and she tightened her hold on his hand. "Do you want to stop for something to eat? My treat," she said in an attempt to change the subject.

"You know I can always eat." He kept her hand in his, and she didn't try to pull away. He wasn't ready to let the physical part of their relationship go. Not yet. But soon. He'd have to do it soon.

She was so sweet and kind and real. And deserving of all the happiness life could give her. He should remind her of the incompatibility of their family plans, but she didn't like it when he brought it up, and he didn't want to bring down the mood.

Instead, he wanted to do something that would make her smile.

Chapter Sixteen

Adam followed Daisy into the kitchen with two bags of groceries and put them on the counter. "That's the last of them."

"Thank you." She made room for the milk in the refrigerator.

"Day-day." Her nephew screeched her name when he toddled around the corner and saw her.

"Hello, angel boy." She scooped Davy into her arms and covered his face with kisses until he was giggling. "Davy, I want you to meet Adam."

Adam smiled at the toddler, and Davy leaned in her arms and reached for the teenager, and Adam didn't hesitate to hold him. "Hey, there, little buddy."

Lizzy came into the kitchen. "Hello, again. I see you've met my son. If he let you hold him this quickly, you must be a good guy. Davy is a good judge of character."

"That's good to know."

"Hey, you only have one dimple," Lizzy said.

Daisy looked over her shoulder. That shared genetic trait was the kind of thing she looked for. Too bad Adam was too old to be hers.

Loren joined them in the kitchen. "Hi, Adam. I didn't

know you were here. Do you want to help me read to Davy and Rose before their nap time?"

"Sure, I can do that." Adam shifted Davy to his other hip and looked at Daisy. "But only if there isn't any work you need me to get done."

"There is nothing pressing right now. Go ahead and help Loren with the little ones."

The teens left the room with Loren chattering away to him about her horse, Mischief.

Lizzy started helping her put groceries away. "He seems like a good kid. I hope it's okay that I let him come in the gate. I probably should've called you, but I was late and rushing."

"I'm glad you sent him my way. I think he needs us more than we need him."

The sound of little boy giggles drifted through the house.

Daisy and Lizzy tiptoed down the hallway and looked into the living room and smiled at the scene.

Adam was sitting on the floor with Davy in his lap. Beside him, Loren held baby Rose. He was reading one of their favorite books and using different voices for each character.

Davy clapped and giggled at the animal sounds.

"That's so sweet," Lizzy whispered.

It sure was. If she never had any kids of her own, at least she had a hand in raising her nephew and nieces.

Finn had gone over to Dalton Ranch to teach Adam how to weld, and he was happy to report that he had picked up the technique quickly. Tonight, all the guys were hanging out at Finn's house, but he didn't want to go home without seeing Daisy. He found her in the home office.

"Hey, Daisy, how's it going?" Her smile was so sweet that he wanted to kiss her.

"Hi. How did the welding lesson go?"

"Good. He's a smart kid." He sat on the edge of the desk.

"I told you he'd be a good addition. Now do you trust my judgement?"

"You have your moments," he teased. "Do you happen to have my watch?"

"I do. I needed to borrow it for the stopwatch feature. It's on the dresser in my bedroom."

"How come you don't take other people's stuff?" he asked.

"I guess you're just extra special."

He couldn't resist tucking a lock of loose hair behind her ear, but then he stood before he did something stupid. Something against the rules. "I'll be right back. I want to ask you about the best saddle brand before I go home."

Upstairs in her bedroom, he saw Daisy's wish list on her bedside table. He started to turn away, but he couldn't resist looking to see if she'd added anything since he'd last seen it. And she had.

Daisy's New Year's Wish List
1) Sleep with a hot guy/Brief, fun affair

They could check both of those off her list. He'd been more than happy to assist with number one

2) Fall _____

Why hadn't she completed it? What was she waiting on? He had a feeling what her wish would be, but he was dying to know for sure.

3) Learn a new skill
4) Have an adventure

Maybe he should offer to teach her how to weld too. And an adventure was something they could accomplish fairly easily.

5) Be a mom

His skin prickled and he backed away from the list as if it was dangerous. And in a way, it was. He couldn't help her with that one.

Finn went downstairs and found everyone in the living room. Daisy was in her blue chair with a horse magazine, and Sage was in her pink one beside her with baby Rose asleep in her arms. Loren and Adam were playing checkers on the coffee table and trying to keep Davy from taking them while Lizzy tried to get his pajamas on.

"Where did Travis and Grayson go?" he asked everyone.

"They went to pick up your pizzas and said they would meet you at your house," Lizzy said.

"Excellent. I'm hungry. Adam, all the guys are getting together at my house tonight," he said. "Want to hang out with us? We're playing cards, watching a game and drinking beer."

Adam glanced at Daisy as if he needed to ask permission, even though it was after work hours. He seemed to realize what he'd done and jerked his eyes back to Finn. "Sure. I'd like to hang out and get to know everyone."

"Good, because you don't want to hang out around here for girls' night," Finn said. "They might try to give you a makeover."

Loren made a move on the game board. "I keep trying to get Aunt Daisy to let us do a makeover on her, but she always says maybe later."

Finn grinned at her across the room. "Come on, Daisy Maisy. Let your niece give you a makeover."

"Maybe I will." She flipped her blond hair over her shoulder.

He clapped a hand on Adam's back. "Are you bringing beer?"

"Only if they will let eighteen-year-olds buy it in this county."

"Oh, yeah. I forgot you're a kid."

"Whatever, old man." Adam stood up and stretched. "You should get the beer because they won't even bother carding you."

Finn chuckled and winked at Daisy.

She stood and called Finn over to her with the universal finger gesture and dropped her voice to a whisper. "Don't get him drunk, please. In fact, don't let him drink at all."

"That's no fun."

"I know. So sad." She lifted her arms as if she'd put them around his neck the way she did in private but then crossed them over her chest instead. "Thanks for making him feel welcome and part of things."

"I think you get the prize for that." He wanted to lean in and kiss her, but instead, he tugged on a lock of her hair. "See you tomorrow."

"Y'all have fun tonight."

On the short ride to Finn's ranch house, Adam seemed to have something on his mind. "You're the oldest brother, right?"

"Yep. Do you have siblings?"

"No. It was just me and my mom. No siblings, no dad."

"Any other family?"

"An uncle who is a bastard. He wants nothing to do with me, and the feeling is entirely mutual."

"That sucks." Finn opened his truck door and got out. This young man really was alone in the world. Daisy had seen that right away, and he admired her for it. He was probably just too jaded and suspicious of people.

Travis and Grayson came in shortly after them with a stack of pizzas they put on the kitchen counter. Everyone started grabbing slices and opening beers. Travis held out a beer to Adam, and the teenager hesitated but took it.

"You know he's not twenty-one, right?" Finn said to Travis.

"No. I didn't know that. No beer for you then. Now that I'm the dad, I feel like I should say that."

"Your son is two," Finn reminded him.

"But he won't be for long."

"Son of a bitch." Jake plowed his hands through his hair. "This laptop is making me crazy. It keeps doing weird stuff."

"Maybe I can help," Adam said, and took his pizza over to the kitchen table where Jake was sitting. "I'm pretty good with computers. Everybody came to me at school for help."

Finn and Travis left them to it and went into the living room to sit on the couch.

"I don't really know Adam yet, but he seems like a good kid," Travis said.

"It's like Daisy adopted him rather than hired him."

"The twins do tend to take in strays, like me. Sage and Daisy started looking out for me years ago. I'm only where I am today because of them. And I wouldn't have my son if Daisy hadn't taken my Lizzy to the hospital to hold babies. She came home with an orphan, and we became a family. My wife definitely takes after her aunts."

"I see what you mean. And now that you mention it, my brothers and I also worked on Dalton Ranch while we saved up to buy this ranch. Those are three amazing women."

"I might've taken Lizzy off the market, and Grayson did the same with Sage, but as you are well aware, Daisy is single."

"I understand single. I plan to *remain* single."

Travis chuckled and patted him on the back before picking up the remote control to change the channel.

I guess Daisy and I aren't being as secretive as we think.

The next day, Finn was still thinking about what Travis had said about Daisy being single. He couldn't quite get a handle on what he was feeling. It was too many conflicting things all at once. He wanted Daisy to have everything she desired, yet he was hanging on to their tryst longer than he should. January was halfway over, but the lust wasn't fading as he'd expected, and they weren't getting back to normal.

He didn't want to hold her back from the future she wanted and deserved, but there was a problem—he didn't want to give her up either. His plan going forward was to make some hard decisions. Spending some uninterrupted time together away from their ranches and the temptation of his house was step one. And that's what had brought them into town for dinner at the new Italian restaurant in Old Town Channing.

But sitting across from her in a dimly lit restaurant with candlelight flickering on her soft skin wasn't helping to decrease his desire for her. Not one little bit.

"You're quieter than usual tonight," she said.

He looked up from his bowl of baked ziti. "I didn't sleep well last night. I guess I'm just tired. How's your eggplant parmesan?"

"Excellent." She forked up a bite and extended it across the table. "Want to try it?"

He made a face. "I don't think so."

"Scaredy-cat."

He grinned and let himself relax, then leaned forward to let her feed him. "Hmm. That's not bad. It's actually pretty good."

"I've been telling you for ages that it's good."

Finn pushed away his worries and focused on enjoying their friendship, because that was the relationship he needed to nurture and protect.

While he waited for Daisy by the restaurant's front door, a couple of women at the bar caught his attention. They were about his age, beautiful and sexy from their sky-high heels to their red lips and carefully styled hair. Exactly the kind of women he would normally make a beeline to talk to, but his lack of a desire to do so surprised him.

And it wasn't only because he was here with Daisy; he just didn't have the urge to bother.

All he could think about was how they wouldn't be able to walk across his front yard with those shoes on. They would be too afraid of breaking a nail to help him work on the ranch. And he'd bet they couldn't ride like the wind as Daisy had done this morning on her horse.

Was it possible he could give her what she wanted?

What do I want? What do I really want?

His palms began to itch, and his throat tightened like it always did at the thought of being a father. Nope. He couldn't be that man.

Daisy stopped to let a family walk by before making her way to the front of the restaurant. Finn was casually leaning against a cedar post by the front door with one boot crossed over the other. Something in the bar across the way had caught his full attention, and she followed his gaze. A heaviness crowded her chest.

He was staring at a couple of beautiful ladies who wore tight-fitting dresses and high heels. She glanced down at her black jeans and boots. Her periwinkle sweater was old and needed to be replaced. She wasn't anything like the glamorous women who held Finn's complete attention. They were more like her sister than her.

Rather than raid her sister's closet now and then, maybe she should get some new clothes of her own.

Was he starting to lose interest in her like he'd said would happen? What was it he'd said? *Our curiosity will naturally burn itself out over time, and then we can get back to normal.*

The weight hanging from her heart grew heavier. The flame of desire wasn't burning out for her.

When Finn rubbed his eyes and sighed, she made her way over to him. "I'm ready if you are."

And that was the whole problem right there in a tidy little package. She was ready for love and a serious relationship, and he was not.

Chapter Seventeen

After watching Finn stare at the fancy ladies at the restaurant the night before, Daisy had been really thinking about the future. She felt like he was drifting away from her. She wanted their future to be shared, so she could either give up and once again bury her attraction to him and move on with her life, or she could try to do something about it.

Daisy stopped in the doorway of the home office where her parents had once worked together at the antique partner desk, face-to-face and laughing much of the time. Now, Sage was set up on one side, and Grayson had architectural plans spread out on the polished oak surface across from his wife. She was so thankful these two had found one another. They were so happy and in love.

Daisy's heart tugged with wanting. She wanted the man she was foolishly falling in love with to love her back in the same way. In the forever kind of way.

Sage looked up. "Oh, Daisy. How long have you been there?"

"Just a few seconds."

Her brother-in-law turned in his chair. "Morning, Daisy. How's it going?"

"Pretty good. Sage, do you have time to go shopping with me?"

Her sister's eyes gleamed. "Makeover shopping?"

"I don't know about a whole makeover, but I do need some clothes and possibly shoes."

"And maybe hair and makeup too?" her twin asked hopefully.

"Maybe."

Sage hopped up from her chair. "Gray, you're in charge of Rosie when she wakes up from her morning nap."

"No problem, honey." He stood, kissed his wife and smiled at Daisy. "You two have fun. And maybe bring home some of that fudge from the new candy shop."

"You got it." They shared one more quick kiss, and then Sage hooked her arm through Daisy's as if she was afraid she'd try to make a break for it.

Fifteen minutes later, they were driving down Main Street in the refurbished part of Channing that was called Old Town. In this area, Main Street traffic slowed to twenty miles per hour. Buildings ranging in age and style from the 1900s to about the 1950s stretched along both sides of the street. There were colorful awnings and sidewalks wide enough for lots of foot traffic. Older but well-tended houses in a variety of styles spread out from this area.

Sage parked her silver sports car in front of Glitz & Glam, the boutique owned by their high school friend Emma Hart.

"Maybe I should get some coffee before we do this," Daisy said. "I'm familiar with your marathon shopping."

"Not to worry. I'll go upstairs to her apartment above the store and make you a cup. You can drink it while Emma and I pick out clothes for you to try on."

"Okay. Let's do this." She moved to open her door.

"Wait." Sage touched her arm. "I hope you know that I don't think you *need* this makeover. You don't need lots of makeup or bling to be beautiful. You are perfect the way you are. I just enjoy doing this."

Daisy smiled. "I know, sis. I think you missed your calling. You should've had a TV program called Makeover Magician."

Sage laughed and opened her car door. "You joke, but I can very easily make a social media video and start a new account. You can be my first client."

"Let me think about it." She pretended to consider it for all of two seconds. "Absolutely not." She followed her sister into the boutique that was decorated in shades of pink with lush velvet curtains framing the plate-glass window. Blingy fixtures hung from the high tin ceiling and artwork featuring flowers gave the place a feminine elegance.

"Hello, ladies," Emma said. "I'm so excited to do this."

"You knew we were coming?" Daisy asked.

"I did. Sage called me."

Her sister put an arm around her shoulders. "It's time to give her wardrobe a boost. But I promised Daisy a cup of coffee before we stuff her into a dressing room."

"That's not helping me want to do this," she said in a sing-song voice.

Sage ignored that and tightened her arm around her twin. "Do you mind if I go upstairs to your apartment and make a cup?"

"Not at all," Emma said. "I'll help Daisy look around while we wait."

She should've known she'd have both of them teaming up on her.

Emma hummed along with the song playing softly on the sound system. "I recently unpacked a shipment of new clothes that will look fabulous on you."

"I'll take your word for it." Daisy smiled to herself. She

wasn't as opposed to this shopping trip as she was leading them to believe. It was more fun this way. And she liked making Sage happy.

Emma held up a maroon dress with a crisscrossing bodice that plunged into a deep V. "This one will look fabulous on you,"

"I'm not sure I can pull off that look."

"Of course you can."

Her sister returned with a steaming mug of coffee with cream and a homemade chocolate chip cookie. "Now you can't say you don't have any energy."

"Thank you." She grinned, lifted the mug higher and blew steam across the hot liquid.

She sat on a stool behind the counter and drank her coffee while the two of them buzzed around the shop gathering way too many clothes. Daisy even rang up a couple of customers for Emma while she waited for them to fill her dressing room.

Right before she was *stuffed* into the small space, Loren came into the shop. "Hi, Aunt Daisy. When I found out you were here, I walked over from my friend's house to help. But I can only stay for an hour because we're working on a school project."

Daisy hugged her niece. "I'm glad you could join us, even if it's just for a little while. But why aren't you at school?"

"It's a teachers' workday."

"Good timing. Sage, what am I trying on first?"

"Start with the dresses." Her sister rubbed her hands together and looked generally pleased as punch.

Daisy pulled off her shirt and caught sight of her plain, white, serviceable bra in the dressing room mirror. *Boring.* She had no desire to be totally pushed up and out like an offering, but she could certainly do better than this. "I think I might need a new bra," she called out to the girls.

"I'm on it," Emma said. "Same size as Sage?"

"Yes, please." She put on the first dress and was not impressed but stepped out for the judging. To her relief, the dress was vetoed by everyone.

"Try on the green dress next," Sage said.

"Here are three bras to try," Emma said.

The black bra had scalloped lacy edges and gave her a subtle lift that she had to admit was an improvement. The emerald green cashmere dress was ultrasoft against her skin and had a scooped neckline and a skirt that hugged her hips then flared past her knees.

She opened the dressing room door. "I like this one."

"Oh, me too. That's gorgeous on you, Aunt Daisy."

She tried on what felt like a million more clothes and shoes. Daisy left Glitz & Glam with two full bags and wearing the green sweater dress and a beautiful pair of brown suede boots with wedge heels.

"I need food," Daisy said when they made it out onto the wide sidewalk.

"Me too. Let's put the bags in my trunk and then eat at the Rodeo Café."

"Perfect."

Sage looked at her watch. "And then we have one other place to go."

"To the candy shop for Grayson's fudge."

"Thanks for reminding me. Make that two more stops. We have appointments for haircuts at the new spa on the corner."

Daisy laughed. "I should have known."

She only got her hair trimmed, but let them curl it, which was something she rarely did. And she even bought some

new makeup and let the beautician apply it for her. She
hardly recognized herself and felt a little like she was playing dress up, but she also felt pretty and flirty and feminine. Like a woman who matched her name.

What would Finn think of her new look? The thought
was dangerous but her urge to see him was overwhelming. While Sage paid, she pulled out her phone and sent
him a text message.

I'm craving pasta. Want to meet me in town for dinner
at Antone's?

His response came quickly. Sure thing. What time?

How soon can you get to town?

Thirty minutes. Meet you in the bar area.

She sent him a thumbs-up emoji, then put her phone
away. "Sage, when you're ready, can you drop me off at
Antone's?"

"Sure. But why?" Her sister grabbed her purse and
headed for the door of the beauty shop.

Daisy started to chew her thumbnail but didn't want to
mess up her burgundy manicure and snapped her hand to
her side. "Because I'm meeting Finn for dinner."

Her twin smiled and grasped Daisy's forearm as they
walked down the sidewalk. "Tell me how it's going. You
haven't said much lately."

"I think our fling is burning out."

"What? No. Why do you say that?"

"Because that's what he does. He doesn't make long-
term or permanent commitments. I went into this knowing

that he was not interested in a relationship." She sighed. "And I see the way he looks at other women."

Sage unlocked the car and went around to her side. "But lately I've seen the way he looks at *you*. I thought maybe he was starting to see the error of his ways. Seeing you dressed up like this might stoke the flames."

Daisy's skin heated, and she wasn't sure if it was embarrassment or anticipation. She was about to find out.

What am I doing?

Daisy waved to her sister and then went inside the restaurant to wait for Finn. She stopped in the restroom to swipe on a coat of her new glossy red lipstick, but when she studied her reflection, she wasn't completely sold on the bold look. She almost wiped it off but stopped herself.

"Be bold. Don't be scared to give it a try," she whispered then smiled.

Her red lips reminded her of the live action movie image of Maleficent, and she suddenly felt sexy. There was nothing wrong with mixing a little bit of Maleficent in with the sweetness of Sleeping Beauty.

She found a seat at the small bar and ordered a glass of red wine. She could see a reflection of the entrance in the mirror above the bar. Right on time, Finn came through the door and was standing in the middle of the room looking around. He didn't know it was her. She turned on her bar stool and called his name.

"Finn. Over here."

"Hi, Sage. Where's Daisy?"

She tipped her head to the side and slowly smiled, her single dimple appearing on her cheek. "You've found her."

His mouth went slack. "Daisy?"

"In the flesh. And makeup and heels." She extended one leg to prove the point.

His eyes tracked down to the suede boots that weren't the least bit Western.

Her pulse began to race. She suddenly felt self-conscious and smoothed her skirt. "You don't like it?"

"No… I mean…" He whistled softly and a slow smile made his eyes soften like they did in the bedroom. "You look gorgeous."

Her skin tingled as warmth spread from her center outward. "It's not too much?"

"It's still you. A little extra shine on something that's already beautiful." His smile was the sexy one that she rarely saw in public.

"Sage will be happy to hear that you approve of her makeover. All I asked her to do was help me pick out a few new clothes, but…" She touched her curls then traced her manicured fingers along her body. "It spun out of control."

"Very nice spinning." His gaze went to her lips. "Can I change one thing?"

"Sure. I guess so."

He grabbed a cocktail napkin from the stack on the bar and began to gently wipe off her red lipstick. "There. That's the way I like you." He brushed a quick soft kiss across her lips.

Her breath caught. He'd kissed her. In public.

If his wide-eyed expression was an indication, he was as startled as she was.

"Dalton party of two. Your table is ready," said a hostess.

He put his hand on the small of her back, and neither of them spoke as they followed the woman to a table. But it didn't take long for them to start laughing about something Jake had done and the antics of the baby goat.

Their meal was filled with laughs and teasing and sexual tension that was more delicious than the food.

On the way home, they kept finding excuses to touch one another. A brush of the arm. A caress on her cheek. Any excuse at all.

"Wow. Look at that moon," she said.

He pulled through the gate of her ranch, but instead of driving up the curving road to the farmhouse, he pulled off to the side and turned off the engine.

Without a word, he got out and grabbed a couple of blankets from the back seat of the truck's cab. "Are you coming? The moon is waiting."

"For once I'm not dressed for this but count me in."

He chuckled. "That's what I was hoping you'd say."

He spread a blanket in the bed of his truck. They climbed onto it and leaned their backs against the cab, and then he covered them with the other blanket.

"You really thought I was my sister?"

"At first. But when you smiled, I knew it was you. Why the change?"

She shrugged and tipped up her face to the moon. "I don't know. My clothes were getting worn out and I needed a few new things. And I guess I'm just experimenting a little bit."

"There's nothing wrong with that." He slowly trailed his fingers through her curls then put his arm around her shoulders and settled her more closely against his side.

The first date vibes kept coming, and she didn't want to admit that she'd longed for this kind of attention from him. Something wobbled inside her, and she sucked in a sharp, cold breath.

Without truly realizing what she'd been doing, had she subconsciously let herself be made over because she'd been testing to see how he would react to her all fixed up? She suddenly felt bad, like she was tricking him into believing she was someone she was not.

"What's wrong?" he asked. "You tensed up. Arè you too cold?"

She shifted toward him and rested her hand on his chest. "I'm warm enough."

He'd kissed her in public, flirted through dinner and now held her under the stars. Even though he hadn't liked the lipstick, was it only the addition of the clothes, hair and makeup that were making him be all romantic and breaking the rules?

"Tomorrow, my camouflage will be gone, and I'll turn back into Cinderella before the ball. A cowgirl Cinderella with dirt on her face."

He tipped up her chin and studied her. "Hey, I might have thought you were your sister for a few seconds, but you *are* identical twins." When she started to speak, he pressed a finger to her lips. "It's not camouflage. Even with the changes, I see you. You're beautiful with or without all the extra fluff."

She felt light enough to float. "Thanks for saying that."

"It's true."

"How many of our rules have we broken?"

"Well, a kiss in public and—" he kissed her, soft and sweet liked he done before "—in the back of my truck. So that's at least two."

She touched his cheek and loved the way his beard tickled her fingers. "What do you think about that expression that says some rules are meant to be broken?"

"I think it's true. Want to make out like teenagers?"

"Yes," she whispered against his lips. "I would like that very much."

Chapter Eighteen

Adam tried to get comfortable on the double bed in his apartment, but his head was throbbing, and he was so hot and achy that he couldn't sleep. Now his throat was starting to burn when he swallowed.

He missed his mom more than ever. He missed the way she used to take care of him when he was sick. She'd always made him soup and hot tea with honey. When he'd had a fever, she'd put cool cloths on his forehead. He'd felt safe and protected. And loved.

But there was no one who loved him now.

Adam pressed his fingertips to his aching eyes to hold back tears. His mom had gotten sick, and then been gone so fast. He hadn't had time to prepare. His life had changed so drastically, so fast. From living on an awesome ranch with the best mom ever to being all on his own. With no home.

When he'd learned his childhood home was about to be sold, leaving school and sneaking back inside had been the right decision. It had been a huge relief to discover the things his mom had left for him in their secret hiding place. The discovery had been way more than he'd expected.

Adam swallowed and winced at the pain. He needed medicine. And help. The only person he could think of to go to was Daisy. In a short time, she had become an important part of his life, and even though he probably shouldn't, he couldn't help it. He cracked open his eyes to look at the clock. It was 10:30 at night, and hopefully she would still be awake.

He got up, pulled his coat on over his sweatpants and walked up toward the farmhouse. The lights were on in the kitchen, and he was happy to see someone moving around. The night wasn't that cold, but he shivered and shoved his hands into his pockets. His whole body was chilled and damp with sweat.

He knocked on the kitchen door and went inside when Daisy called out for him to come in. She was wearing purple pajamas, fuzzy slippers and her hair was in a knot on top of her head.

"Hi, Daisy." The bright lights hurt his eyes and he squinted. "Do you have any aspirin or some other kind of pain reliever?"

"Yes, I do." She put another plate into the dishwasher. "Hey, you don't look so good."

"I don't feel so good."

She dried her hands, came around the kitchen island, felt his forehead and gasped. "Adam, you have a fever. You're really sick. Come with me right now."

"Where are we going?"

"Upstairs to my guest room. You can't be out there in the apartment all alone."

"But I might get you sick."

"Don't you worry about that for one second."

Relief washed over him. He didn't have to navigate being alone and sick. He took a step, but his vision wavered, and he braced his hands on the cool marble surface of the island. He had the urge to put his cheek against the cold stone.

An arm slid around his waist. "Adam, if you're going to pass out, let me know."

He shook his head. "I'm okay now."

"Hold on to me just in case." She pulled his arm over her shoulders, kept hold of his waist and guided him upstairs. "I talked to Finn a little while ago and he said Jake is also sick. I guess going to guys' night wasn't such a good idea."

He sat on the edge of the bed and let her help him get his coat and boots off. "I'm sorry to be a bother."

"You're not. Please don't think that way." She pulled down the blue bedding and waited for him to get under the covers. "Lie down and get comfortable."

He did as she asked and let his head sink into the soft pillow. "Whose room is this?"

"It's the one Sage and Grayson use, unless there are too many people staying here, and then they go stay in that little cabin behind the red barn."

He couldn't imagine having so much family that a house this big was filled up.

"Will you drink hot tea with honey and lemon?"

The backs of his eyes burned with tears. "That would be great. That's just what my mom used to make for me when I was sick."

Daisy brushed his hair back from his forehead. "I'm glad I can be here for you. I'll be right back with meds, water and tea." She hurried from the room.

His throat was tight with more tears he wasn't willing to shed. He wasn't sure if it was because he was sick or because he missed his mom taking care of him or because Daisy was being so nice.

Or because I'm just a runaway kid on a mission who is pretending to be a man.

Chapter Nineteen

Daisy hadn't expected to take care of a sick child tonight, but she was glad Adam had come to her. She reminded herself that he wasn't a kid, even though Finn thought so. He was almost nineteen, but being alone while you were sick was the worst.

She'd given him cold and flu medicine and gotten him to eat a bowl of soup and was about to leave him to rest. "Tell me if I'm hovering too much."

"You're not."

He'd said it so quickly that she got the feeling he didn't want to be alone. "I'm going to take these dishes down to the kitchen, and then I'll be back."

"Thanks for taking care of me." He pulled the covers up to his chin and closed his eyes.

When she returned to his room, she carried the rocking chair from her bedroom, and, as quietly as she could, put it down beside his bed. He cracked open his eyes and gave her a weak smile before falling asleep.

There was a new book she'd been planning to read, and now seemed like a good time to start it. She read the first chapter, but her eyes were getting heavy. When she was sure he was sleeping peacefully, she went back to her own bed to get some rest.

Something woke Daisy, but she wasn't sure what it was. Thinking it might have been Adam calling out, she pulled on her robe and went to his room. He was moaning and his face was damp with sweat. His fever was back, and the forehead thermometer read one hundred and two degrees. She touched his cheek, and he opened his eyes.

"Mom?"

Daisy's heart squeezed, and she brushed back his damp hair. "You're okay. Rest your eyes while I get a cold cloth." In his fevered state, did he really think she was his mother?

She went to the bathroom, held a washcloth under cold water and squeezed it out. His eyes were closed when she returned, but she sat on the bed and bathed his forehead and cheeks with the cool cloth.

He blinked open his eyes and moaned.

"Hey, there. How are you feeling?" she asked.

"Crappy."

"I need you to take some more medicine to help with the fever." She helped him sit up.

He swallowed the pills then eased back onto the pillow and wiped a hand over his face. "Is it hot in here?"

"No. I'm afraid that's just the fever. I'll go get you some ice water." She patted his hand and turned to go. Right as she went out the door, she heard him say something.

"Moms always make things better."

She paused and held a hand to her chest. It was just the fever talking, but it still touched her that he would think of her in that kind of role. She would take care of him the way she hoped someone else took care of hers.

After Finn finished his share of the morning chores, and picked up the slack for Jake and Adam while they were sick, he went in through Daisy's kitchen door to pick up the chicken soup she'd made for Jake. So far, he and Riley weren't sick, and it would hopefully stay that way.

No one was in her kitchen, so he checked the downstairs rooms, which were also empty. Upstairs, he found her in the guest room standing at Adam's bedside. She was holding a digital thermometer to his forehead, but the teenager was sound asleep.

The rocking chair from her bedroom had been brought into the room, and a couple of books were on the floor beside it along with two empty coffee mugs. She'd been sitting at the bedside of a sick young man. A teenager who had no mother.

A mother who had no child.

His chest tightened, and he pressed a hand to the knot in his stomach. He knew in this moment, without a doubt, that she was meant to be a mother, and he needed to help her reach that dream. Not keep her from it.

Like it or not, their time was limited. He would have to let her go…soon.

She looked up, smiled and held a finger to her lips, then followed him out of the room and closed the door behind them.

"How's Adam?"

She started down the stairs in front of him. "Fever, headache and body aches, but his throat isn't bothering him anymore. What about Jake?"

"Moaning and groaning but about the same as Adam. The girl he went out with a few days ago is also sick. She went to the doctor and was diagnosed with the flu, so now we know where this came from and what it is."

"Sounds like it." She slumped onto the couch like she was exhausted. "I wonder why Adam was the only other one who got sick."

He took a seat beside her. "When he was over at my house the other night, he sat at the table with Jake and helped him work on the computer. I would guess that's how. Did you know that Adam is really good with computers?"

"No, I didn't. But it doesn't surprise me. He learns really fast and is a hard worker." She rested her head on Finn's shoulder. "I'm so tired."

"You've been working hard taking care of him. You need to get some sleep so you don't get sick. After I take the soup home to Jake, I'll come back over here, and you can take a nap. I can look after the kid."

She yawned and lifted her head from his shoulder. "You'd do that for me?"

"That's what friends do."

Her expression flickered with something strange, but she looked away and stood before he could analyze it. "The container of soup is on the kitchen island. I'm going to grab a shower while you take it to Jake. I'll see you soon."

When he got back to Daisy's half an hour later, she was already asleep, so he went into the guest room where Adam was also sleeping. He knew the kid wasn't sick enough to need twenty-four-hour care, but he sat in her rocking chair anyway.

The time had come for him to put enough distance between him and Daisy to ease out of their tryst. He'd granted her first wish, but giving up this closeness was going to be way harder than he'd imagined. She might have written down the words *brief fun affair*, but the brief part was tough. Too bad she hadn't written the words *easy to give up*.

Daisy couldn't be "his" forever. He didn't do long-term commitments—other than friendship and brotherhood.

And the thought of being responsible for a child still made his whole body itch.

Adam groaned, brought a hand to his head and cracked open one eye. When he saw Finn, he jerked awake. "What are you doing here?"

"Just came to check on you. Daisy is taking a nap."

Adam cleared his throat. "You know I'm not a little kid, and I don't need constant looking after."

"I know."

He shifted into a sitting position. "I heard Jake is sick too."

"Yep. His date gave him the flu and he gave it to you. I guess that's the thanks you get for helping him with the laptop."

"I feel bad that I'm being a burden on Daisy. I should probably go back to my apartment."

Finn smiled. "You can try, but Daisy isn't going to let you. She's a mama bear about things like this. Just let her take care of you. I'll help her around the ranch while you get better."

"Thanks for that." Adam reached for the glass on the bedside table and took a long drink of ice water. "Did you bring this fresh glass of water to me?"

"No. That would be your fairy godmother."

"Daisy is really nice. She reminds me of the way my mom took care of me when I was sick."

"She does have that quality."

Time's ticking. Finn thought with a twisting sensation in his gut.

Now he felt like he was the one who was sick.

The next afternoon, Finn walked through his front door and heard the clip-clop of Rascal's hooves and the click of Astro's nails on the hardwood floor as they rushed to greet him. He knelt to let the goat hop up onto his thigh and scratched the dog's head. "What kind of mischief have you two caused today?"

Jake was pacing across the living room from the fireplace to the front windows and back again. His face was scrunched into a confused expression.

"Why aren't you resting? What's wrong?" he asked his sick brother.

Jake stopped moving and looked up. "Dad died."

He was confused by his brother's statement. Was this some kind of weird, delayed reaction to something that happened when Jake was fourteen years old? Was he having some kind of weird fever dream? What had happened to make him bring it up now?

"Do you have fever again? That was a long time ago. What has you thinking about it after all these years?"

"Finn, he died a few weeks ago."

It felt as if he'd been hit in the chest. "What? No way."

"I got a phone call from a lawyer in Montana. He said he sent a letter."

He dropped onto his usual spot in the curve of the sectional and the goat hopped up beside him. He remembered the letter going up in flames in the fireplace. "What about the truck accident years ago?"

"Apparently, he didn't die back then."

"But what about the body in the burned up eighteen-wheeler?" Finn asked. "Who was that?"

"I have no idea." Jake sat in one of the recliners and pulled a blanket over himself. "Dad was living in central Montana and died of heart failure."

"This is nuts. Are you sure it wasn't a scam phone call?"

"It's real. And he left you something in his will."

"Just to me?"

"Apparently so."

"You know whatever it is that I'll share it with you and Riley."

"I know. I'm not worried about that. From how I remember things being, I can't imagine that there was much he had to leave to anyone."

"Who knows? He liked classic cars. Maybe he finally fixed one up." Finn leaned forward as Rascal bounced across the back of the sofa.

"You should call the lawyer. I wrote down his number."

"I'll call him later. Where is Riley? Does he know about this yet?"

"Do I know what?" Riley asked as he came in the front door with an armload of groceries.

"You might want to grab a stiff drink before we tell you," Jake suggested as he pulled the blanket up under his chin.

"Let me put the cold groceries up, and I'll be right back," Riley said, and walked away. Only their calm brother could so patiently wait to hear big news.

Finn leaned forward and rested his head in his hands. "You are absolutely sure this is real?"

"As sure as I can be."

Riley returned and sat in the second recliner.

"Tell him what you told me about the lawyer calling."

They quickly brought their middle brother up to speed, and now all three of them sat there in stunned silence. Their father had not died years ago in a fiery eighteen-wheeler crash. Apparently, he'd been living the life of an unencumbered man with no sons to slow him down.

"Do you think he really faked his own death?" Jake asked.

Finn shrugged. "Looks that way. I'll call the lawyer and see what else I can find out about Dad."

A dad they'd assumed had died years ago. A dad who'd been alive and couldn't be bothered with contacting his three sons, proving that he really hadn't wanted them. Finn's feelings of abandonment hadn't just been a young boy's demons whispering in his ear at night.

How could he have left them alone so often and made them feel like they didn't matter? Sure, their father had barely been eighteen years old when Finn was born, but as far as he was concerned, that was a weak excuse. With the terrible example set, Finn wanted to think he'd be the opposite kind of parent, but what if he took after the old man?

"All these years," Riley said, and absentmindedly rubbed the dog's back. "Who does something like that?"

"You were right," Jake said to Finn. "Dad really was a selfish bastard."

"Finn." Riley shifted to face him better. "You've been more of a father to us than he ever was."

His chest tightened with the compliment. "Are you forgetting the time it was my fault Jake got hurt and almost died?"

Jake waved a hand. "We fought, I ran away and got hurt. It wasn't your fault."

It had certainly felt like it was his fault. The memories made him sick. He'd never forget losing his cool, fighting with Jake and then finding his youngest brother bleeding and unconscious under their old tree house. Giving blood and sitting with him at the hospital had been all he could do. He had done the best he could to take care of his little brothers, but had always felt a sense of never being enough.

That had been the moment he decided he would never

willingly become a father. He'd raised his brothers, and it was too risky to be in charge of someone's life in that way.

"You guys okay if I take a walk?" he asked.

"We're fine." His brothers echoed one another.

After pulling on his coat, he put the goat on Jake's lap so she wouldn't try to follow him. "I'll be back in a while."

"Don't worry about us." Riley turned on the TV. "We're having pizza for dinner. Take however long you need."

The sun was setting when he went outside. Finn was feeling raw and confused, his emotions bubbling to the surface, and he absolutely could not fall apart in front of his little brothers. He'd always had to be the strong one. The one who took care of the little hellions. Feeding them, making them take a bath and getting them to school. All of this from the time he'd been about nine years old, and honestly, much of the time even before their young, free-spirited mom had drowned while boating.

Without consciously doing it, he headed straight for Daisy's house. He craved the peace and calm she gave him and needed to be around her for just a little while.

He sighed and kicked a clump of dry winter grass as he stomped across the cold ground. He could not let himself become too needy.

Maybe if he explained all this to her then she would understand his motives for remaining a childless bachelor.

He shook his head. None of this was fair to her. Plain and simple, he couldn't give her what she wanted. Not as a husband or a father to her children. But that didn't mean she couldn't have her dreams come true. Without him.

He growled at himself and walked faster. When he neared the back of her house, he waved to Sage through the window above their kitchen sink, and she motioned for him to come inside. "Hi, Finn. What's going on with you this evening?"

"Not much," he lied. "Is your sister around?"

"She's upstairs in the nursery rocking Rose to sleep, but you can go on up."

"I'll make sure to be quiet." He went up the stairs, taking care not to clomp his boots on the wooden treads, but he could hear Daisy talking before he got to the doorway of the nursery. She was sitting in a rocking chair with her back to him. She resettled her niece onto her lap. Instead of joining them, he stayed where he was, curious to see their interaction. Rose rooted against Daisy's chest.

"I'm sorry, Rosie Posie. I don't have what your mama does." Daisy's sigh was so sad. "I wish more than you could know that I had my own baby who I could feed from my own breasts, but I'm… I'm not a mom." She kissed her niece's forehead. "But I'm not giving up hope. I think things are moving in the right direction."

Finn's gut twisted and guilt hit him square in the chest with the stab of a thousand knives. He hadn't meant to, but he was leading her on. Making her believe he was going to change his mind about being a family man. She shouldn't have to give up her dreams for him.

The time had come. He had to let her go.

Chapter Twenty

Daisy eased Rose into her crib and then startled when she turned around and saw Finn leaning in the doorway. "Hey, there," she whispered, and then tiptoed from the room, leaving the door open a crack.

"I didn't want to interrupt."

He looked so sad, and she instantly knew something was wrong. She couldn't resist reaching up to brush her fingers over the short beard covering his cheek. "Tell me what's wrong."

"Want to take a walk?"

"Sure." Her pulse began thumping uncomfortably, and sweat broke out between her breasts. With the curious way he was acting, she had a bad feeling he was about to end their tryst before the month was over and go back to dating all those much sexier women.

She put on her coat, and they went out the front door. "Tell me what's on your mind."

"My dad died."

She waited for him to continue, but he remained silent. "When you were a teenager, right?"

"No. A few weeks ago."

"What?" She stopped walking and faced him. "How can that be? What about the truck accident?"

He shrugged. "I guess he faked his death."

"Wow. This is…"

"Completely crazy," he said, filling in the blank and then starting to walk again. "I don't know a lot of details yet."

She took hold of his hand and was glad when he held on tight. She'd learned that she could calm him with her touch, and he needed the physical contact as much as she did. Now, if she could just make him see that he would make an amazing dad. "Was your father wanted by the law?"

"Not that I know of."

"Is there a funeral or anything?"

"I assume that's all done. But apparently, he left me something in his will. I don't expect it to be much of anything, but I'll call the lawyer tomorrow."

"I'm here for you. Whatever you need." Finn was a dependable, caring man who rescued animals, but spending time in his arms with only the heat of bare skin between them had been enlightening. She'd discovered a tenderness inside of him that he kept hidden from most of the world. This unexpected news was affecting him more than he'd ever admit.

He remained silent as they walked. There was something else bothering him. Something he wanted to say, but he kept stopping himself. She could feel it.

She'd also learned that he needed time to digest news before he talked about it. The best thing she could do was to give him that time and be there for him. Not to mention, she didn't want to hear him say he was calling an end to their romance.

"We don't have to talk if you don't want to." She squeezed his hand to show her silent support.

The next afternoon Daisy found out that Jake and Riley had gone to San Antonio with her brother-in-law, leaving

Finn home alone. She drove over to his house, but before she could get to his front door, he came out with his keys in his hand.

"Hey, Daisy. I wasn't expecting you." He continued walking, but it was not toward her.

"Going somewhere?"

Rather than meeting her gaze, he looked at his watch. "I'm meeting someone in town. Was there something you needed?"

She bit the inside of her cheek to keep from asking who he was meeting in town, because she knew it wasn't his brothers or Travis. It was difficult to speak around the prickly, foreboding-filled lump that was lodged in her throat, but she forced out a few words. "Nothing that can't wait."

"Cool. I'll talk to you later." He gave her a wave and headed for his truck.

She rushed for hers and got in, unwilling to look any more foolish than she already felt by standing there and watching him drive away. The sound of his truck starting up was like the final bell that marked the beginning of the end of their romance.

Daisy wiped a tear from her cheek. She'd wanted to find comfort and oblivion in his arms, and assumed he would want to as well, but that didn't seem to be at the top of his list.

Her chest felt like it was caving in on itself, and her throat burned. She'd thought that she meant more to him than this. Thought she'd somehow be different than all the other women.

Foolish!

Over the next couple of days, he dodged all of her attempts to talk with one lame excuse or another. She stopped trying, giving him space, but more so, giving herself a chance to lick her wounds. His behavior was more than needing time to think. This was avoidance—of her.

He was already tired of her, just like had happened with her ex-husband. The time had come to fall back on what was left of the 10 percent of her love she'd withheld for this very occasion. The impending heartache was becoming a reality.

Chapter Twenty-One

Dillon Cameron's birthday party at the Dalton Ranch was not where Finn wanted to be, but he'd promised to help man the barbecue pit, and that's where he'd started drinking beer. And then switched to whiskey.

The party was in full swing with lots of eating, drinking and laughing. But Finn didn't feel a part of it. He was on the outside looking in as Daisy moved on without him. Staying away from her had been way harder than he'd expected, and it was unforgivable that he hadn't talked to her about the end of their tryst.

Every time he tried, his mouth refused to cooperate, and his brain couldn't convince him otherwise. It refused to give him the right words.

He knew she was hurt by his withdrawal, but at the moment, she looked pretty happy laughing with Dr. Birthday Boy. The other man's hand was on the small of her back, right where *he* liked to kiss the little dimples above her curvy bottom. But that was something he should not—could not—do anymore.

His gut twisted. He'd thought he was ready to be around her without wanting to kiss her, but that was not the case. As he watched her moving around the party, he still wanted to press his mouth to hers and slide his fingers through her hair. This wasn't just lust. This was…

What is this feeling?

He was miserable. And drunk. He looked down into his glass and tossed back the last sip. He grimaced as the burn worked its way down into his stomach. Making this his last drink would be a smart thing to do. He scoffed at himself. Smart was not something he'd been lately.

All of this was a bad combination on a regular day, but the sight of Daisy enjoying herself with Dillon was not helping. In fact, it was kicking his bad mood up to dangerous. A mood that usually got him into trouble of one kind or another.

Daisy's laugh caught his attention again. Of course it was Dr. Cameron who was making her smile when all he'd been doing lately was the opposite. Dillon could give her things he could not. A family. Not to mention the vet was someone whose bank account balance was a lot closer to hers than his was. He would have to get used to seeing her with someone else. Someone who could give her marriage and babies.

Dillon handed a toy to Davy and smiled at Loren who was holding her baby sister. "I can't wait to have kids of my own," he said. "I've always wanted to be a dad."

Daisy ducked her head, and his insides crumpled.

*I have to protect her from...*me.

Someone called his name, and he turned to see a girl he'd once dated heading his way with a big, bright, lipstick smile. Daisy was also looking his way. Now was his chance—as much as he did not want to—to continue pushing Daisy away. Right into someone else's arms.

His old girlfriend flung herself at him, and he grabbed her up in a hug that lifted her feet off the ground. Daisy scowled and then looked away. Doing this felt so wrong.

He needed to talk to Daisy. He couldn't put it off any longer. On his way over to pull Daisy aside, he bumped into a woman he didn't know. He automatically put out his arms to hold her up.

"Sorry. I wasn't watching where I was going." He'd been laser focused on the woman he had to let go.

The brunette grasped the fabric of his shirt, raised onto her toes and kissed his cheek. "No worries, handsome." She took her time letting go of him.

This time Daisy's scowl was more of a glare, and she turned her back on the sight of him with another woman in his arms. He had a pretty good idea what she was feeling because he'd felt it when he watched her with another man.

As she rushed from the room toward the stairs, he thought he saw a tear slide down her cheek. He couldn't bear to let her go off so upset without at least talking to her, so he followed her.

"Daisy, wait."

She stopped at the very top of the stairs. "You're drunk," she said under her breath so the whole party wouldn't hear her. "Go home and sleep it off."

He rushed up the rest of the steps and followed her down the hall to her bedroom doorway. "I need to talk to you about—"

She spun on him and jabbed a finger toward his chest. "Finn, stop. Our arrangement is over. We're done. You can go flirt with anyone you want. Forget that we have ever been more than friends."

The full weight of the hit to his heart was so sharp and unexpected that he took a step back. "Shouldn't we talk about this?"

"Oh, *now* you want to talk? After days of silence? Just stop this and go home."

He was starting to panic, and he grasped her hand. "Daisy, please."

"Hey! Stop right there!" Adam snapped at Finn, and then stepped in front of the much bigger man, pressing an open palm against his chest. "She told you to go home. Do not treat her like this."

"Boy, do you realize I could pound your scrawny butt into the dirt?" Finn wouldn't hit the kid for a million bucks, because he knew what it felt like to get slapped around, but Adam didn't know that.

"Finn!" Daisy said, and snapped her hands to her hips.

Adam did not back down. "Standing up for Daisy is worth whatever you do to me. She deserves more respect than this."

The kid was right about that.

She put her hands on Adam's shoulders and urged him back from the other man. "Adam, I've got this. He won't hurt me."

Guilt and shame hit Finn and curdled in his gut. He would never hurt anyone. He was screwing things up left and right tonight. He should've gone home hours ago. He could try to smooth things over and make it up to her, but if they made up and ended up in bed and kept going down this romantic road, he'd only be delaying her from finding a man who could give her what she wanted and needed. A man like Dillon.

"You're a brave kid. Respect. And for the record, I would never hurt either of you."

Daisy patted the young man's back. "Thanks, Adam. It's all good."

He shot Finn one more glare and then went down the hall to the bathroom, leaving them alone.

Finn turned to Daisy and met her furious scowl. "I'm sorry, sweetheart. I'm sorry for everything. I'll go away and give you space. I'm walking home."

"Good idea." She opened her door, went inside and closed it without a backward glance.

"I'm such a screwup," he mumbled, and turned to go.

At least he had the perfect reason to get out of town.

Daisy was peeking through a crack in her bedroom door when Finn hung his head and walked away. The look on his face broke her heart but she needed him clear headed for this conversation. They would talk tomorrow and work through this mess.

She stepped out a minute later and was surprised to see Adam standing there with a worried expression on his face. "I'm sorry you had to see that."

"Did you break up?"

His question surprised her. "There is nothing to break up." She said it, but she didn't believe it.

"Oh." He shoved his hands into his front pockets. "Until the last couple of days, you both seemed happy, and I thought things were going well between you two."

She leaned against the wall and sighed. "We are good friends who blurred the lines when we shouldn't have."

"I didn't mean to get in your business. I was just worried about you."

"You're sweet, and I appreciate your concern. Finn and I just have something we need to work through. It will be fine. Don't worry." She crossed her fingers that what she was saying was true.

He nodded. "Okay."

"Let's go downstairs and try to enjoy the rest of the party."

A few minutes later, Dillon made his way over to her. "Everything okay?"

She put on her best smile. "It will be. Sometimes friends… disagree."

"I get that. Want to meet my sisters?"

"Of course."

"There's one of them now." He pointed to a lovely woman with sleek, shiny auburn hair down to her waist. "All three of them came to town to surprise me for my birthday, and now I'll be sleeping on my couch."

His smile told her that he didn't mind a bit.

She met all three of them and did her best to enjoy herself, but when she couldn't fake the smile any longer, she headed for the stairs.

Adam stopped her before she could get there. "Are you going to bed?"

"I am. Will you do me a favor and tell Sage I have a headache and went to bed?"

"Sure." He hesitated and moved from foot to foot. "You know where I am if you need me."

"I sure do. Go enjoy the party and talk some more to that pretty girl who was smiling at you."

He nodded and blushed. "Good night, Daisy."

With a house still full of guests, she grabbed her pajamas and went to take a shower. She stood under the hot spray and let her tears mingle with the water.

Just when she was starting to believe there could be more between them, Finn had to turn into a jerk. "This is my own fault."

She rested her forehead against the tile wall. She should have resisted her attraction to Finn, but she'd thought she could handle a physical relationship. She'd been fooling herself in a big way.

Once she was curled up in bed, her sister knocked on her door and then came inside. "Want to talk about it?"

Daisy shrugged. "Yes and no."

Sage climbed onto the bed beside her and cuddled up to her. "You know I'm here for you."

"What am I going to do?"

"First, you're going to talk it out with me."

She rested her head against her twin's, her tension easing at the comforting contact. "I figured our story was doomed to be a tragedy. This is not an unexpected outcome. I hoped it wouldn't be, but…here we are. An ill-fated romance. Now, I have to deal with the consequences of my actions."

"I'm so annoyed with that man. He has no idea what he's giving up. He can't do better than you."

"I appreciate you saying that, but you're my sister and you have to."

"It happens to be true, no matter who says it. You deserve a great love," Sage said. "You know, it's not a problem with you. It's Finn who won't let himself be happy. Is he punishing himself for something?"

"I don't think so, but it could be I don't know him as well as I thought."

Rose started crying from the nursery, and Sage kissed Daisy's forehead then rolled out of bed. "Get some sleep, sis. I'm just down the hall if you need me."

"Sweet dreams."

Before she turned out the lamp, Daisy pulled her New Year's wish list from the drawer of her bedside table. Number two still said *Fall* with a blank beside it. It felt like the right time to complete the wish to fall in love. Now that her tryst with Finn was over, she would focus on wishing for the person who was meant for her.

Her sister talk with Sage had also made her realize she needed to write down number six on her list.

6) Find someone who loves me the way I love them. The way I deserve.

Chapter Twenty-Two

The next morning, Finn woke with a killer headache and a plan. He threw some clothes into a suitcase and then found his brothers in the kitchen. "I'm going to drive to Montana and take care of the legal stuff about Dad."

"Drive?" Jake put down his coffee. "Alone?"

"I could use the time to…figure things out."

The toaster popped and Riley grabbed the hot bagel. "We have to take a load of cattle to the auction the day after tomorrow and need the new truck, and the old one needs too much work to drive that far. Do you think you can borrow one of the vehicles from Dalton Ranch?"

He winced. He had planned to give Daisy the space she wanted and leave without another confrontation, but he had to be an adult about this. "I'll ask."

"What happened with you and Daisy last night?" Jake asked, and spooned up a bite of frosted cereal.

"Nothing good. But I don't want to talk about it."

"Okay," Riley said. "Drive safe and let us know what's going on."

"Will do."

Finn walked next door to Dalton Ranch. He knocked on the back door and then went into the kitchen where Sage was frying sausages, the savory scent making his stomach rumble with hunger pains. Her baby girl, Rose, was asleep in a playpen near the table.

She narrowed her eyes at him. "Feeling poorly this morning?"

"You could say that."

She mumbled something else under her breath, and it sounded suspiciously like *You deserve it.*

"Is Daisy okay?"

"She's out in the stable with the horses." Sage put down the spatula and leaned against the counter. "I guess you know that she was pretty upset last night."

He hung his head but nodded. "I really hate how things have turned out. The last thing in the world I want to do is hurt her."

"Do you care about my sister?"

"Of course I do. Very much. No question." Recently, in new ways he should not.

"Look me in the eyes, Finn Murphy."

He did as she asked and held her stare, attempting to telegraph all his feelings—as unwieldy as they were—but he wasn't sure what she saw. Even her nod and drawn out sigh didn't clue him in.

She turned back to the stove and flipped the sausages.

"I know you're mad at me, but I need to ask a favor."

She crossed her arms over her chest and seemed to be considering it. "What is it?"

"I need to make a quick trip to Montana. Our old truck needs repairs, and my brothers need the other one to haul cattle to the auction. Can I borrow one of the Dalton Ranch trucks?"

She softened toward him and pushed a plate of blueberry muffins his way. "Daisy told me about your dad. I'm so sorry. You can use the older red one. We can do without it, no problem. When are you leaving?"

"Today. As soon as I can get on the road." He grabbed a muffin from the plate on the island. "I have to clear up some family legal stuff."

Sage lifted a set of keys from a wooden bowl on the counter near the back door. "Drive safe and let us know if there's anything we can do for you here."

"Will do. Thank you, Sage." He put a hand on the door-knob but stopped and looked over his shoulder when she called his name.

"You should use the time away to do some thinking about how you want the rest of your life to look."

A shiver rolled over him. "That is exactly my plan."

Minutes later he put his suitcase into the back seat of the double cab truck then looked toward the stable. He could go find Daisy or he could take a few more days to think things through so he didn't make things worse and completely screw everything up.

Right or wrong, he got into the truck.

As he drove past the Channing city limits sign, he momentarily thought about turning around and going back to find Daisy. Instead, he pulled off the road and called her. If she answered and wanted to see him, he would go back.

The phone rang and rang and rang.

When she didn't answer, he pulled back onto the road.

It was probably for the best. He needed to get his head straight.

Daisy opened the kitchen door and stepped in out of the chilly wind. "Sage, where is the older red truck?"

"Finn took it."

Just hearing his name made her stomach twist. "Where did he go?"

Sage slowly turned from the kitchen sink with her head tilted and her teeth pressed into her bottom lip. "To Montana."

"Montana!" Surely he wouldn't just leave town—hell, leave the whole state—without a single word. Would he?

"You didn't know he was going?" Sage asked.

But apparently...he had done just that. "No."

"I assumed he'd gone out to the stable to talk to you before he left."

"Nope. He did not." Daisy took her frustration out on a piece of junk mail by ripping it in two, then jammed the toe of her boot onto the trash can's foot peddle. The metal lid clanged against the cabinet. Rose sat straight up and started fussing from the playpen where she'd been napping.

She grimaced. "Sorry, sis. I didn't mean to wake her."

"It's fine. She's been sleeping longer than I should have let her."

Daisy went over to pick up her niece, earning a smile that showed off her new tooth. "Hello, Rosie Posie. Did you have a nice morning nap?"

Rose squealed and grabbed Daisy's hair, babbling away like she always did.

"I'll get her food ready," Sage said.

"Since I woke her, I'll change her diaper." She headed upstairs to the changing table. "Cheer up your old aunt, sweetie. Tell me something good."

Rose did not disappoint. She cooed and babbled and made her smile.

But even the baby's charm couldn't completely keep Daisy from thinking about Finn. He had left town without a single word. He had decided to drive across the country while they were in the middle of a… Not exactly a fight, but they certainly weren't in a great place.

I did tell him to forget we were ever more than friends.

She just hadn't expected him to leave town. She'd thought that sometime today they would hash things out and get back to, well, whatever came next for them.

She snapped Rose's sleeper closed then held the clean baby against her chest and kissed the top of her head. Her dandelion fluff blond hair tickled Daisy's cheek. "I love you, precious girl."

At least she had the joy of helping to raise her niece.

Back downstairs, she buckled Rose into her high chair. "I guess Finn wasn't kidding about his curiosity naturally burning out and getting back to normal. But I don't know how we'll ever get back to our old normal."

Sage wrapped her in a hug. "I'm so sorry, sis. Maybe there can be a new normal between you two. A better one."

"I hope you're right." She let her twin's comfort start to mend some of her heartache. "It was ridiculous of me to think I could turn off my feelings like that."

"Want me to whip Finn's butt the next time I see him?"

"Yes, please," Daisy mumbled into her sister's blond curls. A few tears escaped, and she lifted her head to wipe them away.

"Ma-ma-ma-ma," Rose yelled and banged on her high chair tray.

"Sorry, baby." Sage kissed the top of her daughter's head and spooned a bite of apple sauce into her mouth. "I'm not very happy with Finn at the moment, but don't completely give up on him yet. I think there's something there worth fighting for."

She sighed. "Me too, but now I'm questioning if I'm ready to talk to him yet. He called me earlier."

"What did he say?" She wiped food from Rose's cheek.

"I didn't answer, and he didn't leave a message. I need time to think and make a plan. I'm trying to go through all the scenarios in my mind and figure out what I'll do in different situations."

"You're going to make yourself crazy doing that."

"Entirely likely." She looked at the clock above the table. "I need to get back out to the stable. I have work to do, and later Dillon is coming for a routine check of the horses."

"Titan is as healthy as a horse." Dillon chuckled at his bad joke and patted the horse's flank before stepping out of the stall with his vet bag. "I'm starving. Will you go into town with me for dinner? I hate to eat alone in a restaurant, and I have no food in my refrigerator."

Daisy's initial reaction was to decline so she could eat ice cream in front of the television, but she forced herself to say yes. "Sounds good. I'm hungry too." She was surprised to discover that she actually was.

"How about that new Italian restaurant? It's pretty good," he said.

Her chest ached. She didn't want to go to the restaurant where she and Finn had enjoyed such a romantic evening. "I just had Italian for lunch." She wouldn't tell him it was a frozen dinner she'd popped into the microwave. "Do you mind if we eat at the Rodeo Café?"

"Not at all. I love their fried chicken."

"Give me about ten minutes to change my clothes, and I'll be ready to go."

"I'll meet you at my truck."

The cat followed her into the house and upstairs. In her closet, she grabbed a pair of clean blue jeans and tossed them onto her bed, but when she caught sight of the big blue handprints covering both back pockets, she groaned. Getting away from things that reminded her of Finn was going to be next to impossible.

She placed a hand on top of his much larger print and remembered what it was like to have his calloused palms sliding over her bare skin. Going forward, wearing those would be the only time his hands were on her.

The cat bumped her head against Daisy's hand, and she scratched her under the chin. "You know what, Lady, I'm not wearing jeans tonight. I'm going to wear some of my new dressier clothes. I bought them for me, not for Finn."

At least that was what she was going to continue to tell herself. She picked out a wrap-style dress in a cool shade of blue. She paired it with suede boots that zipped up to her knees and a black angora sweater in case she got cold. She was glad Sage and Emma had talked her into buying all of it.

She dressed before brushing her hair and swiping on a coat of mascara. She leaned in close to the mirror to apply lip gloss.

Was the wish she'd completed last night already starting to work?

She wasn't sure how to feel about that. It would be, it was time to turn her attention to a man who didn't have hang-ups about being a father or a husband. It might not be Dillon who was meant to be hers, but she was going to put herself out there.

I can do this. I don't have a choice.

The familiar and casual ambiance of the Rodeo Café relaxed some of her nervousness. Daisy slid onto one side of a booth near the back, while Dillon slid onto the other.

"I'll have an iced tea, please," Dillon said to the waiter.

"A large chocolate shake for me." At least she was indulging while out in public and not home alone in the dark. She'd count that as progress. She couldn't be expected to get back to her usual self on a dime.

"I'm sorry I didn't get to spend more time with your sisters at the party. Tell me more about them. Or something else about yourself," Daisy said.

"They're younger than me. All three of them are artists, but they're also very different. One is a student, another travels a lot and the third is a journalist. We had a single mom who worked long hours as a surgeon, so they looked to me for a lot of stuff."

"That must be why you're such a good listener. Are you an artist too?"

"I am."

"What kind of art?"

"I like to sketch portraits. Charcoals and pencil mostly."

"I'd love to see some of your work."

The waiter returned with their drinks, and they ordered food.

Daisy was enjoying herself more than she'd thought she could, but she still wasn't getting any tingles from the handsome man across from her.

Dillon leaned back against the red vinyl booth and stretched out one arm. "Do you love him?"

The question startled her, but she sighed and put down her chocolate shake. There was no use denying that she knew what he was talking about. She propped her elbows on the table and her chin on her fists. "I do."

"I thought so. What are you going to do about it?"

She scoffed and flicked a hand in the air. "There is nothing to do. As embarrassing as it is to admit, it's one-sided. We want completely different things."

He shook his head. "It's not one-sided."

She sucked in a quick breath. "Did he say something to you?"

"No. Still just giving me the same old glares whenever I touch you or laugh with you. Hell, even look at you."

"You aren't just saying that to make me feel better?"

"I wouldn't mislead you in that way."

"Even if he does like me, it doesn't change the fact that he and I want completely different things. He never wants to marry or be a father."

"That surprises me."

"Yeah, it does me too. But try telling him that."

Dillon sat forward and lowered his voice. "I'll tell you what. I won't give up on love if you don't."

"Deal."

"You're friends with Emma Hart, right?"

"I am." Now she leaned forward. "Are you interested in Emma?"

"I might be." His smile was adorable. "Will you tell me more about her?"

"I would be happy to." It was a relief that this was not a date. He was interested in someone else, and she was happy to do a little matchmaking. "What do you want to know?"

The miles continued to slip by in a blur, but Finn's foul mood had not improved, and his head wasn't any clearer than when he'd left home without talking to Daisy. The long drive and solitude were not helping as much as he'd expected them to. But it would hopefully give him enough time to sort his unruly emotions and feelings back into their appropriate boxes.

And getting a taste of his old life in Montana would remind him why he stayed away from serious relationships.

He'd left his relationship with Daisy in a messy kind of limbo. It had all turned out just as he feared. He'd hurt Daisy and made her cry.

With every mile, he missed her more and more, and when he stopped for the night, he called her for the fifth time. The phone rang and rang and then went to voicemail. He wasn't completely surprised, but he had hoped that she would want to talk to him by now. She wouldn't answer his calls or texts, and the idea that he had not only lost a lover but also a valued friendship was making his chest hurt.

He still wanted to take her in his arms and press his mouth to hers. Not just in a pleasurable way that made his body burn, but also in an emotional way. Why did his feelings have to get so mixed up with his body? But what he wanted and what was good for the woman he…

His breath faltered and blood whooshed in his ears. The feeling that was swallowing him up from the inside out couldn't be love.

Could it? It was only a touch of panic about losing her friendship. That had to be all it was.

Chapter Twenty-Three

When he arrived in Montana, Finn called Brown & Taylor and then drove straight to the law office. He followed the skinny, elderly lawyer into his brightly lit office and took a seat in one of the leather high-back chairs.

"Thank you for coming all this way, Mr. Murphy."

"Sorry I didn't get the letter and it took me so long. What is so important that I needed to come in person?"

Mr. Brown unbuttoned his suitcoat as he sat in the chair behind his desk. "Did you know your father had married again before he died?"

"I did not." Women had always liked him, so he wasn't surprised. "Wouldn't that mean his wife would get anything he had?"

"She would, but they divorced when she ran off almost two years ago."

If it had ended, why had he bothered to mention the marriage? A band of tension around his chest was tightening. Something big was coming. He could feel it in his bones.

"I'm sorry to tell you that there is no money. That all went to medical bills. But there is something." He hit a button on the intercom on his desk and talked to his secretary. "Mary, please send them in now."

Them? This got weirder and weirder.

The office door opened before he could ask what was going on, and an older woman entered with a blond toddler on her hip. She was too old to be the mother, but the child was curled close to her and sucking her thumb. When she saw Finn, the child lifted her head and looked at him with huge blue eyes.

"This little girl is two and a half years old, and she is your half sister, Ivy Murphy."

"Sister?" Finn stood as if he'd been shocked by a cattle prod.

"Yes. Mr. Murphy, you are her legal guardian."

Finn blinked a few times as if that could clear up the bizarre situation that he'd suddenly found himself in. The inheritance was not money—which would've been shocking—or a collection of baseball cards or even a run-down classic car.

It was a child.

The toddler pulled her thumb from her little rosebud mouth with a popping sound. She whispered something he couldn't make out and then leaned out of the woman's arms as she reached for him.

Finn was stunned, but he was used to holding babies around Dalton Ranch, so he moved closer and took Ivy into his arms. She looked a lot like his little brothers had at this age. She looked a lot like all three of them.

The child studied him with confused curiosity, and her lip began to tremble.

The woman stepped forward and rubbed the little girl's back. "It's okay, Ivy. You're safe."

He cradled the back of her tiny head, her riot of blond curls soft under his hand.

"She was a daddy's girl, and you look a lot like your father. I think Ivy sees it."

His throat tightened, and he smiled at the toddler. "Hi. My name is Finn. I'm your big brother. Everything is going to be okay."

But on the inside, he was freaking out in a major way. He couldn't promise everything would be okay and had no idea what to do next. He wasn't even sure how to take his next breath.

Ivy yawned, returned her thumb to her mouth and rested her head on his shoulder. Since his legs had gone numb, he sat back down.

The woman took the other chair beside him. Her smile was kind, and she was wearing a bright fuchsia blouse and gray slacks that matched her silver-gray pixie haircut. "I'm Sara. I've been taking care of her these last few weeks."

"Tell me more about her. Was my dad actually a hands-on father to her?" Having firsthand knowledge of being his father's son, he was doubtful.

"He was. Especially after her mom left and then lost custody."

This was surprising news, and he wasn't sure how to feel. He was of course grateful that Ivy had been cared for, but that old childhood feeling of abandonment was filling him up.

He looked down at the helpless little girl who was falling asleep on his chest. "And you've been taking care of her?"

"I have. I was your father's neighbor, and since she already knew me, I agreed to look after her until you could get here. But I'm seventy-five and too old to take care of her long-term."

"What happens now?" Finn looked helplessly between Sara and Mr. Brown. "Am I just supposed to be an instant...father?"

The lawyer came out from behind his desk and leaned

against the front of it. "You have a couple of options. You can find her a family here in Montana, put her in foster care or you can take her home and be her guardian. You can also make other arrangements for her once you get to Texas." He reached behind himself for a stack of papers. "Here is some paperwork to look through and sign. Don't hesitate to ask any questions you have. Why don't you take the night to look these over and maybe call your brothers."

"I think I'll do that."

"Where are you staying?" Sara asked.

"I'm going to find a cheap motel."

"You'll come to my house," she said. "I have two extra bedrooms, and there is no reason for you to spend money on a hotel."

He started to decline her offer so he could be alone to make some kind of sense out of this, but as he adjusted the two-year-old on his lap, she clung to his shirt as if she never wanted him to let her go.

If only Daisy was here. She would know what to do and say and how to navigate this shocking situation. "Thank you, Sara. I'd like to stay with you."

"Good, because it looks like someone doesn't want to let you go."

Out in the parking lot, he put Ivy in the car seat in the back of Sara's car. She woke up and reached for him, and he knelt to her eye level. "Ivy, you need to ride in your seat, and I have to drive my truck. He pointed to it parked a few spots away. I'll follow you to the house. Is that okay?"

She nodded and hugged an old brown teddy bear.

Sara patted his arm. "It's a small town, so you'll have no trouble following me to my house. It's only a few miles away."

"I'll be right behind you."

He tried to call Daisy as soon as he started the truck. It rang and rang over the Bluetooth speakers, but once again went to voicemail.

"You've reached Daisy Dalton's phone. Please leave me a message." Beep.

"It's me again. Please call me back. I really need to talk to you."

They drove by an area of local small businesses and then into a neighborhood that was old but well-tended. The trip was so quick that he didn't even have time to get his thoughts organized. Sara's house was a midcentury ranch that was painted a soothing shade of yellow. Not the mustard color that Daisy hated. It was surrounded by mature trees, and there was a For Sale sign in the yard of a little white bungalow next door. Was that where his dad had lived?

It was a hell of a lot nicer than the house they'd grown up in.

He parked in the driveway beside her car and met the older woman and the toddler on the small front porch. Ivy stood beside Sara but stared up at him with the most expressive eyes he'd ever seen. He followed them inside and to a guest room where he put his bag. His little sister trailed after him from room to room. When he came out of the bathroom, she was waiting outside the door for him.

"You two can sit in the living room where the toys are while I get supper on the table," Sara said, and turned on the television to a cartoon and then hummed as she made her way to the kitchen.

Finn was still dazed by the day's news and didn't know what to do or say. He wasn't used to kids being this quiet. Davy and Rose didn't let you forget that they were around. "Will you show me your favorite toy?"

Ivy went over to a plastic tub beside a green corduroy chair, pulled out a tattered copy of a book and brought it to him. She climbed up on the couch and settled herself beside him, her tiny red boots not even reaching the edge of the cushion.

Guess I'm reading a book.

He opened it to the first page. She scooted closer and closer as he read about woodland animals.

"Supper is on the table," Sara called to them.

He stood, and this time, he reached for her. "Let's go, little miss."

The corners of her mouth tilted up and then turned into a shy smile, and if he wasn't mistaken, she was batting her long eyelashes.

Aw, man. She's trying to melt my heart. Just like Daisy does.

This was the first real emotion he'd seen her express. He picked her up and settled her in a booster seat at the kitchen table.

He accepted a plate of chicken with rice and green beans. "Thank you. This smells wonderful." It reminded him of something Daisy made.

"Ivy likes it, but you have to make sure to cut everything up really small for her," she said, while demonstrating exactly what size was acceptable.

"Is the house that's for sale next door the one where my father lived?"

"He rented it from me, but having a rental property has become too much work for me alone, and the market is good for selling. Don't let me forget that I have a box of his things in my garage that he wanted me to give to you."

"Okay." He wasn't sure he wanted to look in the box. What other shocking discoveries would he make?

She sprinkled pepper on her food. "You know, he talked about you three boys. He was a complete mess until his wife left. Only then was he able to stop drinking and pull himself together. He said he couldn't bear to fail a fourth child."

"We thought he was dead."

"He told us about that. He came forward years later to clear it all up. That's how my husband met him. He was his lawyer and then later became his AA sponsor when Ivy was born."

"Did he say why he faked his death?"

"He didn't want to drag you down or be a burden on your lives. He didn't want to embarrass you like his father had done to him."

Finn barely remembered his grandfather. He'd thought the old man was funny, but looking back, the man had probably been drunk. Finn's emotions were all over the map, and he made a decision to drink less and maybe stop all together.

After dinner, Finn went out into Sara's shady front yard to call his brothers.

"Hey, Riley. I have news. Is Jake with you?"

"He's right here. I'll put the call on speaker."

"Hey, bro," his youngest brother said. "What did you discover? Did dear old dad get rich and leave us a fortune?"

"Nope. Dear old dad left us a kid."

There was silence on the line, and he could picture their stunned expressions.

Riley's deep voice broke the silence. "Did you say kid?"

"Dude," Jake said. "He wouldn't leave us a kid."

Finn shook his head when they started arguing. "Shut up, the two of you. Listen. Dad had another child. And he listed me as her guardian."

More silence filled the air. Finn turned toward the house and saw Ivy watching him through the window. Her elbows were braced on the windowsill and her chin was propped on her hands as she stared at him. Her sad little face tore at his heart. He waved to her, and she perked up and waved back.

"Are you putting us on?" Riley asked. "This is a joke, right?"

"No. It's no joke. Her name is Ivy. She's two and a half years old, an orphan and she doesn't want to let me out of her sight. I don't know what the hell to do."

"Do you need us to come to Montana?" Jake asked.

"No. At least not yet."

"We'll be on standby if you need us," Riley said.

Finn walked in a circle around a tree. "I can't just leave her behind. They'll put her in foster care. I know that's not always a bad thing because I've seen the Daltons be great foster parents, but I just can't abandon her here to an uncertain future."

"Agree," they both said.

"You should call Daisy," Riley suggested. "She'll probably know what to do."

He had the same thought, but she wasn't even talking to him.

Once Ivy was asleep, he sat at the kitchen table to read a letter from his dad and to look through the stack of legal paperwork.

Finn,
I hope you get this letter. Let me start by saying how proud I am of the man you have become.

Finn's anger was making his stomach sick. He remembered a few times as a kid when his dad had told him he was proud of him for taking care of his little brothers. Doing *his* job as the parent.

> *The last time I left you, I went into rehab. I let a*
> *drifter I'd met in a bar deliver my last load down*
> *south because he wanted to get to that city. I didn't*
> *find out about the crash and him being assumed to*
> *be me until I left rehab early. Because I couldn't even*
> *get through rehab, I knew you three were better off*
> *without me in your lives. I've been keeping an eye on*
> *you and your brothers all these years, and I'm im-*
> *pressed and proud. Only in the last few years have*
> *I been able to pull myself together. And then I found*
> *out my heart was giving out on me. Finn, you did*
> *real good with your brothers when you were just a*
> *kid. Better than I was able to, so I figure you can do*
> *it again. Your sister is sweet and very shy and has*
> *already had a hard life. I hope you'll consider being*
> *a better father to her than I ever was to you. At least*
> *find her a good home. I'm sorry I failed you and your*
> *brothers. I'm proud of you, son.*
> *Dad*

He was too numb to know how he felt. This whole situation was so entirely unexpected. The letter seemed like too little too late. What was the proper response? Ripping it up and tossing it away? Getting all nostalgic and forgiving?

He shook his head and moved on to the stack of legal papers. He kept rereading sentences, trying to interpret the legal jargon. And getting more frustrated by the second.

He glanced at his phone on the table beside him. Daisy still hadn't returned any of his calls or responded to any of his text messages. If he didn't hear from her in the next couple of hours, he'd send the SOS message they'd agreed upon to distinguish one of their jokes from a true emergency. And in his mind, his current situation definitely fit the definition of a true emergency. Alarm bells were clanging at a very high decibel.

Sara sat across from him. "Would you like some help? My late husband was a lawyer, and I was his legal secretary."

"Yes, please." He pushed the pages across the table.

She went through it page by page and told him what he needed to know. "Do you know what you want to do? About Ivy."

There was no way he was going to be able to drive away while watching her sweet face get smaller in his rearview mirror. He couldn't bear to leave this quiet little girl behind to an uncertain future. But driving across the country with a toddler seemed too daunting to face alone. The Dalton family knew all about fostering kids. They would help him figure this whole thing out—if Daisy would ever answer his calls or texts.

"I know I can't just leave her here in foster care." He rubbed his eyes to fight the fatigue setting in.

"Go get some sleep, Finn. A decision doesn't have to be made tonight."

Finn lay on a mattress that was way too soft, but that wasn't what was keeping him awake. The idea that had been trying to take shape all day would no longer be ignored. He knew the perfect mother for this orphaned little girl. The answer to his problem was obvious.

Daisy wanted to be a mom, and when she met Ivy, she wouldn't be able to resist the cute toddler. This was a way for him to give Daisy one of the biggest wishes on her list while also giving his baby sister a chance at a good life. But he couldn't just spring this on Daisy without careful consideration. Not when they weren't even speaking.

He grabbed his phone from the nightstand and groaned. Still no response. He'd thought their friendship was strong enough to handle the risk they'd taken with it, but more and more he worried that he'd been way off target.

It was time for a Hail Mary.

Maybe a child would help her forgive him for not being what she needed and get over the heartache he'd caused. He crossed his fingers and sent the one text message he knew she would answer.

The cowboy is in the henhouse.

Daisy woke with a gasp. She was still in the fog of a dream that she couldn't remember, but it had left her wanting to cry.

Her phone chimed from the nightstand.

Finn?

She groaned and covered her face. Couldn't she wake up without him being the very first thing on her mind? Was it her phone or the dream that had awakened her? It was still dark, but there would be no going back to sleep. She had to know who was texting her in the middle of the night, so she rolled over in bed and looked at her phone screen.

The cowboy is in the henhouse.

She sat straight up in bed. It was their SOS message. The one message she couldn't ignore.

She knew him well enough to know he would only send

this message they'd agreed on if it was necessary. She called him, and he answered after the first ring.

"Daisy. Thanks for calling me back."

"What's the crisis?" she asked, getting straight to the point.

"I have a little problem, and I could really use your help." His voice sounded tense and slightly panicked. "Can you fly to Montana?"

She swung her feet onto the floor. "Are you hurt or in jail?"

"No. Nothing illegal. I want you to come here and drive back home with me. Please."

Finn was always so confident and self-sufficient. She'd never heard him sound this desperate. "You're sure you don't need bail money?"

He cleared his throat. "I just need you."

Her mind started spinning with what his request could mean. He'd used their SOS because he needed her to come be with him. Did he miss her and want to spend time with her? Was he trying to make things up to her?

"Daisy? Are you still there?"

"Why do you want me to come all that way only to turn around and ride home with you?"

"I'd rather tell you and show you in person when you get here."

Her skin tingled. With time alone to think, had he changed his mind about remaining a single, fatherless bachelor?

She didn't want to work through their issues over the phone. They needed to see one another face-to-face. The long drive would give them the uninterrupted time they needed to talk through everything that had happened between them—in depth. Their true feelings and desires and goals. How they'd move forward. What came next. Even though it would be impossible for her to completely return to her prelove feelings for Finn, they could find a new normal.

"Please, Daisy Maisy. You're the only one I want with me right now." His voice softened and held a note of longing.

And if she wasn't mistaken, a note of panic. "Send me the information about where to fly into, and I'll be there as soon as I can."

"You're the best, sweetheart."

He'd only called her that name a handful of times, and every time it gave her hope that was too risky to have. "I'll see you tomorrow."

When she landed in Montana and got to the baggage claim area, she spotted Finn over the top of a group of travelers. The other people moved away and...

The breath was knocked from her lungs. An adorable toddler was perched on his hip, clinging to his shirt as if he was the only one who could keep her safe. She was very petite with blond curls and big blue eyes. And she looked a whole lot like Finn.

Daisy's whole body went cold. She remembered the letter he'd accidentally burned the day he'd jumped into the icy pond to save a baby goat. Could that have been about this child? When was the last time Finn was in Montana? She didn't think it had been within the last several years but...

Could this little girl with the same blue eyes be his daughter?

Chapter Twenty-Four

A large group of people moved past the baggage claim area, and Finn caught sight of Daisy. His pulse jumped with another powerful flash of that big unnamed feeling. The one that threatened to swallow him up. It made his insides quiver and his brain short-circuit.

He'd left Texas with a goal of controlling his attraction to Daisy and setting his mind to what needed to happen. Not to miss her more every day. He hadn't even realized just how much until he'd seen her gorgeous face in the midst of a faceless crowd.

When did I start thinking of her as gorgeous?

She stared back at him as a myriad of emotions moved across her face, but she remained frozen in place, other people weaving around her.

He made his way over to her. "Hello, Daisy Maisy."

"Finn." She rubbed the base of her throat as if she was having trouble speaking. "Who is this precious little angel?"

"This is Ivy Murphy." He patted the toddler's back. "Ivy, say hello to Daisy."

The little girl tucked her head under his chin and popped her thumb into her mouth.

Daisy looked even more startled than before but forced

a smile. "Hello, sweetie." Her expression wobbled when she met his gaze. "Her last name is Murphy?"

The way her voice rose in pitch on his last name revealed her thoughts. With his free hand, he took hold of hers. "She's not my daughter."

"She's not?"

"She is my half sister."

"Oh." Her shoulders relaxed into their normal easygoing position. She stroked the back of Ivy's tiny hand that clung so fiercely to his shirt. "Ivy, I'm very happy to meet you."

The toddler curled closer to him, and he cradled his sister's head, doing everything he could to make her feel safe. "She's shy."

"That's okay. We can take our time getting to know one another."

He hoped it didn't take too long because he was really counting on the two of them hitting it off. If Daisy didn't want to be her mom, he didn't know what he'd do. He was so unsure about everything to do with taking care of a little girl, and as much as he liked to be in control, this was a very uncomfortable feeling.

"Do you have any luggage to claim?"

"No." She rolled her carry-on bag forward. "Just this."

"Then let's get out of here, and I'll tell you all about it."

As they crossed the parking lot, Daisy got an odd look on her face. "Is she your only other sibling?"

"As far as we know."

"Your father must have been near fifty when he had her."

"Yep. And he had a wife who ran off on them. He lived more years without us than he did with us," he whispered over the top of Ivy's halo of blond curls.

She put a hand on his shoulder, but only gave him an awkward pat. She didn't slide her fingers along his back to massage the tension in his neck or run her fingers up into his hair. He'd lost that privilege when he decided they were over but hadn't had the courage to talk to her about it.

"All this time he let you…" She kept walking, not completing the question he'd been asking himself ever since he'd been to the law office.

Why had their father let them believe he was dead? "There is one more thing. He named me as Ivy's guardian."

Her mouth opened as if she'd speak and then closed again until they stopped beside the truck. "What about her *m-o-m*?"

He shook his head. "Completely out of the picture. Legally and otherwise." He buckled Ivy into her a car seat. "Are you hungry, little miss?"

She nodded and reached for her tattered teddy bear. She hadn't uttered a single sound all day. Not even when Sara had cried and hugged her before they drove away.

There was a box of items on one side of Ivy's car seat that was secured in the center, so Daisy put her suitcase on the floorboard by Finn's bag and then settled on the front passenger seat. "I could eat too."

"I saw a café not far from here." He glanced in the rearview mirror to back out of the parking spot. Ivy was stroking her teddy bear as she hugged it to her chest. Her vulnerableness broke his heart.

"This is all so unexpected," she said.

"That's putting it mildly."

"So…" She swallowed a few times and then cleared her throat. "She is why you wanted me to come to Montana and drive home with you."

There was a note of something in her voice that he couldn't quite place. But as he looked at her, he suspected it was disappointment. He thought about how his phone call and request to come meet him might have sounded from her side of the conversation. Had he led her to believe that he had changed his mind about their future relationship? He felt sick and ashamed.

"Are you mad at me for not telling you about Ivy over the phone?"

She shook her head. "You could have told me, you know. I still would have come to help you."

"It wasn't my intention to trick you. I promise. The thought of driving across the country with a toddler sent me into a panic. And there is no one else I want to make this trip with."

Her sigh was long and drawn out. And sad.

"Daisy, I'm really sorry about that night of the party and the way I've withdrawn. Basically, for my behavior lately."

"What was with all the flirting with multiple women and basically..." She fiddled with a tassel on her purse.

"Acting a fool?" he asked.

"You said it, I didn't."

"But you were thinking it."

"You know me so well."

They shared a smile and a small bit of his tension melted away. He pulled into the parking lot of the café and parked near the front door. It was a rustic building with a covered patio off to one side.

"I like the looks of this place." Daisy attempted to get Ivy out of her car seat, but she wouldn't go to her.

Ivy shook her head and arched toward him, so he once again lifted her into his arms. "You're safe, little miss."

They were seated at a booth with Ivy in a booster seat beside him. His sister hadn't said a word, but he had a feeling that her big blue eyes saw everything.

He scanned the trifold plastic menu. "I'm not even sure what to order for her to eat."

"Let's check our options." She looked at the kid's section. "Ivy, do you want pizza?"

The little girl shook her head and scrunched up her face.

"Do you like chicken nuggets and macaroni and cheese?"

That brought a small smile to her rosebud mouth, but she looked to Finn before nodding.

"I think we have a winner," he said. "Let's get both."

Daisy handed her a red and a purple crayon and the coloring sheet the waitress had put on the table. "So, the three of us are driving back to Texas?"

He lowered his voice. "My choice was either leave her here in foster care or take her with me."

Ivy chose that moment to look up and grin at him with a flirty tilt of her head. He tweaked her little button nose.

"You made the right choice. She's irresistibly adorable. Who has been looking after her?"

"My dad's neighbor, but she is seventy-five years old and only agreed to do it until they got ahold of me."

"Once we're home, what's the plan?"

He met her gaze and saw vulnerability and uncertainty in her eyes. "Honestly, I'm still working on it all out. I'm reeling from the surprise and trying to absorb everything, but you're the only person I want helping me navigate all this."

"I'll do what I can to help you."

"Thank you, Daisy Maisy."

After lunch, Daisy got into the back seat with Ivy and read books to her. The fact that she'd so quickly taken on a caretaker role didn't surprise him. It reinforced his decision. It was important to find the right time and the right way to tell her his idea about her raising Ivy. But he also couldn't put it off for too long—like he'd been doing with their conversation about the state of their relationship.

Stop being a chicken.

When she stopped reading, he glanced in the back to see that Ivy was asleep. But even then, Daisy remained behind him. "How's it going back there?"

She climbed into the front and buckled her seat belt. "She is sound asleep. I did get a few smiles out of her while I was reading."

"I knew you two would make friends quickly."

She had nothing to say to that. Their conversation wasn't their normal easygoing banter. It was stilted with long pauses and tension. And he hated it.

They drove for several hours before stopping at a motor lodge in a small Montana town. The kind where your car was parked right in front of the door to your room and one large window looked out over the parking lot.

The woman at the front desk smiled at Ivy. "Your daughter is adorable. She looks just like you."

"Thanks." Finn forced the word through the constriction in his throat. The idea of being a father who was responsible for someone else's life had its usual effect. Panic threatened to burst its way to the surface, and his skin prickled. The stress of looking after his little brothers was something he did not want to repeat.

"Would you like a room with two double beds or one king?"

Finn didn't know what the answer should be, so he turned to Daisy.

"One king," she said, and shot him a don't-even-think-about-it look. "So Ivy can sleep between us and not roll off the bed."

Her message was clear. One bed was not so he could cuddle up to her. She wasn't forgetting or forgiving anytime soon.

He couldn't grant her wish to be her husband or a father to her children, but he did have a way to grant another wish on her list.

Chapter Twenty-Five

Room number 7 was small, with a sink and laminate counter straight ahead, and behind a flimsy door was a postage-stamp-size room with the toilet and bathtub. The only piece of art on the wall was a snowy mountain scene that made her think of their holiday hideaway. It instantly made her long for that magical time when they'd felt separated from the rest of the world.

On the airplane, Daisy had convinced herself that this long drive would be a similar bonding experience and help them find their way forward. So much for her hope that he'd seen the light.

She put her carry-on on the floor beside the bed, relieved that the room was clean and that the motel had adopted the practice of wrapping the comforter between two white sheets the way they did at large hotel chains. There was no germy bedspread to deal with.

Finn lifted Ivy from his hip and put her on the center of the bed. "I'm going to go get her suitcase and the other stuff from the truck."

"I'll take her to the bathroom." She held out her arms to the child. "Can I help you go to the potty?"

Ivy nodded, but not quite ready to accept Daisy, she scooted to the edge of the bed and slid off feetfirst. She followed Daisy to the bathroom and let her help with her purple sweatpants and Pull-Up.

"Your Pull-Up is dry. Good job, Ivy. You're such a big girl," she said as she lifted her onto the potty. She received a sweet smile that emphasized the toddler's high cheekbones that were very similar to her three big brothers'.

"Do you want me to order takeout from that hamburger place next door?" Finn said on his way back inside with the last bag.

"That works for me." She propped the child on her raised knee and helped her wash her hands. "I would really like to take a shower, and then I'll give Ivy a bath."

"I'd appreciate that," he said.

Daisy opened her suitcase and pulled out her pajamas. The grime of a day's travel clung to her, and she was exhausted.

"Ivy and I will walk over to get the food while you shower. What do you want?"

"If they have it, a lemonade and a cheeseburger. You know the way I like it. And onion rings, please."

"Got it." He reached out a hand as if he would touch her face but dropped it to his side instead. His attempt at a smile didn't reach his eyes or have the same sparkle as Ivy's had only moments ago. "I'll see if they have anything sweet for dessert."

The toddler peeked over his shoulder and moved her little fingers in a bye-bye wave as they went out the door.

"See you soon, sweetie." Her cuteness made it hard to stay sad.

This dejected mood wasn't productive. On a deep inhale, she raised her arms above her head then slowly let it out as she folded forward to touch her toes. She made the decision to throw off her downer mood, be the best friend she could be and find happiness in every moments that she could.

"I'm choosing to look on the bright side."

They were back with dinner when she came out of the bathroom, and they ate at the tiny round table by the window with the toddler on his lap.

"Guess what I have in my suitcase." Daisy grabbed one of Finn's french fries and handed it to the little girl. "Bubble bath. Is there anyone here who likes to take a bubble bath?"

"Bubble," Ivy whispered so quietly that she almost missed it.

"Oh good. As soon as we finish eating, I'll run your bath."

The toddler dipped the french fry into Finn's puddle of ketchup then smeared it across her cheek on the way to her mouth.

"Good thing the bath is after dinner," he said with a chuckle. "And apparently, I should've ordered more french fries."

Daisy swiped another fry and nibbled the tip of it. "Why do you say that?" She couldn't hold a straight face and giggled.

"Gosh, I wonder."

"I'll share my onion rings with you."

His full lips moved slowly into his bedroom grin. The kind that made her toes curl. It was so hard to keep an emotional distance from this man.

Once Ivy was fed, bathed and read to, she was sound asleep in the center of the big bed. Her hands were tucked under her cheek, and she looked like a cherub.

Daisy wasn't as relaxed, and was sitting in one of the chairs by the window while Finn showered. The thick curtain was pulled back just enough for her to see a sliver of the sky and parking lot. She hated the awkwardness between her and Finn. But they'd had moments throughout the day that gave her hope they would be able to work things out. It might take a while, but they could get there. They had to.

She was unsure of what would or should happen next, but she needed to find out if he planned to be a father to Ivy.

And without getting her hopes up, what he saw her role being, if any.

A cloud of steam escaped the bathroom right before Finn stepped out. In a pair of pajama pants, and no shirt, with wet hair falling over his forehead, he was a treat for the eyes. She flashed back to the moment he'd stepped out of the icy pond in nothing but a pair of boxer briefs.

Daisy put a finger to her lips. "She's asleep."

He turned off the light above the sink and spoiled her view, but her eyes adjusted, and she could see him in the light coming in around the curtain as he pulled on a T-shirt and then sat in the other chair.

"You are so good with her," he said in a low voice.

"I've had lots of recent practice with Davy and Rose."

He worked his mouth around like he'd say something but only slumped down in the chair instead.

The silence was making her want to jump out of her skin. "This is usually something Sage or Lizzy would say, but we're going shopping tomorrow."

"For what?"

"After looking through Ivy's suitcase, I've discovered she needs a few new things. Some clothes, a new pair of shoes and more books and toys so she can entertain herself on the long drive. We're also going to run out of training pants."

"Good point. Today, before you got here, was the first time I was all on my own and completely in charge of her. I wouldn't admit this to many people, but it was kind of terrifying."

Feeling antsy, she put one foot on the windowsill and bounced her leg. "I've watched you with Davy and Rose, and now with Ivy. You are really good with them, and they all adore you."

"I'm funny. Like another kid. Or a big brother."

"I know this is something that was not in your plan, and you're nervous, but you can do this. You are going to be okay. You will be a great dad."

He sat up straight, shook his head and rubbed his palms together. "No. I can't do it, Daisy. I know all about boys, but girls... I don't have the foggiest idea how to raise a little girl. Can you imagine her being raised by her three much older brothers? It would be a disaster."

"Well, she'll know how to hunt and fish and raise cattle and horses."

He groaned. "See what I mean? What about all the pink and the dolls and other girl stuff? Especially when she's a teenager."

"You're not alone in this. I'll be right next door." She wanted to scream at him to see her as a partner. As someone who could be a parent alongside him. As a woman he could love the way she loved him.

He leaned forward and spread both hands on the table like he needed to brace himself. "I was going to wait to say anything until you two got more acquainted and we were on better speaking terms, but I have a way to make one of your dreams come true."

Is he finally seeing what we have together?

"It's perfect," he said. "You can adopt her."

Daisy's heart swelled, and she wanted to throw herself into his lap. Finally. He wanted them to be a family.

"I can turn over guardianship as soon as we get home,

and I can be the fun big brother next door, and everyone will be safe."

Her heart that had just soared now plummeted as if all the blood had rushed from her body. He wasn't asking her to build a family *with* him. He wanted her to take a responsibility off of his hands.

Ivy chose that moment to whimper in her sleep then sit up and cry out. They both moved toward her and bumped into one another. Daisy reached out to comfort her, but the toddler turned to Finn. He picked her up and she instantly calmed and settled against his chest.

With a strong aching in her own chest, she went around to her side of the bed, climbed in and rolled to face the wall. He was the most frustrating man on the face of the planet, and she was working hard not to throttle him.

He whispered soothing words to the child, and a few minutes later, she felt Finn put Ivy down and climb in on his side of the bed.

When he whispered her name, she pretended to be asleep. He did not want to hear what she would say to him if she opened her mouth.

If you can't say anything nice…

The next morning, Daisy wasn't feeling much better about the state of things. She knew he had the ability to be a good parent, but *he* didn't believe it. She needed to make him see it. Somehow.

Maybe it was time to review her wish list and make changes. It might be foolish, but it had worked in the past.

They had eaten breakfast, and Ivy was having a morning nap in her car seat while they drove along a rural stretch of highway, but Daisy felt numb and was quieter than normal.

With hurt feelings, she didn't know what to say to him, so she answered direct questions and said little else.

But when one question kept spinning around in her mind and wouldn't let go, she finally asked, "Finn, why did you suddenly pull away from me? Was it just time because the excitement wore off?"

He jerked his eyes from the road to her then refocused forward before answering. "No. The excitement did not wear off."

"Just time to date more women?"

"No." He reached across the console and rubbed her arm. "That's not it either. It all kind of snowballed. I knew that our time was limited. Then I found out my dad died after letting us believe he was dead all these years. I started remembering stuff from my childhood. My parents' rotten marriage. Their parenting skills—or lack thereof. Then I heard you talking to Rose about being a mom."

"So, you did hear that. I suspected so."

"I did. And then I saw you laughing with Dillon like you always do and he said he can't wait to have kids of his own. He wants what you want, and you like him. And it all made me realize yet again that you deserve more than I can give you."

She shifted in her seat and stared at him for a moment. "Were you jealous?"

He growled, "Yes. Even though I have no right to be."

"It that why you were flirting with every female at the party?"

"In my inebriated state, I thought it would make me mad enough to push me away and help put needed space between us. I did it to give you a chance at having everything you want."

Something shifted inside her. "You did it to give me a chance to have a husband and a child of my own?"

"As hard as it was, I did."

"Now see—" she put a hand to her chest "—when you go and say things like that, it makes my insides get all warm and melty. Makes it harder to stay mad at you for pulling away without a conversation and running off without a single word."

He smiled, but it was sad. "Does that mean I'm on the road to forgiveness?"

"You really pulled away for my benefit, not yours?"

"Yep."

She studied his profile. "I think if you examine that a little harder, you'll discover it benefits you too. It gets you out of being tied down."

He sighed. "Guess my brothers are right about my ability to be an ass."

"Even so, my heart is urging me toward forgiveness."

"You should probably listen to your heart."

"Maybe you should do the same, Finn."

He glanced in the rearview mirror, and she could tell he was looking at Ivy.

She motioned with her hand. "Oh, pull into that shopping center up ahead on the right. We can get everything we need there."

Ivy refused to sit in the cart and remained securely in her favorite person's arms.

As they made their way through the store, Daisy studied their profiles and could see the family resemblance. "When you met Ivy, did she take to you right away?"

"Yes. I look a lot like my dad," he said.

"He must have been a very handsome man." She picked

up a couple of different shirts and held them up. "Which one do you like, sweetie? The pink one or the yellow one?"

Ivy pointed to the pink one.

"Good choice." Daisy put that and several other items of clothing into the cart and then pushed it to the toy section.

Ivy sucked in a breath and leaned from her spot in Finn's arms to grab a toy goat off the shelf. It had a soft, velvety white body, pink satin in its ears and tan leather hooves.

The toddler kissed the toy goat's head and then hugged it to her body. Daisy and Finn smiled at one another.

"I think we've found a winner," he said.

"If she likes this, imagine when she sees Rascal."

"This is a baby goat," he said to his sister. "Can you say goat?"

She smiled at her new toy. "Baby."

Daisy's cheeks hurt from smiling as she watched the two of them interacting. She was proud of the way he was stepping up to a situation he hadn't expected and never wanted. She could so easily see the three of them as a family. She just needed him to see and want the same thing, and pushing him wouldn't work. Finn Murphy was too strong-headed. This was a realization he needed to come to on his own.

But that didn't mean she wasn't going to help things along.

He just needs time and some gentle prodding in the right direction.

Once they were back on the road, Finn was feeling better about how things were progressing. Daisy sat in the back seat with Ivy and read books to her. Finn listened to their interaction, and although Ivy didn't speak, he heard a couple of soft giggles. The sound made his worries feel just a little bit lighter.

Daisy climbed over the seat into the front and smiled at

him as she buckled her seat belt. "Did you hear her adorable little giggle?"

"I did. She's warming up to you quickly."

"She really likes stories about animals."

"We've got enough of those at home."

"Finn, did we just enter Utah?"

"Yep."

"Why are we cutting through the corner of Utah? This
is going out of our way."

"To see a few sights. You wanted an adventure, and it's
the least I can do to grant your wish," he said, and then bit
the inside of his cheek. Had he just given away that he'd
read her list?

She narrowed her eyes. "When did I tell you I wanted a
big adventure?"

"Can't remember exactly."

"Finn Murphy!"

"Okay, okay. I might've seen your list."

She gasped. "You read it? When?"

"Um…it fell out of your pocket the night I put my handprints on your butt."

"Butt, butt, butt," Ivy said from the back seat.

He looked at Daisy, and they tried not to laugh. "Oops."

"Have you noticed that she likes to say words that start
with the letter B?"

"Not until you just mentioned it." They'd heard her say
bubble and baby and now one he had not intended to teach
her.

"I'm so embarrassed that you read my silly wish list."

"Don't be. It benefited both of us." He grinned but kept
staring straight ahead.

She pulled her hair up into a ponytail and secured it
with the band she always wore on her wrist. "Is that why

we started sleeping together? Because I said I wanted to sleep with a hot guy?"

He rubbed his mouth, trying to hide his grin. "Did that wish come true?"

"I suppose if I really stretch my imagination, you fit that criterion. I bet the part about a brief fun affair caught your eye, didn't it?"

"I can't lie. It did."

"Wait a minute. The adventure wish wasn't written until *after* the handprint incident, yet you know about it."

"It was on your bedside table when I went upstairs to get my watch."

"And your eyes just happened to fall on it?"

"Something like that. It didn't say private or keep out." He grinned in a way that he hoped would make her do the same.

"You are a mess, Finnigan. Hey, look." She pointed to a colorful billboard. "There's a zoo in the next town. We have to stop. Ivy will love it."

He had a feeling both of them would love it. He surprised himself with the desire to go as well. "That sounds like a good idea."

When they walked up to the zoo and Ivy saw all the animals painted on the entrance, she smiled and patted Finn on the shoulder as if to tell him good job.

Daisy chuckled. "Stopping was a great decision. Let's rent one of the wagons to pull her around in."

"And hope she'll ride in it."

"I bet she will if you put her in it and pull her."

Thankfully, she loved riding in the wagon. They bought snacks and set off toward the bears. Daisy walked beside Ivy and handed her a piece of cookie. And to Daisy's delight, Ivy reached up to hold her hand as she walked along beside her.

Their growing connection chipped away a bit more of the tension that was constricting his ribcage.

When they went through the primate habitats, Ivy was the most excited they'd seen her be. One of the gorillas held her baby upside down and kissed his tiny face before draping him over her shoulder.

Ivy bounced her knees and clapped, her precious giggle making everyone around them smile.

"You like that, little miss?"

She raised her arms for him to pick her up. Finn scooped her up but then held Ivy upside down by her ankles like the gorilla. She laughed harder than they'd heard her yet.

"Daisy, take my hat, please."

She put it on her own head, and he seated Ivy on his shoulders. Her tiny hands clasped the sides of his head as they moved to the next exhibit. At least they were getting a few words out of her. It was all progress. The smiles, the giggles, the hand holding with Daisy. All of it.

"What animal should we see next?" he asked her.

Ivy made a meowing sound.

"I think there's a new lion cub," he said. "Want to go see the baby lion?"

"Baby." She kissed the top of his head with a noisy smack.

"Aww." Daisy put a hand to her heart. "That's the cutest thing ever. You make her feel so safe."

The constriction was back to choke off some of his breath. Keeping her safe was his responsibility.

In the hotel room that night, Finn opened the bathroom door but paused when he heard Daisy singing a lullaby to Ivy. She didn't have her niece Lizzy's amazing voice, but the way she was using it was beautiful. He pressed the heel of his hand to the center of his chest. Dang it, there was that feeling again. Ready to engulf him. He waited for the usual foreboding feeling. But it didn't come.

He braced his hands on the sink, closed his eyes and took a few slow breaths. When he opened his eyes, he was looking at Daisy's cosmetics bag. Sticking out of the top was her blue New Year's wish list, now tattered from time and many handlings. Had she left it where he could see it on purpose?

He pulled it out and unfolded it. She had completed wish number two. *Fall in love.* He'd known that's what she'd meant it to be, but what had taken her so long to write it? She had also filled in number six. *Find someone who loves me the way I love them. The way I deserve.*

"Oh, sweetheart." Was it possible? Could he give her what she wanted and deserved?

He put the piece of paper back where he'd found it, stepped out and peeked around the corner. Daisy was curled up on her side with her back to him. Ivy was facing her and staring at her with wonder, kind of the way he liked to do. She was an amazing woman who deserved everything her heart desired.

He watched them until Ivy's eyes fluttered close, and Daisy kissed her forehead. When he went to her side of the bed and sat on the edge, Daisy sat up.

"Are you okay?" She cupped his cheek and brushed her thumb through his beard.

Her touch sent a warmth all the way through to his core. "I'm good. I just wanted to tell you good night before I went way over there onto my side of the bed." He slid his fingers into her hair to cradle the back of her head and brushed his lips against hers.

"Can you be patient with me? Please."

Chapter Twenty-Six

The next day they only made necessary stops—which were frequent with a toddler—but Daisy was enjoying every minute of it. They were back to their normal easy flowing conversations, and after what Finn had said about being patient with him, she had more hope that he was seeing the light of what could be. Good thing patience was one of her virtues.

She reached into the back seat to hand Ivy a small container of dry Cheerios. "Here you go, sweetie. Do you still have water in your cup?"

Ivy picked up the spill-proof cup and shook it to demonstrate the water sloshing inside.

"Good. We'll get some real food soon."

"My stomach agrees," Finn said. "You know, if we keep driving after we eat, we'll arrive in the middle of the night."

"We need to find a hotel." It was a delay tactic, but one more day on their unplanned adventure would give both of them a little more time to adjust to a new reality. A reality with a child involved. Because as soon as they got to Channing, real life would once again be upon them.

He took the next exit off the highway. "I was just thinking the same thing. Up ahead I see a couple of hotels and a shopping center with restaurants."

"Perfect." They shared a knowing smile. They both knew the truth of why they were stopping, and she was glad they were in agreement.

The hotel was nicer than the ones they'd stayed in for the past two nights. There was even a playground where Ivy got to run around and get some exercise. But she was still very timid, even around other kids. She made sure she could see Finn and Daisy the whole time, as if she was worried about being left behind. It made Daisy want to gather her up and never let her go. In only a few days, this precious child had stolen her heart. Just like her big brother had.

The toddler climbed up a short ladder with surprising skill, and they moved to the bottom of the slide.

"With those climbing skills, she's going to need to be watched like a hawk," Sage said.

He groaned.

Ivy slid down to them, her blond curls ruffling in the wind and her eyes bright.

Daisy held out a hand to her. "Want to swing?"

Ivy nodded and took hold of her hand, making Sage's heart sigh, right along with Snow White and Maleficent.

Once she was in the baby swing, Daisy stood behind her to push while Finn leaned his back against one leg of the swing set.

A little boy was giggling in the swing beside her. "Mama, higher. Push higher, Mama."

Ivy studied the mother and son then tipped back her head to look at Daisy. When she smiled at the toddler, she received one in return.

"When we get home tomorrow, which one of our houses do you think would be better for Ivy?" he asked.

She pictured his house. Their guest room was full of workout equipment and would take a lot of work to turn into a little girl's bedroom. Paint and furniture and all the little touches to make her feel at home. "There is already a kid's room set up at my house with a crib and a toddler bed, so that makes the most sense. At least to start. But if she is at my house, then you will have to be too."

He put an arm around her waist. "I was hoping you'd say that."

When it got dark, they were all in the hotel room bed watching a movie in their pajamas. Ivy was curled against his side with her head on his shoulder, her tiny fingers twining through his beard as her eyes fluttered closed.

Daisy propped up against the headboard. "Did your dad have a beard?"

"Yes. Sara told me Ivy did this to him too."

"You're a comfort to her. It's so sweet."

"You do the same thing," he said.

"What thing?"

"You absentmindedly run your fingers through my beard when we're lying in bed.

"I guess I do, don't I." She frowned. "At least I did." And if everything fell into its proper place, maybe she would once again.

He settled the sleeping child on the mattress between them and smoothed her curls. Carefully so he wouldn't wake her, he propped his back against the headboard like Daisy. "I miss this. Being in bed with you. Talking and hanging out."

"Just the talking?"

He reached for her hand. "I miss all of it."

"So do I." Whispering made it feel like they were telling secrets.

"Remind me why we have to be friends only," he said.

She shook her head, smiling. "I can't. I might have written that I wanted a brief fun affair, but now that I've had that, I want more. I want back what we had."

"What if I screw it all up?"

"What if *I* do?"

"I can't imagine that. Are you willing to take another chance on a guy who can't get his act together?"

"That depends. Are you putting a time limit on us and planning an end like we did before?"

"No. I'm just…" He brought her hand to his lips and kissed her knuckles. "I don't know how to be away from you. Can we take it day by day, and I'll try to earn it?"

She leaned his way and kissed him. "You've earned a kiss. Want another?"

"Absolutely." He cradled her cheek and kissed her deeply.

The next morning, they started out on the last leg of their adventure. They'd driven through scenery that wowed them and supported the title America the beautiful. Her camera was filled with snowcapped mountain peaks, open valleys where sunshine slanted across the land and pictures of Ivy and Finn.

Daisy looked into the back seat. "Ivy, we're almost to my house. There are going to be a lot of people who want to meet you, but they're all very nice."

"There is another kid for you to play with and lots of animals," he said.

The toddler's smile brightened at the mention of animals, and she hugged her toy goat.

When they pulled up to Dalton Ranch around lunchtime, everyone was gathered on the backyard patio. The Murphy brothers, Sage's family, Lizzy's family and Adam all waved, but because they had warned them of her shyness, they didn't rush over. Except for her adorable nephew.

Davy wasn't having any of the staying away and toddled over to Daisy for a hug.

"Hello, my sweet angel boy." She swung him high into the air and made him giggle.

Finn got his baby sister out of her car seat and called his brothers over to join them. Ivy curled against him. When Riley and Jake smiled at her, she raised her head, but she kept her thumb in her mouth and didn't release her tight hold on Finn's shirt.

"We're your big brothers," Jake said. "Welcome to the family."

"I'm Riley, and that's Jake."

"What do you think of that, little miss?" Finn asked. "Now you have three big brothers."

Daisy joined them with Davy on her hip. The little boy reached out to patty Ivy's back. Her thumb popped out of her mouth as she smiled back at him.

"Let's go meet everyone else," Finn suggested.

There was a potluck meal laid out on the patio table, and they all filled their plates and eased Ivy into meeting their extended family group.

The toddlers took to one another right away and played happily side by side on the patio while the cat soaked up their attention.

Davy tugged on Lizzy's skirt. "Mama, mama, mama. Up, pease."

She lifted her son into her arms. "Ready to go inside for a nap?"

He shook his head. "No, no, no. Play."

Ivy stared at them then turned to Daisy and raised her arms, and she picked up the toddler. "Let's go inside and play with Davy until naptime."

"She is so precious," Sage said as they made their way

through to the living room. "You have got to catch me up on the status of your relationship."

"I'll give you the highlights. The long version will have to wait until we're alone."

They put the children beside the basket of toys and sat across from them. Davy gave his new playmate a yellow dump truck with a Barbi and Ken doll in the back of it.

Daisy propped her feet on the edge of the coffee table. "The man is making me nuts with his hangups, but he asked me to be patient and give him a chance."

"How patient does a woman have to be?" Sage asked.

"I don't know, but he is wearing on mine."

"But you love him."

"Heaven help me, I do."

The whole group had been a little overwhelming for Ivy, but now Adam was the only one who remained. He was on the couch watching the end of a movie he couldn't get on the TV in the apartment. Ivy was on the floor beside Davy's toy basket. She looked precious in a new set of pink pajamas with her hair still damp from her bath.

Finn came in the front door with a load of logs in his arms.

"Need help?" Adam asked him, and got up.

"You can get the next load. This is good for now."

Daisy was just happy to be home and relaxing in her comfy blue chair with a glass of white wine. She let contentment spread through her. This was the kind of life she dreamed about. A family of her own. Her dream was within reach and right here for the taking.

Oh, Finn. Why can't you see that you deserve a family of your own?

He just needed to get out of his own way.

He put another log on the fire and closed the screen. His muscles bunched as he put his hands on his thighs and stood in one fluid motion. She inwardly sighed. She loved watching him move. He took a seat in the chair beside her. She grinned at the sight of a cowboy dressed mostly in black sitting in her sister's pink velvet chair.

Adam was focused on the end of the movie, but when Ivy brought him a book and crawled up beside him, he didn't hesitate to turn his attention to her. "Do you want me to read to you?"

The shy little girl nodded and smiled while batting her eyelashes. He was one more person who had fallen a willing victim to her charm.

He opened the book and began to read to her. He used different voices for the characters and made animal sounds that made Ivy giggle and imitate him.

Daisy and Finn shared a smile.

"Someday, she's going to have guys eating out of her hand," he whispered.

"Someday?" Daisy chuckled. "She already does. You, Adam, Riley, Jake and even Lizzy and Sage's husbands. And it's not just men."

"True. I'm so glad I didn't leave her behind, and that she has you in her life."

"She has you too." She reached across the little round table between them and put her hand on top of his. "You know how much she adores you."

His next breath was deep, and his exhale was long and slow as if he needed time to gather his thoughts.

"Finn, because you brought her home with you, she is coming out of her shell and making connections that she will get to keep forever."

When the book was finished, Adam stood. "I have to go back to my own place now, but I'll see you tomorrow, Ivy."

"Morrow?" she asked, and stood on the couch cushion.

"Yes. Tomorrow maybe I can show you the horses."

Daisy followed Adam to the door. "Thanks for being so sweet with her."

"No problem. Thanks for letting me hang out with y'all."

"Anytime. Good night."

"Night, Daisy."

Finn held out his arms. "It's bedtime, little miss."

Daisy went upstairs with them. The nursery had a crib and a toddler bed. The pale blue walls were soothing, and the light fixture looked like a bouquet of brightly colored flowers. The bedding was horse themed and there was a packed bookshelf along one wall that was flanked by crates of toys.

"Ivy, which bed do you want to sleep in?" he asked.

The little girl went over to the toddler bed and climbed on. "You." She pointed at Finn and then to the small bed.

He knelt beside it. "I won't fit in this bed. I'll be in a different room that is just down the hall."

She poked out her bottom lip.

"Let me show you where I'm sleeping, and then you'll know where to find me." He scooped Ivy up but then paused and looked at Daisy. "I didn't ask, but will I be in your room?"

"Do you want to be?"

"Of course."

She turned and smiled over her shoulder. "Then follow me."

In Daisy's bedroom, Ivy climbed up onto the big bed like the little monkey that they'd discovered she was. She lay down in the middle.

Daisy and Finn looked at one another. "This idea might have backfired," he said. "Ivy, this is where I will be tonight. Just down the hall from your room. Now you know where to find me."

She didn't look convinced, but after Daisy rocked her, they eventually got the little girl to sleep in the toddler bed.

When the two of them finally climbed into Daisy's bed—minus a toddler—they were exhausted.

"Adam is so sweet with Ivy," she said. "I knew he would fit in well around here."

"He's a good kid."

"So, you no longer think he's up to something or has an ulterior motive for showing up here?"

"No. He kind of reminds me of myself. Poor kid." He pulled her closer, and she rested her head on his chest.

"Being like you is a positive in my book."

He kissed the top of her head. "Not long ago, you would've agreed with me and teased me."

"You're probably right." She tipped up her face to smile at him. "Give me a few days and I'll be back to teasing you. Promise."

He kissed her. "Thanks for having faith in me."

She could see the changes in him. He seemed a little more settled every day. More open to the kind of life he'd given up on. As she held him in her arms, she remind herself not to rush things, but rather to trust that they would get where they were meant to be.

He nuzzled her neck. "You smell good."

Her body was coming alive under his hands. "You do too."

"Do you think it's okay if we close and lock the door for a few minutes before we go to sleep?"

She chuckled. "I think that's a very good idea."

* * *

Finn woke when something tickled his ear. When it happened again, he cracked open one eye and immediately grinned. Ivy was at his bedside. Her cherub face was on his level, her chin propped on her hands that were folded on the edge of the mattress.

"Good morning, little miss." He made a big show of stretching and groaning and being silly.

She giggled and clapped for his performance.

Daisy sat up. "Good morning, sweetie. Want to come up here with us?"

She nodded and climbed up with a little help. Instead of settling down between them, she started jumping on the bed. Her blond curls floated about her head as she bounced.

He chuckled and flopped back onto his pillow. "I think she and Rascal are going to get along just fine. And I have a feeling I'm going to have to learn to function on less sleep."

Chapter Twenty-Seven

Finn parked in front of his house on the Four Star Ranch and waved to Riley on the front porch. Astro and Rascal were frisking around in the front yard.

"Ivy is going to love this," Daisy said.

They both turned in their seats to look at the little girl who had an old teddy bear under one arm and a toy goat under the other. "Are you ready to meet two more animals?" he asked.

"Yay." She clapped her hands.

As soon as they got out of the truck, the goat saw him and bounded in their direction. Ivy squealed so loudly in his ear that he winced, but her joy made him smile. He knelt to introduce her to the goat and the dog. "This is Astro, and this little girl is Rascal."

"My baby," she said, and plopped onto her bottom to cuddle the baby goat on her lap. She giggled when Astro licked her cheek and Rascal nibbled at the ruffle on her shirt.

Daisy sat beside her, so he went over to talk to Riley while they played with the animals. "Did you have a chance to look through the box of Dad's stuff that I gave you last night?"

"I did. There are some good pictures in there, but I haven't been through all of it yet." His brother crossed his arms over his chest and studied him. "So, are you going to do it? The whole dad, mom and kid thing?"

The question didn't send him into an immediate panic like it would have only days ago. But there was still a level of discomfort that made his pulse jump. "I'm working on figuring out how everything will look. I don't know how to be a good father."

"You idiot," Riley said. "What do you think you've already been doing with Ivy, and the way you teach Adam stuff? What do you think you did with me and Jake from the time you were a kid yourself?"

"Man, when we were young, it was constant stress. I barely got us from day to day."

"But you did. And I didn't turn out so bad."

"That's somewhat true." He slapped his little brother on the back.

Ivy ran across the yard with Rascal on the leash, and Daisy smiled at him. "I have a feeling that little girl and baby goat are going to be hard to separate."

"I think you might be right. If you take the goat over to Daisy's, you'll probably have to take the dog too. Every family needs a dog," Riley said, and chuckled.

Over the next few days, Finn worked on his ranch, helped Adam with some maintenance chores on the Dalton Ranch, worked on his relationship with Daisy and parenting skills with Ivy. All while playing the part of a family man.

While Ivy was with Lizzy and Davy, Daisy, Finn and Adam were getting the horses ready to ride out and check all the fences after a big rain.

"We need to look at every section of fence very carefully," she said. "We especially need to check both locations where the creek cuts through the property."

"Hey, Daisy," Adam said. "I saw an old motorcycle in the red barn. Does it run?"

"No. It hasn't run in many years." She mounted her horse and patted her neck. "It belonged to my older brother. Lizzy's father."

Finn flicked a stone from his horse's hoof then lowered its leg to the ground. "We can pull it out and take a look at it, and I can probably help you get it running."

"That's not a good idea," Daisy said. "My brother got hurt riding that old thing."

Adam swung into the saddle. "It's not just horses that I know how to ride. When I was a kid, I had a motorbike, and I rode it all over our property."

"Well, that old motorcycle is trash. We should've thrown it out ages ago."

"I don't think it's trash," Finn said. "But if you're throwing it out, I'll take it. Adam, do you know anything about working on them?"

"No, but I'd like to learn, if you'll teach me."

"I think we can find some time for that." Finn was now on his horse as well, and they all rode toward the back of the property. "I need to buy some supplies to work on one of the tractors, and we can grab what we need for the motorcycle too. If you'll help me with the tractor, I'll help you."

"You have yourself a deal, old man," Adam said.

She chuckled at his nickname for Finn. The guys started discussing how they would pull the bike out of the barn and look it over so they would know what to buy. They were completely ignoring her safety concerns, but she was happy to see them bonding, and she hated to spoil their fun.

Adam had no family to count on—other than hers. No one to teach him things like mechanics or repairing things around the house or how to be a man. No one to spend holidays and birthdays with. And all of this was no doubt why she felt so protective over him.

Finn and Adam working on something together would build their relationship. And maybe they could help heal one another, because she knew both of them had demons and doubts that they were fighting.

"Put me down as being against the whole motorcycle thing, but I won't try to stop you."

"Cool. Thanks, Daisy." Adam hooked a thumb over his right shoulder. "I'll ride in this direction and y'all can take the other."

"We'll meet you at the front gate," she said, and smiled as Adam spurred his horse."

Finn watched him ride away. "In some ways he seems more mature than his years, and in others…"

"He seems younger," she finished for him.

"There's something about him that I can't put my finger on. Something he isn't telling us."

A few days later, the motorcycle was close to done. It was getting late, and Finn was hungry, but they'd gotten a lot of work done on it this evening.

"You did good, kid. Let's go get some supper."

Adam walked beside him as they crossed the backyard. He held his left hand against his chest. "Don't tell Daisy that I hurt my hand working on the motorcycle. She might want us to stop before we finish it."

Finn stopped walking. "How bad is it? Let me see."

The teenager held out his hand. There was a scrape across the top from his wrist to his knuckles, and it would surely turn into a bruise. "It's not so bad. Doesn't hurt much."

"Adam, did you break your little finger?"

"No." He wiggled all his fingers to demonstrate their

working order. "It's always been like that. They've both been bent for as long as I can remember."

The back door opened, and Daisy stepped out. "Are you two hungry?"

"Yes," they said in unison and followed her inside.

"Go wash up. It will be about ten more minutes until it's ready."

After they had clean hands, they sat at the kitchen table, the savory scents making his stomach growl.

Ivy came into the kitchen with dolls clutched in her arms. She went straight to Finn and handed him the Ken doll. "Daddy."

A rush of emotions hit him, but the toddler wasn't done surprising them yet.

She went over to Daisy and handed her the Barbi. "Mama. Baby," she said, and then hugged the little child-sized doll.

Daisy met Finn's eyes, telegraphing similar emotions to his.

Ivy had just announced what she expected going forward.

The oven timer went off, beeping almost as fast as his heartrate.

Since neither of them were moving, Adam chuckled and went over to the oven. "Is it just me, or does the timing of this alarm seem like a sign that today is the start of something new?"

Chapter Twenty-Eight

Finn had discovered that although they'd gotten the motorcycle running, it wasn't safe to ride until they replaced a part on the front suspension. He'd been looking for Adam so they could go to town to get it, but he couldn't find him. There was one more place to look.

He went into the apartment behind Daisy's stable, but Adam wasn't there either. The kid kept the place clean, as far as floors and the tiny kitchen and bathroom were concerned, but his things were scattered about. Papers around his laptop on the table, clothes hung in layers over a chair and books tossed here and there.

When he turned to go, the toe of his boot caught the corner of a box that was sticking out from under the couch. It slid farther out across the floor, and when it hit the leg of the coffee table, the lid popped off. The first thing he saw was cash. A lot of cash.

"What the hell? Where in the world did he get this much money?" His skin went cold. Were his initial thoughts about Adam right?

He *was* hiding something.

He picked up the box and sat on the couch. It wasn't small bills like you'd have if you'd been saving money over time. They were large bills bundled together in neat, banded stacks. Underneath was a file folder, and when he saw what was written on the tab the hair stood up on the back of his neck.

Daisy Dalton.

He pulled it out from under the cash and flipped it open. An old photo of Daisy was on top. Beneath that were pages of information about her.

"This doesn't make any sense."

Adam didn't seem the grifter type, but his intuition had warned him that something wasn't right when the young man first arrived at the ranch. Adam really was hiding something big, and he had a lot of questions.

"What the hell are you doing getting into my stuff?" Adam shouted.

He looked up into the green eyes of the scowling young cowboy. "Did you steal this money?"

"Hell no! I got it from my mom."

"I thought your mom was dead?"

His eyes narrowed into slits that could shoot arrows, and he stormed closer, once again not intimidated by a much bigger man. "She is, dumbass. She left it for me, and you have no business snooping through my stuff."

Finn instantly felt bad that he'd brought up the kid's mom, but there was a more immediate problem to deal with first. He held up the photo of Daisy. "What about this? Are you going to tell me you got this from your mom too? Why do you have a dossier on Daisy?"

"I don't have to tell you anything, old man. Screw you. I'm out of here." Adam stormed out of the apartment, slamming the door behind him.

Finn jerked off his hat and slapped it against his thigh so he could plow his other hand through his hair. Why did Adam have all this information about Daisy? Was he a grifter here to get her money? Is that why someone his age had thousands of dollars in cash?

Daisy liked this kid so much, and so did he. She'd taken him under her wing. She was going to be crushed when she discovered the truth.

He heard the old motorcycle start up, and his heart leaped into his throat. He ran outside, but Adam had already taken off down the driveway toward the front gate. If he got going too fast or made any sharp turns, things could go wrong in a hurry.

Finn ran to his truck, jumped in and took off after him. He caught up to Adam right as he pulled out onto the road…

And his heart tried to jump out of his body as he watched the scene play out in sickening slow motion. Adam laid down the motorcycle and slid across the asphalt right in front of an oncoming truck.

Finn skidded his truck to a stop in the gravel along the roadside, threw it into Park and leaped out, leaving his door open as he raced to Adam. Dropping to his knees, he put a hand on Adam's shoulder to keep him still and started checking his head for injuries. "Hold still. Don't move."

"Hurts," he groaned.

"I know, kid. I've got you. Just breathe nice and slow."

A pool of red blood was spreading out from under his pinned leg. He had to see where the blood was coming from and get the bleeding stopped. The rush of adrenaline was making him tremble.

This can't be happening.

The driver of the truck appeared with a cell phone pressed to his ear. "The ambulance is already on the way. He pulled right out in front of me. Thank God I didn't hit him."

Adam groaned and tried to push the bike off himself, but Finn stopped him.

He pulled off his flannel shirt, popping off a few buttons in the process. "Can you lift the motorcycle very slowly so I can see where the bleeding is coming from?"

"You got it," the other man said, and did as he asked.

Finn put his head close to the ground to make sure the motorcycle was safe to move. "Okay, you can lift it all the way off of him." He quickly pressed the wadded shirt to the wound on the teenager's thigh right above the knee.

Adam gritted his teeth and put a hand over his eyes.

"You're doing good, kid. Just hold still, and we'll have you to the hospital in no time."

It was all his fault that Adam had taken off on the motorcycle. His fault he'd been so upset that he'd pulled out onto the road without looking while on an unsafe motorcycle and almost been hit by a truck.

Finn's stomach lurched.

This was way too much like the time he'd carried his little brother who'd been unconscious and bleeding after falling from a tree house. Once again it was his fault that someone was hurt.

This was proof that he should not be a dad.

"Am I going to die?" the teen said through gritted teeth.

"Absolutely not." *Please, God. Let him be all right.*

Adam groaned. "I need Daisy."

"I'll call her. Just let me take care of you first." What was this kid's fascination with Daisy?

"I'm not a thief." Adam lifted his head but dropped it back onto the folded-up towel the other man had put under his head. "It's my money. I promise."

"I know. I believe you. I'm sorry I messed with your stuff."

The ambulance siren grew louder, but before it reached them, Daisy's truck came from the opposite direction. She pulled over, jumped out and ran to them.

"What happened? Oh, my God."

"He's going to be all right," Finn said.

She dropped to Adam's other side and took his hand. "Did you hit your head?"

"Don't think so." He hissed as Finn adjusted the pressure on his leg.

She shot Finn a furious glare that cut to the bone. "Why did you let him ride this stupid motorcycle? I knew something like this would happen."

He should've known too.

His muscles tightened, making him feel as if he was caving in on himself. He didn't answer, because what could he say? This was all his fault.

The ambulance arrived and the paramedics took over.

Time was moving in both hyper speed and slow motion. He held up his hands and looked at the blood. Someone handed him a wet towel, and he cleaned them the best he could.

They got Adam strapped onto a stretcher and wheeled him toward the ambulance. "There's not much room," said one of the paramedics.

"Can my...mom come? Please?" Adam said, surprising both of them.

A female paramedic patted Adam's arm. "Yes, your mom can come."

She looked at Finn, her wide eyes revealing her emotional state. The kid didn't know what it meant to Daisy to be used as a pretend mom. "You got this," he said. "Go with him."

"Ivy is with Lizzy and Davy." She climbed into the back of the ambulance. "Finn, you're meeting us at the hospital, right?"

"I'll be there." If she wanted him there, he would suck it up and be there. And do his best not to make things worse.

Daisy was able to breathe once the paramedics assured her Adam was out of immediate danger. He was woozy from blood loss and drowsy from something they'd given him for the pain, and if she hadn't driven up when she did, he would be going through this all alone.

She wasn't sure why she felt so protective over this young man. He was too old to need her as a mother, but she would be here for him anyway.

At the hospital, they wanted to get an X-ray of his leg right away, so she sat in a small waiting area.

Finn arrived a few minutes later. She had planned to fuss at him about the motorcycle, but he looked so devastated that she just wanted to hug him instead. The problem was, he wasn't getting close enough to touch.

"How's Adam?"

"They're X-raying his leg."

"He took off on the motorcycle before I could stop him." Finn started pacing. "You were right. Working on that old bike was stupid. "

The anguish wafting off of him was palpable. "You were just trying to connect with Adam and teach him something."

Finn came to a sudden stop. "This is the kind of thing that happens when I form a connection with people. Tell him I'm sorry." He turned to go back out of the ER doors.

"Where are you going?"

"I need some air. Before I screw something else up."

She growled under her breath. The last thing she needed right now was him doing his distance thing.

He walked out into the parking lot.

"Maybe he really can't handle fatherhood." She sat in

an uncomfortable plastic chair, sick to her stomach and sick at heart.

"Hey, Daisy," Jake said as he sat down beside her a few minutes later.

"How did you know we were here?"

"Finn called me."

"He left. I don't know where he went."

"He's sitting outside. He didn't go far."

Jake handed her a cup of coffee. "It's because of me that Finn is so upset."

She took a sip and waited for him to explain, but he only stared at the wall in front of him. "How is any of this your fault?"

"When I was about ten years old, we got into a fight." He stretched out his legs and tilted his head back. "I can't even remember what it was about, but my usually coolheaded big brother lost his temper. I threatened to run away, he said good, and so I did. I climbed up into an old tree house in the woods near our house. One of the boards was rotten, and I fell. I got hurt pretty badly."

The image made her cringe. "And of course he blamed himself for his little brother getting hurt."

"He said he should've fixed the tree house or kept me from running away or whatever else he could blame himself for."

"You almost died." Finn's voice came from behind them, and they both turned around.

"Can I talk to Daisy alone?"

"Yep." Jake got up and patted his big brother on the back as he walked by.

She stood and grasped his hands. "I'm sorry I made it sound like I was blaming you for the accident. This is not your fault."

He shook his head as if she'd told a lie. "You weren't wrong. It is my fault."

A young nurse walked over to them. "You can follow me to Adam's room. The doctor wants to talk to both of you."

Their discussion would have to wait.

They followed the nurse down a short hallway and into a sterile, white exam room. Adam was in the bed, and a doctor with red hair and wire-rimmed glasses was standing at its foot. "Good afternoon, I'm Dr. Smith. Thankfully, Adam's leg is not broken, but we do need to perform a minor repair surgery."

The nurse opened the door and stuck her head into the room. "Dr. Smith, that call you've been waiting for just came in."

"Please, excuse me for a minute. I'll be back with some paperwork. Since Adam is only fifteen, one of you will need to sign it." He turned in a rush and left the room.

Daisy and Finn shared a shocked expression and then turned their stares to Adam. "Fifteen?" they said in unison.

He winced. "Yes."

"Did you run away from home?" she asked.

"No, I ran away from boarding school."

The ramifications of what this could mean began flashing in her mind. She'd been employing an underage runaway. If only she'd completed the background check. "You have some serious explaining to do, young man."

Finn stopped pacing the small room and stood at the foot of Adam's bed. "Why did you show up at the ranch with a ton of cash and a dossier on Daisy?"

She gasped. "A what?"

"I can explain everything," Adam said.

Chapter Twenty-Nine

Finn braced his hands on the foot of the hospital bed. "Let's hear it, Kid."

Adam tried to sit up but winced and lowered himself back onto the bed. "It's not as bad as it sounds. I'm not a con man or a thief. After my mom died, my great-uncle who I barely know became my guardian. She had no idea what a big jerk he really is. Instead of moving onto the ranch like he was supposed to do, he sold my home and sent me away to boarding school."

"Where does he think you are now?" Daisy asked.

"Still at school. I'm good with computers and imitating voices, and I might have sent some emails and made some calls. The school thinks I've gone home while my uncle thinks I'm still there."

"Adam!" She momentarily covered her face with her hands. "You're going to get all of us in trouble over this. You should be in school, not working all day on a ranch."

"I'm sorry, Daisy. I promise I'll make it right and make sure you don't get blamed for anything." The teenager moved his leg and hissed with his eyes squeezed tight.

Daisy chewed her thumbnail and sat on the side of his bed. "You traveled to Channing all by yourself?"

"It wasn't hard to do."

Finn hated the worry and distress on her face, so he turned away. "And what about the folder full of information about Daisy?" he asked from his spot by the window.

"Well… I have a good reason for that too."

The doctor rushed back into the room before he could answer. "Sorry about that. Since Adam has a rare blood type, I wanted to make sure the blood bank has what we might need, just in case."

Daisy's gaze snapped to the doctor. "What blood type?"

"AB negative."

"That's *my* blood type," she said.

Finn looked at Daisy and Adam side by side. He gasped and then cursed under his breath. All the little things that had been spinning around in his mind finally added up. Their shared single dimple. Their laugh and some mannerisms. And now that he knew his true age, it all fell into place.

Adam must be—

"I'm your son," Adam said.

"My son?" Daisy's vision swam and she swayed. Finn was beside her in a moment and put his hands on her shoulders to keep her steady.

"You're my biological mother."

So many feelings and thoughts came at her all at once. Shock. Confusion. Joy mixed with sadness for the time lost. Daisy leaned forward and cradled both sides of his face, searching for some piece of herself in his eyes.

The doctor frowned. "I'm confused. You didn't know that you are his mother?"

"I'll fill you in," Finn said to the other man, then looked at Adam. The hospital is going to need your uncle's phone number."

"He won't care, but it's in my contacts list. I guess there's no way around calling him?"

"Nope. Sorry, kid." Finn picked up Adam's phone from the bedside table. "Pull it up for me."

"We will definitely need to talk to your guardian," Dr. Smith said.

With the information he needed, Finn kissed Daisy's forehead. He might have to slip away to catch his breath now and then, but no matter what happened next, he wanted her to know he was here for her. "You two talk, and I'll go see about what needs to be done."

The men left the room, and Daisy pressed a hand to her pounding heart. "Is this for real? You are really my son?"

"I have a folder full of information and a letter from my mom that says so.

She always told me how I was born, but it wasn't until after she died that I found the information she had on you. She put it with some cash in a secret hiding spot where she knew I would look. I also have a trust fund."

"The fertility clinic had a description of me, but it was supposed to be anonymous. How did your mother know it was me?"

He shrugged. "Maybe because she had a lot of money and knew people? You're not mad at her, are you?"

"No, honey. I'm not mad at all. However she did it, I owe her my biggest thanks." She squeezed his hand. "You've been through so much. You have no idea how long and how many times I have wondered about a child of mine somewhere out there in the world." A tear rolled down her cheek.

"Don't cry. I had a really wonderful childhood. And a great mom."

"I'm so glad to hear that. Is it just you? No brothers or sisters?"

"Just me. And according to the paperwork from the fertility clinic, I'm your only child."

She pressed her lips to his forehead for a quick kiss and couldn't stop the tears. "I'm glad you came to find me."

"I think my mom chose you because of your love for horses."

"I'm overwhelmed." She laugh-cried. "And happy. So happy."

"So, even though I screwed up, I get to stay around?" he asked.

"Well, there is the matter of your guardian and you running away. It won't be simple, but we'll have to deal with all that legal stuff before you get to come back home."

"Home?"

"Absolutely. I want you to think of Dalton Ranch as your home. Let's just hope we don't have to jump through too many legal hoops to make it happen."

"I'm pretty sure Uncle Pete will be happy to have someone take me off his hands. He has fancy lawyers who handle all that kind of stuff for him."

The crestfallen expression on his face made her chest tight. "Why didn't you tell me who you are when you first arrived?"

"I was worried it would freak you out, and I wanted you to get to know me first. And then maybe you'd…" He shrugged.

"You fit with us from the very first day. As soon as we get things settled, you're going to have to start school. You've already missed too much."

"The same school where Loren goes?"

"It's the only high school in Channing. I can't believe I just found out who you are, and now I have to worry while you have surgery."

His eyes were glazed with pain and medication, but he grinned enough to show his dimple. "Sorry... Mama Daisy. Can I call you that?"

She swallowed the lump in her throat. "I would like that."

A few minutes later, they came to take Adam for his outpatient procedure and left her and Finn alone in the room.

Daisy sat on the bed and let out a slow breath. "Tell me what you found out about his uncle. Is he on his way here?"

"No, he's not. The hospital called him and got permission for the procedure, and then I talked to him. He didn't even seem all that concerned about him leaving boarding school. He was more worried about getting his money back than where Adam had been."

She gasped. "He sounds horrible. Does he want Adam back with him or to return to the boarding school?"

"No. He's eager to hand over guardianship and is calling his lawyer right away to expedite the process."

"That's just what Adam said would happen."

"Since you are a registered foster home, it should make things a little easier. You're going to need to call and talk to him soon, but it looks like things will go the way you want."

She got up and walked his way. "How do you know what I want?"

He met her halfway and opened his arms to cradle her against his chest. "Because I know you."

"It's such a relief that his uncle is getting the process started, but it also makes me want to find the man and smack him." She lifted her head from his shoulder. "Who treats a grieving child like he did?"

"There are those mama bear claws I was talking about. I kind of pity the man."

That made her grin just like he'd been hoping to do.

* * *

Adam's outpatient surgery went well, and after he woke up, they took him home to the Dalton Ranch with permission from his uncle. With Finn on one side of him and her on the other, they got him upstairs and settled into bed.

Standing in the hallway outside of the bedroom, Finn pulled Daisy into a hug. "You've had a big day."

"One of the biggest."

"I'm going to go over to Travis and Lizzy's to get Ivy."

"Hey, old man," Adam called from the bed. His words were slurred from the anesthesia and pain meds. "Where do you think you're going?"

"Just next door for a few minutes."

"You need to stay here and take care of my mama Daisy." He shook his head unsteadily as if trying to clear his vision. "She cried, and I need a nap before I can take care of her."

Finn moved to his bedside. "You've got it, kid. Close your eyes and get some rest."

Adam was so drowsy that he fell asleep still mumbling something about how he'd make things right.

In Daisy's bedroom that night, Finn flopped back on the bed and plowed a hand through his hair. "What a day. I can't believe Adam got hurt."

"Want to know what I've noticed?" Daisy asked.

He tucked his hands under the back of his head and stared at the ceiling. "Sure."

"The first time I met Ivy, she was frightened and curled against you. You were looking at me, but you cradled her head in a move so protective and paternal that it melted my heart."

"I did that?"

"Yep. And you've done lots of similar things since then."

He shook his head. "Adam could've been killed because of me. And then you never would've known that you have a son."

"Stop beating yourself up about it, or I'm going to have to give you a spanking."

He chuckled. "I'd like to see you try."

"Mama, where you?" Ivy called from the hallway.

"In here, sweetie."

Ivy peeked around the corner and a smile spread across her face before she ran to them.

Daisy lifted her up onto the bed with them.

"Give me a hug, little miss."

Ivy put her head on his chest and tried her hardest to wrap her short arms around his broad chest.

"That's just what I needed." He kissed the top of her head.

Ivy stood up on the bed and then leaned in to kiss his cheek. "Wuv you."

He sucked in a breath. "I love you, too."

Daisy's tears spilled over once again.

A second later their adorable toddler was jumping on the bed between them.

"I'm going to go check on Adam."

Daisy suspected he also needed to wipe a tear from his eye. She scooped up the toddler and covered her cheeks with kisses until she giggled. "All right, you little jumping bean. Let's go get a bath."

Finn went downstairs to check Adam's medication and wound cleaning schedule attached to the front of the refrigerator with butterfly magnets. It was time for his antibiotic and a pain reliever. He put them in a paper cup and poured a fresh glass of water.

When he went into the guest room where the youth was

recuperating, Adam was sleeping. Now that he knew the kid was only fifteen years old, he could see it. He could also see Daisy in his features.

Adam had been more alone in the world than he had ever been. But he had faced his struggles head-on. He'd come up with a brilliant scheme to leave boarding school without his guardian's knowledge. He'd traveled alone and found his way to the Dalton Ranch and convinced them he was an adult.

Finn admired this kid's grit. "You're one smart, tough kid," he said under his breath.

Adam opened his eyes and blinked a few times. "I know I am," he said in a quiet, hoarse voice.

"I thought you were asleep."

He winced as he shifted himself up on the pillows.

"It's time for your medication. How are you feeling?"

"I could use one of those pain pills."

"It's in here." He shook the paper cup, poured the pills onto Adam's palm and gave him the glass of water. "Need anything else?"

"A truck would be nice."

"Keep dreaming. First you have to get a driver's license." Finn sat in the rocking chair.

"Are you going to teach me to drive?"

"You really want me to teach you?"

"You've taught me lots of other stuff already."

"Aren't you mad at me for what happened to you?"

"No. I should've said something sooner about who I am. Or been better at hiding my stuff."

"I shouldn't have been looking at your stuff."

"Why were you in there?"

"Looking for you to tell you that the motorcycle needed more work before it could be ridden."

"Oh." Adam grimaced. "It was stupid of me to jump on it and take off."

"I won't argue with that."

Adam shifted again and gritted his teeth. "Thanks for being there with me when I got hurt. You kept me calm when I was freaking out."

The tension in Finn's chest loosened. "I'm glad I was there, too."

He still couldn't help but blame himself for the accident. There were things he could have and should have done to prevent this near tragedy. He could've listened to Daisy and not helped him work on the motorcycle. He shouldn't have come down so hard on him about the money and information about Daisy. If he hadn't been so hot-tempered and jumped to conclusions without really listening, Adam wouldn't have taken off.

While holding Adam's bleeding body in the middle of the road, gripping fear had wound tight around his insides, and he wasn't even his kid.

But he is Daisy's child.

He hadn't known that fact at the time of the accident, but looking back, he should have figured it out. They shared their one dimple, the way they tapped their thumb to their pinkie when they were thinking, and the crooked fingers just like Sage and Daisy. If it hadn't been for the false age thing, he would have put it all together.

It didn't seem to matter whether it was his child or someone else's, he still felt protective. And now he knew there was no escaping connections and relationships. And love.

"You and Daisy are good together," Adam said, interrupting Finn's thoughts.

His head snapped up to look at the young man. "I would've thought you'd want me to stay away from her."

"I used to think that. Until I saw how much you care for her. You'll make good parents for Ivy."

"You think I'll make a good father?"

"I've never had one, so I don't have a comparison, but you seem like a good dad to me."

Finn leaned forward, propped his elbows on his knees and stared at the floral pattern on the rug beside the bed. Daisy had been telling him the same thing, and so had both of his brothers. He'd been fighting all of them. Fighting himself.

He was no longer the scared kid taking care of his brothers when he was just a kid himself. He was an adult. A grown-ass man with a ranch and people and animals depending on him. What difference did a title make? Whether he was a brother or an uncle or a friend, he'd already been taking care of everyone around him.

He could be a dad to Ivy and to this fatherless child beside him. To Daisy's child.

He could be the man Daisy needed him to be.

"Hey, old man. Did you fall asleep on me?"

He sat up straight and grinned at the kid. "Just thinking about some important decisions."

"I could really go for a cheeseburger and french fries," Adam said. "Seems like a perfect chance to get on Daisy's good side and make it up to me."

Finn chuckled. "Is that right? Lucky for you, I was already planning to go into town. I'll pick up some food for you."

"Thanks. Wait, before you go, close the door and hand me that duffel bag."

Finn did as he asked, and put the bag beside him on the bed. The teenager dug around in it, pulled out a ring box and flipped it open to reveal an emerald cut diamond ring.

"This was my mother's ring," he said. "I know she would want Daisy to have it, so if you ever need to use it—hint, hint—you know where it is."

He squeezed Adam's shoulder and nodded but couldn't talk around the lump of emotion lodged in his throat.

If even this kid believed in him, then shouldn't he believe in himself?

Chapter Thirty

While Finn went to get the food, Daisy set up a card table by Adam's bed so all four of them could eat together. As Finn headed back into the room with the drinks, he stopped to watch Daisy steal two of his french fries, eat one and give the other one to Ivy. He smiled and a lightness filled him. How had he ever thought Daisy wasn't the sexiest woman in the world?

She was…everything.

He never got tired of her company, she made him laugh and they rarely fought. And when they made love, they were in sync in the best way. What more could a man ask for?

In a spur of the moment decision, he let his heart guide him. He walked forward and sat in the folding chair beside her.

She cocked her head and smiled at him. "What's up?"

"I see that you're teaching the next generation to steal my fries."

"Us girls have to stick together, don't we, sweetie?"

"Girl stick." Ivy giggled and then reached for another one of his french fries.

Daisy kissed the top of her head and beamed a big smile that showed her dimple. Just like the young man in the bed beside her. Her son, who he'd taken under his wing long before he'd known the truth of his parentage. He looked at Adam and a silent understanding passed between them.

He turned his attention back to the woman who held his future in the palm of her hands. "Daisy Maisy, you've not only taken my food and drinks and T-shirts and who knows what else, but you've also taken something much more important." He took her hand across the small card table. "You've stolen my heart."

"Heart," Ivy said, and patted Daisy's chest.

He smiled and stroked her head of curls. "That's right, little one." He put a hand to his own chest. "This heart right here."

"Finn, do you mean it?" Daisy asked with love shining in her eyes.

"Oh, I definitely mean it. I think of you before I fall asleep and when I wake up each morning. I thought I wanted the life of a single, unencumbered man, but you make me see everything in new ways. You came into my life and stirred up my world in a most wonderful way. You are my inspiration and my joy. My conscience. My encouragement. You bring out the best in me and make me see myself as more capable than I gave myself credit."

"It was easy to do. You're a good man, and you have changed my life for the better."

He glanced at Adam, and the teenager tossed him the small box. Finn got down on one knee, making her gasp. "I love you, my sweet stubborn Daisy Maisy. And I have one more thing you can take." He flipped open the ring box. "Will you take my heart? Forever? Will you marry me and build a family with me?"

"Yes. I absolutely will. I love you dearly."

He slipped the diamond ring on her finger. "I had help with the ring, so I can't take all the credit for it."

"It was my mom's," Adam said. "She would want you to have it."

"Oh, Adam. It's gorgeous. That is the sweetest thing ever and so special." She stood and hugged Finn, and Ivy squealed when they squashed her between them. Daisy wiped tears from the corners of her eyes. "We're going to be a real family. You have helped me complete my wish list."

Finn kissed her and then Ivy's rosy cheek. "We've already got two kids, so I think we're off to a good start."

"Two kids?" Adam asked.

"I know you're almost a young man, but I think you could use a dad as well."

"You mean it? You really want to be…my dad?"

"Absolutely. If that's what you want as well."

Adam's grin widened to show his dimple. "Can I still call you old man?"

"Sure thing. But let's retire calling me grandpa…for now."

"Daddy." Ivy got his attention by patting his cheek. "Wuv you."

He cuddled her close and smelled the baby shampoo in her hair. "Love you too, little miss."

Daisy was full on crying now as she wrapped her arms around his waist and whispered in his ear. "I'm so proud of you. I love you."

"Thank you for showing me how to open my heart."

Epilogue

Everyone was at the Dalton Ranch for Sunday dinner, and Loren was excited about the artwork she'd had framed. She unwrapped the brown craft paper and held the painting of a woman in a garden.

Dillon stopped behind her. "Where did you get this painting?"

"We found it hidden in a secret drawer in our house in town. The house used to belong to my great-aunt Tilly DeLuca. But as hard as I've tried to find out, I don't know who the artist is."

Dillon stepped closer and squinted at the initials in the bottom corner of the painting. "I think I might know. I think it was painted by my great-grandfather James Kenneth Cameron."

"No way! Really?"

"I'm not positive, but I have a sister who knows a lot more about his artwork than I do. Can I take a photo of this and send it to her?"

"That would be great," Loren said. "This isn't the only one. I have more paintings and sketches by the same artist. Do you know the name Tilly DeLuca?"

"I don't think so, but one of my sisters might."

"This is so cool," Loren said. "Hey, Mom. Guess what I just found out." She raced off to spread the news.

A while later, everyone was in the backyard eating and playing and visiting, but Finn stood behind Daisy with his big hands spread across her baby bump.

"Did you feel that?" she asked.

"Was that the baby moving?"

"Yes. Oh, there it is again."

He came around in front of her, dropped to one knee and kissed her baby bump. "Hello in there, tiny one." He looked up at her with a huge smile. "We're going to have three children."

"Can you handle that?"

"Yes, ma'am." He stood, cradled her face and kissed her. He glanced around at their extended family. "With this crew to help out, I know I can."

"The man who never wanted a wife or child is now a husband and soon to be a father of three."

"Isn't it great how things work out?" he said.

"The best."

"Daisy, come sit with me," Sage called over to her.

"I'll go make a plate of food for you while you talk to your sister. You have a baby to feed." He kissed her and headed to the table.

She went over to sit by her twin in a pair of lawn chairs off to the side. "Remember when it was just the two of us here on this big ranch?"

Sage glanced down at Rose who was asleep in her arms and kissed her baby girl's cheek. "How things have changed. We are two lucky ladies."

"I agree."

Ivy's giggles drifted on the warm breeze as Finn lifted her high into the air so she could pretend to be an airplane as he flew her over to her Riley and Jake. Adam was teaching Loren how to rope, and Grayson and Travis were at the grill laughing. Lizzy placed one hand on her own pregnant belly and used the other to wipe ketchup off Davy's cheeks.

"I wish Mama and Daddy were here to see what we've built," Daisy said.

"I think they are. They're up in heaven hand in hand and looking down with smiles."

"Family photo time," Loren called to everyone. "Gather under the tree, please." The teenager rounded everyone up, set the timer then ran to join the group.

All of them crowded together and smiled for the camera. After they dispersed, Loren went over to check the camera and showed the photo to Daisy. "What do you think? Do we need to take another?"

Adam was making bunny ears behind Loren's head, and Jake was holding Ivy upside down—much to the little girl's delight. Travis and Lizzy were kissing, Finn had one big hand splayed on her stomach and Grayson was making a funny face at his baby daughter. And the cutest thing of all was Davy, who had his back to the camera but was bent over smiling at the camera from between his own legs.

Daisy felt a flutter in her belly and was so filled with love she thought she'd burst. She put an arm around her niece. "It's the most perfect family photo ever taken."

* * * * *

   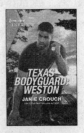